...right © 2023 by Kathy Iandoli
...ed in the China

...Rights Reserved, including the rights to reproduce this book ...ortions thereof in any form whatsoever.

...information address Kingston Imperial
...ghts Department
...5 Sheridan Ave, #360
...ami Beach, FL 33140
...nail: info@kingstonimperial.com
...ww.kingstonimperial.com

...irst Edition:
...ook and Jacket Design: Kingston Imperial
...Manufactured in the United States of America

Cataloging in Publication data is on file with the library of Congress
Title: King of New York
ISBN 9781954220539 (Hard Cover)
ISBN 9781954220546 (Ebook)

KING O
NEW YO
A NEW MAFIA TA

KATHY IANDO

For my Mother Anna,
my Capo Donna.

UNO

Jimmy felt the cold steel on his forehead.

As the gun's muzzle burrowed deeper against his skin, the pressure inside his skull intensified to the point where he couldn't tell where he began and the piece ended.

He was getting a headache, which, ironically, the coolness of the pistol soothed.

"You know what I'm thinking?" A deep voice echoed in the background. "I'm thinking you need a better view. We're talking best-seat-in-the-house kind of view. How does that sound to you?"

The gun then moved from Jimmy's forehead and slid slowly into the space between his eyes.

"Now, isn't that better?" the phantom voice continued. "Plenty of people would kill for that view. You know what I'm saying?"

The muzzle had left an imprint on Jimmy's forehead. It resembled a third eye in the middle of his skull.

Jimmy couldn't make out the face and didn't recognize the voice.

All he knew was that this was the end.

He patted his pockets one last time in desperation, but the result was the same as the last time and the time before that. They were empty.

"This is your last shot, Jimmy," the voice mocked. The man had a husky laugh. Dirty. "*This* one right here." The muzzle jostled against his skin, pressing up against the bone, and the more it moved, the more the gunman laughed.

The world of the unlit room narrowed to the gun itself. He couldn't make out much about the hand holding the grip or the finger on the trigger. Jimmy tried to focus on a faint light, confused about where it was coming from. He shuffled his legs a little, hoping to edge into a position that offered a better angle, anything that might provide more than a glimpse of features that could just as easily have been a mask. He wanted to see who was about to end his life.

That didn't feel like a big ask.

That was the thing about Jimmy Martello: He might've gotten himself into trouble, but he was—and would always be, well, at least for a second or two more—a man of honor, like his family raised him.

He wanted to look his killer directly in the eyes before drawing that final breath.

In a way, he was showing respect to them both, the hunted giving kudos to the hunter. A morbid sort of congratulations. A high-five of the damned.

He moved his legs some more.

"Oh, you wanna dance?" the voice crooned. "Let's bust a move then. Cue the music!"

Life didn't flash before his eyes.

Instead, Jimmy was met by a chorus of his dead relatives, flanking him on both sides: his *nonna*, Giuseppina, and her brother Alfredo. His *bisnonna*, Carmela, and her sister Maddalena, his great aunt.

The mysterious voice cut through the gathering of ghosts. "Let's hear the choir sing!"

With one slight breath, they all joined in, voices raised, joyously belting out Dean Martin's "Volare."

Volare meant *to fly*, and Jimmy was about to take the longest, highest flight of them all.

That, or fall.

And it was a long way down to where that fall ended in fire and brimstone.

"Father, forgive me," Jimmy mumbled in a prayer that was never going to be answered.

Given all he'd done in life, a smarter man would have begged for forgiveness, but Jimmy was not a smart man. He wouldn't beg anyone. Not even the Big Guy. He always said, "The Big G, then me"—asserting his divine dominance.

His final thoughts began racing blindly in panic through his skull, punctuated by the harmonizing of his ancestors.

"Say good night, Jimmy," the voice slid through the singing.

He heard the dull *click* of the trigger, and then . . .

#

"Volare" was still playing as Jimmy opened his eyes.

He almost choked on a deep gasp of air.

He rose shakily from his tortured slumber and looked around his room.

Spears of sunshine poked through the holes in the afghan blanket hung across his bedroom window. Jimmy hated the morning light. He was the only member of the Martello family with hazel eyes, and they'd teased him mercilessly about it. The only other person in the clan with light eyes like his was his least favorite uncle, and he hated that connection.

Jimmy's *nonna* used to call him *il vampiro* out of sarcastic endearment.

She'd crocheted that afghan for his sixth Christmas. He wondered how she'd have felt knowing it had become a curtain years later.

"Doesn't the garlic make you sick, little Jimmy?" she would tease in Italian while she cooked every morning.

"Wrong monster, *Nonna*. The only thing that can take me down is a silver bullet. I'm a werewolf," Jimmy would always reply with a laugh, playing their game. She'd scratch the scruffy shadow of stubble that sprouted from his jaw.

And every time, she'd shake her head as she stirred her wooden spoon in the deep steel pot. "*Vampiro!*"

He missed her.

Nonna passed away four years ago, and last night was the first time he'd seen her in a dream since.

Dream?

Nightmare.

Jimmy sat up straight in the bed, taking stock of his surroundings. As Dean Martin completed his next looping chorus, he picked up his phone and turned off his alarm's music.

The room was dark and cold and made him think of a coffin.

Yet he was still alive.

And today was his twenty-fifth birthday.

He pushed himself up out of bed, and with a swift tug, pulled his *nonna's* afghan from the curtain rod. The August sun seared through the window's glass and the screen to beat against his face. Jimmy smiled. The outside world looked different today. He shook his head and ran his fingers through his jet-black hair, a final farewell to the residue of last night's dream.

He slipped his black Gucci slides on over his white socks, but he didn't bother changing out of the teal basketball shorts he'd slept in.

He threw on a wifebeater, which they crudely called a *guinea tee*. It was an obvious look for a dark-skinned Sicilian man, but Jimmy was all for stereotypes. He had family from Tunisia, as did many of his friends. Calling them *guineas* was the kind of casual racial slur he'd been hearing all his life. It wasn't going to make him change his look. More often than not, Italian men like him wore white ribbed tank tops, whatever the weather. To Jimmy, it was more like a mark of belonging.

It was appropriate attire for today. The summer block was hot in more ways than one.

In the bathroom, Jimmy splashed cold water onto his face and brushed his teeth before he went out, opening the door to his brownstone. He stood on the steps overlooking his street—Doctors' Row.

Bay Ridge, Brooklyn, had a different kind of vibe today. The air was crisp and clean, and there wasn't a cloud in the sky. It was like the whole world was celebrating his birthday with him. That was the kind of love he could get on board with. There was even a part of him that believed he deserved it.

Jimmy surveyed his neighborhood, standing tall and toned,

like a Roman statue.

He had the kind of muscular build that came from playing a lot of pickup ball in Brooklyn playgrounds. Born and raised in Bay Ridge, he was a wanderer at heart. He enjoyed venturing out to other parts of Brooklyn to play ball and talk music—hip-hop—with the guys in Bed-Stuy. It was a nice change of pace. Otherwise, all day and every day, he was surrounded by Italians. His whole block was flooded with them, second-generation, third-generation Italians, from the top of the boot down to Sicily and Sardinia.

His neighborhood could double as a map of Italy.

Jimmy walked over to the corner store and grabbed his favorite coffee-flavored soda, Moka Drink, from the refrigerator, earning the scorn of the owner, Giuseppi, from behind the counter. "Why do you always drink that Calabrian piss juice?" Giuseppi quipped. It was their regular banter. It wasn't funny, but it was a little ritual. "Drink Manhattan Special like a real Sicilian. I'm telling you, the espresso in it will put some hairs on your little beanbags."

Jimmy laughed and grabbed a second bottle of Moka Drink out of spite.

"Just for you, 'Seppi, I'm gonna drink *two* today. One for each hand. It's my birthday!"

As Jimmy handed Giuseppi the five-dollar bill for his sodas, Giuseppi pushed the money right back to him. "Your money's no good here, birthday boy. And here, have some of this . . ." He slid a tiny bottle of sambuca into Jimmy's hand. "This'll *really* make you grow hair on your beanbags."

Jimmy stepped outside of the store, cracked the cap off his first Moka Drink with his teeth, and took a sip. He had no idea if there was any real caffeine in the soda, but it woke him up every morning without fail, so real or not, it was good enough for him.

"Ay, *cugino*, it's not even eight o'clock, why the hell are you up? On your *birthday*, no less," his cousin Nicky hollered as he approached the front of the store. With Jimmy seated and Nicky standing, they were almost the same height. Nicky was shorter than Jimmy, with a fuller face and more pronounced nose, yet they were cast from the same genetic block.

"Come on now, Nick, what did Nas say about waking up early on my born day?" Jimmy replied with a smile. They weren't just family; they were best friends. In the Martello family, it was rare to venture outside the safety of the clan and make real friends, and with good reason.

Jimmy's father, Italo Martello Jr., was the don of the Martello crime family, close cousins to the Bonannos, one of the more notorious crime families of New York City and New Jersey. Jimmy's grandfather, Italo Sr., had retired to the position of underboss a few years back. As the newly minted boss, Italo Jr. handled most of the day-to-day now. Italo Sr. had developed lung disease from the twin killers of a lifetime of puffing on thick cigars and the lungfuls of asbestos he'd inhaled when he'd served in the navy at nineteen and they were pulling the stuff off ships.

"I gave them my heart, and the bastards took my lungs too," Italo would say through his hacking cough.

He was industrious, though. Over the years, he found new ways to make money. Lots of them. And while he was always tied to his family—who were neck-deep in racketeering and other crime—that didn't make him a gangster. He was one of them, but he wasn't one of them.

It wasn't until Italo found his way to the doorstep of his cousin, Santo Bonanno, that all that changed, and his tenure with the Mafia truly begun.

He entered by running numbers for his distant family, which meant taking part in the Mafia lottery—highly illegal, but with scope for netting a huge reward. Italo had a gift for numbers. Had he stayed in Palermo, maybe he could have done something with his gift; studied and become a math professor at

Catania University, maybe. Instead, he became a human calculator for the Mafia. He earned a reputation for both impressively quick calculations and an unmatched memory of numbers.

Jimmy inherited that gift with numbers, though he made a point not to ask questions about the other side of his family's business. He didn't want to know. Questions meant you risked getting answers, and just like with his bedroom in the morning, he liked to be in the dark.

Jimmy had a lucrative job managing the family's finances and putting his MBA from Fordham to good use. He'd developed a system for dealing with it that he liked to think of as numerical ignorance; every transaction was reduced to the bare numbers, nothing else. He didn't need to know what had been bought and paid for, or what had been sold. They were just numbers, not crimes. He could almost believe that. One day he'd be made, though, because it always came back on the numbers guy, but he was a long way down the line, and he didn't want to think about it.

His uncle Domenico was a capo, but Domenico's son, Domenico Jr., known affectionately to most as Nicky, wasn't made yet, either. Italo and Domenico's youngest brother, Salvatore, was, technically, next in line. They called him *Sale*, though they pronounced it *Sally*, which was short for *Salvatore* but translated literally to *salt* in Italian. It was an inside joke. Sale was always salty about something. He was obsessed with learning the intricacies of the family business, but no one trusted him with the information.

The Martello family owned one of the largest construction companies in Brooklyn, where they funneled most of their money before it circulated through poker tables. The closest Sale got to the secrets was answering the phones at the front desk and making copies of blueprints whenever he got fired from whatever job the family had lined up for him. He wasn't exactly a gifted kid.

Everyone had known Sale would wind up in prison one day. There was a tragic inevitability to it, but none of them had thought it would be because he'd become a drug mule for some local gang. He was an idiot. He'd stuffed kilos of cocaine into Magnum Trojans and swallowed them one by one. Someone snitched, telling the cops to "Check Salvatore's ass . . ." If Salvatore's family didn't have any faith in him, why should the Nineteenth Street Crips? That was the logic.

Salvatore was sentenced to six years at Rikers Island. He'd served only three so far.

Italo Jr. and Domenico hoped he'd shank somebody and end

up staying there for life.

Now, Jimmy and Nicky sat on the stoop outside of Jimmy's brownstone. Jimmy passed Nicky his other Moka Drink, and Nicky cracked the cap off with his teeth and sipped at it.

"Any idea why *Zio* wants us all at the house today?" Nicky asked, referring to his uncle—Jimmy's dad.

Jimmy's father had a home on Bay Ridge Parkway that was big enough for all the family to gather on Sundays. At 2:00 p.m. every Sunday, Jimmy's mother, Anna, would finish rolling the meatballs and fry them before putting them into the sauce for dinner. It was tradition. Family time. Only today was Saturday. That wasn't tradition. That was unnerving.

"Dunno, surprise party for pretty boy here," Jimmy cracked, pointing at himself with his two thumbs.

They both laughed and clinked their Mokas together before taking another sip.

"*Salute*, bro," Nicky said.

Jimmy stood up from the steps. "A'ight, bro, I'm gonna head to the barber shop, get a shape-up. But I guess I oughta shower first," he said, lifting up his arm to expose his hairy armpit.

Nicky pinched his nose. "You smelly scumbag!" he joked. "I'll see you at two."

But two was optimistic; Jimmy was running late for his

father's house, but he wanted to look as sharp as ever. He broke out his midnight blue Brioni suit and paired it with Bontoni brown leather shoes. He wore his Patek Philippe Nautilus on his wrist. It was more than a watch. It was a timepiece. The gold crucifix from his confirmation hung around his neck, along with a gold chain holding the Italian horn protecting him from the evil eye—or *Il Malocchio*, as *Nonna* had called it. His barber, Johnny, did an extra good job with his shape-up today. Jimmy felt like a million bucks, and he looked twice as good. It was rare that he got dressed up, but he always felt great when he did.

Finally, his iPhone chirped that his Uber Black was approaching.

Jimmy locked up and walked outside, fixing his diamond-studded cuff links on the way. He felt like he was auditioning to be the next James Bond. He had it in the bag.

"Hoot-hoot!" Mrs. Maita yelled from her open window next door. "Don't you look dashing, little Jimmy! If I was thirty years younger, you'd be in trouble, young man!"

Jimmy looked up at his elderly neighbor and smiled. *Thirty?* he thought, grinning. *More like fifty*. "*Grazie*, Mrs. Maita. You're looking beautiful, as always."

Mrs. Maita brushed the gray hair away from her face. "You really are a little charmer, that's for sure and certain, Mr.

Heartbreaker."

"That's me." He flashed her a grin.

The black Escalade rolled up.

Jimmy hopped inside.

It was less than ten minutes from his father's house, even in traffic, but that forty-seven-dollar Uber ride was worth every cent.

He jumped out of the SUV, pleased to see his mother, Anna, was waiting outside to greet him.

Wrapping him up in a big embrace and kissing his forehead, she said, "Happy birthday, my baby."

He slid his hand into his coat pocket and pulled out a tiny wrapped jewelry box.

"Thank you for bringing me into the world, Ma," he replied with a big smile. "This is your day as much as it is mine." Jimmy loved his mother more than anything, and every birthday, he would buy her a gift as a reminder of the day her life changed forever. That was the thing about birthdays to Jimmy: They were big for two people, not just one. Yet people tended to forget the woman who became a mother on that day all those years ago, so it felt good for him to make a fuss.

"Always my sweet boy," she said, as they walked inside the house. "Your father's in his study."

"I'll go find him."

Jimmy approached his father's study and knuckle-knocked on the heavy cherrywood door before he pushed it open a crack.

"That you, my boy?"

"Sure is, Pop!"

"Come on in," his father yelled from the other side of the study, out of view.

Italo and Jimmy were mirror images of each other, only Italo was older and grayer. He had that same Sicilian skin, though it was slightly darker. The genetic line was strong. Italo's father, Italo Sr., looked like an even older and grayer version of the pair, pruned by all of those years in the sun.

Nicky's father, Domenico, had a stronger nose and chiseled jaw that made him movie-star handsome. Nicky inherited the family nose.

His father wasn't alone in the study. Jimmy's *nonno*, *zio*, and *cugino* were all there.

Jimmy first kissed his *nonno* on each cheek, followed by his father, and then his *zio* and *cugino*.

His father walked back to Jimmy.

"Happy birthday, my boy," he said, holding Jimmy's face in both of his hands.

His smile was warm. As warm as he'd ever seen it. There was

such obvious pride in his eyes.

Italo dropped his hands and clapped them together.

"OK, we've got a little family business to attend to. Shall we?"

Jimmy half expected people to jump out from under the desk
and yell, "Surprise!" But very quickly, it was obvious that wasn't
happening. His father walked behind the desk and opened a
drawer. He pulled out a travel humidor that held Cohibas lined
up like soldiers. He turned toward his hidden liquor cabinet and
pulled at the accordion door, displaying two bottles of red wine
with the Martello family crest on the label.

The Martello family never made a business out of selling its
own wine, but it was a beloved tradition to make a few bottles
every year to keep them connected to the earth and the old
country.

During their first big trip to Sicily, back when Jimmy was
nine and Nicky barely seven, they'd stayed in *Zio* Edoardo's villa.
He'd cracked a joke that Jimmy had never forgotten: In order to
earn their keep, they had to make wine. "Rinse your feet,"
Edoardo had told them in a thick Italian accent. "And climb in
Don't be squeamish. Come on, in, in." He'd ordered them into a
giant tub full of red grapes. Jimmy and Nicky had giggled like it
was the funniest thing, but they'd climbed over the side and
dropped down into the tub, merrily stomping their feet, much

to everyone's amusement.

"That's it! That's it! You've got it!" Edoardo had said proudly.

The kids laughed as they danced around, turning their feet progressively more and more purple.

When Nicky and Jimmy had returned home to the States, Italo had a whole system setup in their backyard so they could tread their own grapes to make wine. It became a weekend tradition during their Brooklyn summers. The aim was to have enough grapes squashed by Jimmy's birthday on August 7 so that they could "earn their keep" back home too. The grapes would yield enough wine to carry them to the Feast of the Seven Fishes on Christmas Eve.

As the boys got older, the joke didn't hold up as well. Both boys ran the daily operations for Martello Construction while their fathers handled the other side of the business. So, in the end, his father gave in and started relying on technology to crush the grapes.

Still, every time he saw the Vino di Martello label, he remembered that first summer in Sicily and for just a moment forgot about the world and how they had gotten here.

"First, let's have a little vino," his father said, pouring the deep red into small glasses that he passed around the circle. "You and Nicky failed again this summer. Not a single grape ready."

His father shook his head, chuckling.

The rest of the room joined him, like it was the funniest thing.

"OK, *aspetta*. I've got a few things to say." Italo raised his glass. "Jimmy, I've waited twenty-five years to celebrate this moment. To celebrate you, my son. You know, I'm proud of your sister, Gina, but her study abroad in the Cilento Coast is making my wallet scream for mercy, so you are looking better every day."

Everyone laughed, still holding up their glasses of wine.

"You have the heart of a lion, my boy. You ask me, that's why you were born a Leo. The stars already knew. I'm not sure I ever told you this, but we named you after Saint James, because he knew how to make his way out of persecution. I want you to be that same kind of man, Jimmy. You're a noble man. And that is all a father could ever ask. But today? Today you're going to be a made man. *Salute!*"

Jimmy's eyes widened as they all took a sip of their wine.

He turned and looked over at Nicky, whose eyes were as wide as his wine-stained grin.

Everyone put their glasses down.

Jimmy cupped his hands together, nervously wondering what was happening next.

His *zio*, Domenico, lifted the leather portfolio on the desk, revealing a prayer card of Saint James.

Italo turned to his father, Italo Sr., who handed him a knife from his blazer pocket and a gun from his waist.

Jimmy instinctively held his hand out to his father.

Italo gripped Jimmy's index finger and pricked it with the knife.

He squeezed a few drops of Jimmy's blood onto the picture of Saint James.

Domenico pulled a Zippo from his back pocket, ignited the spark wheel, and used the flame to light the card of Saint James on fire.

He handed the flaming card to Italo Jr., who handed it to Italo Sr.

He passed it over to Nicky, but the heat made him recoil.

Nicky quickly threw it to Jimmy, where the flame died in his hand.

"My son," Italo said in Italian. "You live by the knife and the gun now. And that is how you will die. We all will one day. It is the family way."

Jimmy nodded. The ceremony was complete, and Jimmy was now made.

Italo picked up the box of Cohibas and handed one to each

of the men. He then passed around the guillotine cutter to clip the ends so that they could suck in the smoke as they lit them.

This was a moment the old men intended to savor.

As Jimmy held the Zippo to light his cigar, a desperate scream from Anna, out in the kitchen, shattered the moment of serenity and joy.

The men froze, each listening hard for the sound of footsteps beyond the door before hands started reaching for weapons.

The door slammed open, and bullets sprayed, ripping into Italo's desk.

Fire from an automatic weapon tore through the wall, exploding plaster in a shower that filled the room like smoke. The brutal explosion of violence had their attention.

Three men in ski masks stormed into the study.

The slaughter went in age order.

They shot Italo Sr. first, the bullet punching right through his rib cage into the lungs, piercing the tube that connected the oxygen tank to his cannula. He took a single gasp of suffocated breath even as the oxygen continued hissing, then hunched over.

Italo Jr. took a bullet in the heart.

He collapsed into Jimmy's arms.

Third man down was Domenico, snuffed out with a clean

shot between the eyes.

Three shots that were delivered so quickly, yet their landing points were strangely symbolic. Italo Sr. breathed life into the Martello family, and now he had none left. Domenico was the watchdog who lived to protect, always a watchful eye, and Italo Jr. was the heart of the family.

The heads of the Martello family had fallen, one by one.

Nicky started convulsing. He dropped to his knees, pretending to be shot, as his father flopped down and landed with his body over Nicky's. Nicky closed his eyes, playing dead. It didn't matter that there hadn't been enough shots. He wasn't thinking about anything but trying to survive.

Jimmy grabbed the gun off the desk and started shooting back. He used his father's lifeless body as a shield.

His aim was shaky in the moment.

He shot one of the men in the knee, the other in the shoulder.

Italo had taken his son to the range every Sunday morning after church since his twelfth birthday. Jimmy had never imagined he would ever need to use those lessons on life and death. He naively expected his father to live forever, and even then in the harsh reality of death, his *Zio* Domenico would take the lead. Now they're both gone. Jimmy was skilled yet sheltered. He never fathomed this disruption of his peaceful life.

Fear and adrenaline made his hands shake.

Two more bullets punched into his father's lifeless body, the killers backing out of the room. They dripped blood as they went.

Jimmy was alive. And so was Nicky.

Jimmy stood there for a few seconds longer, holding the gun in one hand and supporting his dead father's weight with the other. Time stopped—or at least his place within it. Tenderly, yet to feel the sheer weight of grief come crashing down on him, Jimmy lowered his father's body to the floor. He couldn't make sense of all the blood. Then time snapped back into place, and reality came cascading over him in a tidal wave of pain.

"Mamma!" he yelled, racing out of the study and flying down the stairs to the kitchen.

He found her sitting on the floor, sobbing against the cabinets. He couldn't see any blood. Leaning in, he kissed the top of her head.

"Stay right here, Ma." It was gentle, but it was an order too. "You don't need to see any of this."

Jimmy walked back into the study to find Nicky standing over his father's body. He looked over at both fallen Italos.

Tears filled his eyes.

They both looked at their *nonno*'s dead body, without exchanging a word.

Jimmy locked eyes with Nicky, but Jimmy couldn't cry.

It was as if the tears were gone, scorched by the fires of pain he felt smoldering deep inside.

He wasn't sure he'd ever cry again.

He looked over again at his *nonno*, gone.

His *zio*, gone.

His father, gone.

Every generation of Martello men before him, gone.

Extinct.

He took his father's hand and removed the gold ring from his index finger, then slid it onto his own. It was symbolic, a transfer of power, a coming into his birthright, a real making of the man.

He kissed his father's forehead and whispered into his ear: "I've got it from here, Papa. I promise."

#

Salvatore tapped at the bars of his prison cell nervously. He was not slowly going out of his mind. He let out a primal yell and pushed away from the bars. He couldn't take being caged.

He paced the concrete floor.

To his brothers, he was Sale, mocked for being the salty baby of the family, the butt of jokes and the constant sighs, frowns, and disappointments of a child who couldn't get it together.

To the inmates of Rikers Island, he was someone else entirely. He was *SB* (short for *Salvatore Boss*), one of the only Italian guys to make good with all of the diverse populations and affiliations inside.

It had been easier than he had expected.

A surprising number of people wanted to know him.

He had his nickname initials *SB* tattooed on each corresponding ring finger by Julio, the prison tattoo artist. The day he had them done, Julio burned the end of a paper clip and dipped it in ink, carefully dotting the letters into Salvatore's olive skin while he sat there motionless and equally emotionless.

Unbeknownst to his own family, Salvatore had begun taking courses in prison. It had been his lawyer's suggestion. For every course he passed, he'd get three months taken off his sentence. Salvatore was crazy, but he wasn't dumb. He'd spent six months straight breezing through classes until he'd accumulated thirty-six months, making his parole date in two weeks. Not a single soul knew this but Sale and his attorney.

By his own logic, he figured if he could knock down his father, brothers, and nephews, the other members of the crime family would *have* to make him a made man. It was just a numbers game. And SB had game. He'd made promises to the gangs in Rikers, brokered deals and truces, and opened lines of business. If you weren't a criminal when you went in, you sure as hell were one when you came out. His proposition was elegant in its simplicity; as soon as he was made, he'd bring localized drug dealing into the family business, and under the Martello umbrella, everyone would win.

"You see, it's simple," he'd told Randy, a Blood from Los Angeles who'd wound up in Rikers after a double homicide while visiting Yonkers. "I just line them up." SB carefully placed dominoes one right next to each other. "You know what happens then? Then I knock 'em down." He'd smiled as he carefully flicked one domino onto the next and watched as one by one, the rest toppled over. "We'll rebuild this bitch how we want it. Our image; the only limits, our imaginations."

Randy had nodded in agreement. "You think ya family's gonna agree to this new . . . business plan, SB?" he'd asked.

"They won't have a say in the matter, trust me, my friend. I'm cutting their tongues out. Silence is fuckin' diamond, forget golden. Trust me on this."

Salvatore had continued to line up and knock down the dominoes, like he couldn't stop himself. Over and over all morning, compulsively, and into the afternoon, the sound of tumbling dominoes haunted the cellblock.

He figured everyone would be at Italo's for cake and coffee, given it was Jimmy's birthday. That was the thing about the family. They were predictable, which was unhealthy in their line of work. It would be easy to hit them all at once.

So, why hadn't he heard a peep from the guy he'd paid off to handle it?

Three years ago, when the cops had taken him in, they'd shoved laxatives into his mouth and suppositories up his ass to force out the cocaine he was smuggling.

SB had done his damnedest to resist the shits but managed to unload two feces-covered condoms full of cocaine. "That's all I got." The lie was easy, but the longer it took to get out of there, the more chance the laxatives would do their thing, and he'd be shit out of luck, literally.

Later that night, in the darkness of his cell, the gut cramps hit properly, and there was no holding back as it flowed out of him like a geyser.

Two more condoms full of coke splashed down.

He'd fished around in the bowl, wiped them down, washing

his hands, and hid them under his pillow.

They were better than gold dust in this place.

He'd held on to them, knowing there'd come a time when he'd need what they could buy—a Trinitario in the prison, Lito, and the order to have his entire family whacked. Three years of holding, of hiding, of biding his time.

But Lito was taking forever.

He was in the visitor's section meeting the outside messenger, and SB was in here, practically chewing at the walls in his impatience. The last thing he wanted to do was jeopardize his early release, but there were so many times he could dream of their faces—his father, his brothers, and their bastard sons, ruined.

The plan was good. He had the best kind of alibi. No one would put it on him while he was still behind bars.

At long last, SB saw Lito come strutting down the hall. He was flanked by two prison guards. As he approached, Lito looked over at Salvatore, opened his mouth to say something, then stopped himself short.

"Did the cakes get baked?" SB asked, desperate for confirmation it was done.

"Hey! Quiet, Martello!" one of the guards barked.

Lito lowered his head slightly and shook it. "Some didn't

make it into the oven," he whispered.

#

An hour had passed.

For Jimmy and Nicky, it felt like an eternity.

Jimmy sat on the living room sofa, trying not to think about the fact that the patriarchs of his family lay dead in the study above his head.

His clouded brain was attempting to think.

"How do we handle this?" Nicky asked.

"Dignity first," Jimmy said, not thinking beyond the immediate moments ahead of them. "They deserve that. No body bags. Ma . . ." He turned to his mother. "Who's that EMT that we know? Maybe we can pay him off, get him to put oxygen masks over them, make it look like they are fighting for their lives while we go looking for their killers."

Nicky shook his head doubtfully. "You think that'd work? I mean . . . gunshots. Someone's going to get the cops involved."

Jimmy fired a look at Nicky. "We're going to have to make sure that doesn't happen, cuz. Because they'll be looking for the killers, and we don't want them getting in the way. This is family business. We find them and kill them ourselves."

Nicky looked down at the ground and nodded. He understood.

It was taken out of their hands, though.

Police sirens filled the air, rising as they shrieked closer until they were deafening. The cars pulled right into the driveway. One of the neighbors must have called the police, despite that long-standing agreement of see nothing, hear nothing, say nothing that had been fostered by Italo Jr., bought and paid for with money, zeppole, and wine every holiday season. There were new neighbors down the block. They'd moved onto the street in July, meaning the Martellos hadn't delivered their welcome basket yet.

The first police officer came in through the smashed kitchen door.

As soon as Jimmy saw who it was, he rolled his eyes.

"Well, now, if it isn't Rico Suave," the officer said, offering a crooked smile and tombstone teeth. Detective Phil Mulligan had had it out for Jimmy since Jimmy turned sixteen. It wasn't exactly a friendly rivalry; it was an obsession.

The NYPD had a whole task force carved out for the Mafia, and since most of them were scared of the higher-ups, they took to picking at the low-hanging fruit, like Jimmy.

It wasn't the first time they'd called him *Rico Suave* to his face. The *Rico* part was a direct reference to the Racketeer Influenced and Corrupt Organizations Act (RICO, for short), which was the only way the task force could hope to take down the Mafia once and for all. If they could prove that these businesses (including the Martellos' construction company) were nothing more than fronts for Mafia activity, they could dismantle the crime family root and branch.

That was the plan.

So far, it had proved impossible to hit the Martellos because Jimmy kept the books clean. Not just clean, pristine. He'd been too clever for them. The cops knew he handled the finances and insisted on calling him *Rico* to remind him his day was coming: the one fine day they'd nail him and his family.

It was pathetic, and right now, a gloating Mulligan was the last cop he wanted to see.

"Don't you have some rapper to wrongfully accuse? Or maybe some innocent dude crossing the street who's in need of a beatdown that you'll just deny ever happened? Why the fuck are you even here? We're mourning," Jimmy said with a snarl.

"Mourning? What the fuck's that supposed to mean?"

"Dumb fuck."

Four officers crowded into the house behind him. They were all holding, their weapons aimed right at Jimmy. But Mulligan read the look on Jimmy's face and understood. He lowered his gun and told the others to do the same. The last thing anyone wanted was for this to spiral out of control. That was almost enough to make Jimmy laugh, like it could be less controlled than it already was.

"Want to tell me what's going on, Jimmy?" The use of his given name wasn't lost on him, either. "Your door's busted up, and we've had reports of gunfire."

There wasn't much point denying it, unless they wanted to give a bunch of bent cops the opportunity to pin the murders on them if they didn't cooperate.

"I'll show you," Nicky said, reading him right.

Two of the cops walked past Jimmy, nodding at Anna, who was sitting stone-faced at the kitchen table as they headed for the stairs.

Two stayed, keeping an eye on things.

Jimmy knew what they'd find—the carnage first, but then the smaller stuff, the chunks of cherrywood missing from the doorframe, the blood from the man he'd shot.

Mulligan walked out of the doorway as one of his men came back down to report. "I'm calling in the coroner," Mulligan said to Jimmy. "Getting a forensics team in here, and you're going to tell me everything. You understand, Jimmy? Every fucking thing."

"That's not going to happen," Jimmy replied, reaching for his pocket, trying to think what his father would have done. His mind was all over the place. He might have been a lot of things, but his father he was not.

"Kid, let me save you the embarrassment. You're either about to shoot me or try and pay me off. Believe me when I tell you neither is going to work," Mulligan said. He didn't sound angry or even surprised, like he'd expect this from them because they were less than human in how they valued life. Everything had a dollar and cents value, even an old man gunned down while still attached to his oxygen tank.

Jimmy had no idea what to do, so he pushed his wallet back into his pants.

"Good man. Now, my condolences to you both," Mulligan said to Jimmy and Nicky as he turned to leave the room. "And to you especially, Mrs. Martello. I'll be back to ask some questions soon, while things are fresh in your minds. Right now, just try and remember everything you can, every detail, no matter how small it might feel. There's nothing insignificant in cases like this."

And just like that his family, *the* ultimate crime family, was reduced to a case.

Jimmy didn't want to have his Brioni suit dry-cleaned.

He wasn't going to get rid of it, either.

The blood of his father was on that suit, and as morbid as he realized that was, he couldn't part with that bit of his father. The blood had dried and was held within the fibers of the midnight blue material. It would be there forever.

He held the arm of the suit jacket hanging in his closet, inspecting the stains. He ran his fingers across them, but there was no magic in the blood. No connection that suddenly flared to life between the old man and his heir.

They'd held the bodies of Italo Sr., Italo Jr., and Domenico for two weeks while their family back in the old country sorted their visas for the funeral.

Word traveled fast through the underworld. By the morning after the triple murder, all the crime families knew that the main Martello men were gone, and in turn, that Jimmy was made.

The funeral would be Jimmy's first outing as a made man, a reintroduction to the others who shared a lifelong bond with him now. It wasn't just that he was made; tragedy meant he was the newly crowned don of the Martello Family. There would be those who didn't respect that and would look to gain an advantage. That was just the nature of this world of predators and prey.

Jimmy pulled his black Canali suit from his closet.

He still wore the Bontoni shoes, conscious of the fleck of his father's blood on one tip. He hadn't taken off his father's ring since putting it on, despite the fact there was blood on the metal as well.

His mother walked into the room and watched him from the mirror, pride and pain in her eyes.

Anna had stayed in Jimmy's brownstone with him since the murders.

Jimmy wasn't prepared to let her sleep at home, not yet. It wasn't so much fear of the gunmen returning as it was fear of the ghosts trapped within those four walls. Thankfully, his sister, Gina, had been granted permission to finish her summer semester remotely back home in the States, and she'd return to NYU in the fall.

"You look just like him when you're getting ready," his mother said. She fluffed her light-brown hair and smoothed her black dress over her petite frame.

Jimmy looked at his mother through the mirror and smiled. "We'll do him proud today. Promise."

They went down to the street as the limo pulled up to the brownstone. Nicky and his mother, Rosaria, were seated on one side. Anna and Jimmy got in, taking up places on the other side. The plan was for Rosaria and Anna to move into Anna's home after the funeral. Nicky and Jimmy intended to sell Rosaria's home and use the money to keep their mothers comfortable while they figured out the business. Gina would eventually move into the dorms at NYU with their cousin, Nicky's sister, Evelina, but they would both stay at home when school wasn't in session. Jimmy had twenty-four-hour security in place for when his mother and *zia* moved back into the house. But it still felt like it wasn't enough. That he could be somehow doing *more*.

As the limo approached Saint Andrew the Apostle church, Jimmy saw a sea of men in suits standing in the street outside. Some faces he recognized; others, he didn't. There was a huge amount of them, so many that the sea of faces all became weirdly featureless.

Once the limo came to a stop, his father's consigliere, Vincenzo Amato, opened the car door. Everyone called Vincenzo "Enzo," and the Amato family was a direct line of the Bonannos, meaning in essence that Enzo was like a brother to Italo and Domenico.

Jimmy even called him *Zio*.

A month earlier, Italo had told Enzo his plan for Jimmy to be made.

"He's a little wet behind the ears, Italo," Enzo had cautioned.

"Weren't we all at one time, Enzo? My boy's got heart," Italo had replied. "He'll take action when he needs to. I have faith. And let's face it, my father won't be around much longer the way his lungs are deteriorating. Dom and I are slowing down. Now is the right time. He needs to learn the family business while we're still here to help him figure it out."

Time wasn't on their side.

Enzo and his brother, Luca, were supposed to be at the house for the induction ceremony. Had it not been the day of Luca's granddaughter's christening, he would have been. It was only Italo's insistence that Jimmy be made on his twenty-fifth birthday, not on any other day, that saved them from being wiped out along with the rest.

Enzo grabbed Jimmy by the shoulders and embraced him hard.

The summer sun reflected off his silver hair. He looked at Jimmy with both sympathy and love. "Listen to me, kid. I'm here for you, whenever, whatever. We are blood," Enzo said, looking Jimmy right in the eyes. "But we don't have time to feel sorry for ourselves or nurse our pains. We have work to do, capisce? Monday morning, nine a.m., meet me at Zambetti's. Enter through the back entrance." He kissed both of Jimmy's cheeks. "Welcome to your new life."

Jimmy nodded.

All three coffins stood side by side.

The family had chosen porcelain white boxes with gold etchings, each bearing a large crucifix and their respective initials. The church was full of flowers from every family across the city, plus everyone who knew, loved, or paid homage to the Martellos.

As Jimmy reached the church doorway, he saw Giuseppi from the corner store in the last row, kneeling against the pew with tears in his eyes.

Gina had wanted to get ready with Evelina, so they arrived in a different limousine.

They both emerged and hugged their brothers.

Zio Edoardo had arrived from Sicily, along with his daughters, Ginetta and Laura. They were in the limo with Gina and Evelina.

The whole family assembled at the front of the church, as the priest—Father Geno—walked in, releasing incense from the gold urn as he proceeded slowly down the aisle.

He reached the front as Jimmy and his family were seated.

"It is a morning for sorrow and for joy, though it is hard to see now, through the tears," Father Geno said. "Today, we gather, as the Lord has called home three noble and God-fearing men. Good men. Family men. Men with love in their hearts. Love for the people around them, love for the streets they were brought up on, and those they now made their homes. In all of this, they never forgot whom they were or where they came from. Today, we may mourn them, but we know our Lord has a bigger plan in mind. That, we must believe."

The strong odor of the incense transported Jimmy to his *nonna*'s funeral years back, when he had sat in that same pew and ached beyond words with the sheer immensity of her loss. Jimmy remembered how he'd wondered if he could ever endure that much pain and sadness again, and now here he was, enduring. But the pain he felt now was different. This pain was underpinned by a foundation of rage. Jimmy had no intention of grieving.

He wanted vengeance.

Father Geno was deep in recitation of the Nicene Creed when the church's huge timber doors slowly opened.

The creaking sound echoed around the walls and under the vaulted cathedral ceiling as the doors opened wider, filling the church with light.

Jimmy turned around.

A man's silhouette stood dramatically posed against the sunlight.

The newcomer didn't move until everyone was looking his way. Then he walked forward, stepping into the light.

Salvatore pulled the handkerchief from his cheap suit pocket and instinctively started dabbing his green eyes. His eyes had always possessed a crazy look to them, so much so he seemed demonic at times, especially now, when he was faking grief.

"*Famiglia!*" he wailed, walking down the aisle and dabbing his eyes some more. "*Famiglia!*"

Nicky looked over at Jimmy, who in turn looked over at Enzo, looking to the old man to take his cue. Enzo shook his head at Jimmy, acknowledging the fact that he had no idea of Salvatore's prison release and was every bit as surprised as they were.

#

Salvatore loved the idea of leaving everyone speechless.

All the better to surprise the family, and he really wanted to savor that surprise more than anything. The thought of those whispers and rustles of shock passing among them, all crowded in there to pay their respects to the dead, made his ego dance the tarantella.

When he'd returned home from prison, he'd made his way to the doors of the only crime boss who hated his kin more than he did: Angelo Massino.

Salvatore tried to play dumb with Angelo, acting as if he didn't know that his father and brothers had died or that his nephews made it out alive, with little Jimmy taking his place in being made. He'd stood in Angelo's living room, forcing tears he didn't want to shed and choking out an unconvincing, "No! It . . . it can't be!"

Angelo read him like a book, "Listen, Sale. That grief is bullshit, I've seen more convincing tears from a crocodile. So shut the fuck up, trying to lie to me. I ain't your fool. If I am going to entertain your *pazzo* head, then you have to be completely honest with me. Now, be straight, or get the fuck out of here."

Salvatore stopped crying and looked Angelo dead in the eye. "Fine," he hissed. "You got me. I've got a proposition for you."

"Speak your words."

"Business with your hookers is drying up, has been ever since the city put all those laws into place for legitimizing a lot of aspects of sex work, or whatever they're calling it these days." He made aggressive air quotes as he talked. "I know that your family needs more money, and I know how to get it." He'd had good inside information on this only recently. Prison life had been kind to Sale.

Angelo nodded. "Keep going."

Salvatore rubbed his hands together. "OK, so I have an in now with the Bloods over in Canarsie, where we can get pure heroin. I'm talking the rawest you've ever seen. Plus, I've got the options on crystal meth and coke, even oxy, if that's what floats your boat. We hide the merch in your salt bins for your salt trucks; only thing is, we don't use them to salt the roads in the winter, ya get me?" He let out a throaty laugh, but Angelo wasn't amused.

"And how did all of that fall into your lap?" he probed.

Sale shrugged. "Like I said, I've got connects, good ones too. I'm a good man to do business with." And that was the most honest thing he'd said in a while. He'd been surprised by just how keen people were to do business with him, but Sale wasn't going to tell anyone else that. He wanted the world to think that his change of fortune came down to his personal qualities, not so much to fool them as to fool himself. He desperately wanted to believe that was true, so much so he never questioned the opportunities that came his way. He kept talking.

"OK, OK. So, we go sell the good stuff over here in

Manhattan and Los Angeles. Then we go down to Florida, and we sell the stuff we couldn't move here, plus we move the crystal meth and oxy down there, to all those rednecks and swamp-dwellers. Hell, the South Beach kids in Miami will eat it up too. Well, snort it up, smoke it up, shoot it up. Whatever fuck they do with that shit, and we'll be the supplier making all their dreams come true. Cut the shit with fentanyl to stretch it out, and as a bonus, get the rep for bringing the ultimate high. Whaddya say? Show me the money, right?"

Angelo waved his hand at him. "*Aspetta*," he said. "We don't bring drugs into this thing of ours unless it's high-end trafficking. The streets are an ecology, see. Everything living in careful balance, like nature. They let us keep our women and our casinos; we don't mess with their drugs. We feed off each other, symbiosis."

Salvatore doubled down. "Nah, Angelo, see, that's where you're wrong. It's not symbiosis; it's parasitical. But all that's about to change. We never had an *inside guy*." He jammed his thumb into his chest. Everything had lined up to make this possible for him.

Angelo raised his hand again. "*Aspetta, aspetta*. Who is *we*? Last I checked, nobody *made* you a *we*."

Salvatore felt the bruise to his ego like the slug to his gut from one of the inmates on the night he'd gone went into prison.

He took a deep breath. "Just because my own flesh and blood never took me seriously doesn't mean a thing. I've got friends, believe me. Tight friends, closer than blood. So, let me prove myself. I can make this happen for the Massino family. I won't stamp your name on it until you see it's a success."

Angelo slowly nodded. "And what's in it for you?"

Salvatore smiled and opened his hands. "Me? Easy. You make me a made man," he replied.

"Fine. You've got a deal," Angelo said skeptically. "If you bring us the kind of business we need to bounce back, I will do what I can to have you made. You have my word, Sale."

Salvatore nodded. "Good. Good. I trust you, Angelo. I know you're good for every promise out of your lips. But, one thing . . . it's only a little one, but I would greatly appreciate it if you'd stop using that word. Call me *Salvatore*, or *Martello*, or even better, *SB*. The *B* is for *boss*."

"The name makes the man," the mafioso agreed.

#

Salvatore continued marching down the church aisle, still wiping his eyes. He was a terrible actor, right down there with the B-movie characters. He saw Angelo raise his eyes upward and smirk, head still down in prayer. Angelo didn't think Sale could do much for him, but he'd enjoy watching the upstart making a mess of what was left of the Martello family.

Salvatore slid into the row of pews where Nicky prayed and sat beside him and Rosaria. She shifted uncomfortably. As the priest moved through the ceremony, Salvatore made sure everyone knew he was grieving, with his exaggerated sniffles, snots, and constantly dabbing at his eyes, cutting through the silence of the congregation and looking around to make sure everyone saw him.

#

Jimmy made eye contact with his uncle. A teary-eyed Salvatore kissed his fingers and waved his hand.

Jimmy faked a smile and nodded. Theatrics aside, Jimmy found it incredibly difficult to gauge the sincerity of Sale's grief. He knew that two of the bodies in the boxes—Italo Jr. and Domenico—had believed he was a lost cause, but they loved him because he was blood and would always be their baby brother. Blood counted for a lot. There was no getting away from the truth of that. Sale had lost his whole family. Salvatore let out another piercing wail, buried his head into his hands, and leaned forward, his forehead against the back of the pew in front of him.

While Sale's head was down, he artfully teased his phone out of his inner pocket and texted Angelo: *Jimmy needs knocking down a peg or two. Or over. Immediately. One less problem.*

#

The repast was held at Gennaro's catering hall. Even more people showed up wanting to pay their respects and eat one last meal in the elder Martellos' honor. Jimmy and Nicky stood at the entrance, taking a moment to greet everyone in the place of their mothers. It was ritualistic theater. It was the family saying the old ways are preserved, the old ways live on, flesh is flesh, blood is blood.

Nicky leaned over to Jimmy. "You think we got enough penne for all these assholes?"

"They can have my plate," Jimmy responded flatly as yet another nobody came to press the flesh. "This whole charade is all making me sick to my stomach."

Salvatore walked in, shoulders back, head up, looking as if he'd never been away. "*Nipoti,*" he called to his nephews.

"*Mi dispiace*."

Jimmy and Nicky both nodded in unison. "*Grazie, Zio. Grazie*."

Salvatore leaned close to Jimmy and whispered, "Maybe now is not the time. I'd hate for you to think it inappropriate, nephew, but congratulations on your new status, young Jimmy. Well earned, kid." Jimmy nodded, as Salvatore continued. "Listen, it goes without saying, but sometimes you need to say it anyway: You have a father in me."

Jimmy squinted as Salvatore put a hand on each of Jimmy's shoulders.

Jimmy looked down and noticed the *S* tattoo on one finger and the *B* on another. Prison ink. Crude. Ugly. Infected at one point.

He couldn't help but wonder why Sale would want to mar his flesh like that.

"My promise to you, Jimmy. I'm here to help you be the best Martello man you can be," Salvatore said. "Capisce?"

It took everything in Jimmy not to punch his uncle right in the throat in that moment. He felt nothing but repulsion for the man. He was slime.

"Thank you, *Zio* Sale," he said instead, swallowing the revulsion down, and walked away before Salvatore could correct him on his name.

Jimmy headed over to Enzo's table. "Nine a.m. Monday, right?" Jimmy asked.

"Nine a.m.," Enzo confirmed.

#

Jimmy walked over to the rear parking lot of Zambetti's, looking for the dented screen door that encased a solid metal one.

He opened the screen door, the hinges crying out for mercy.

He barely knocked on the metal door, and it swung open.

A big man in a beanie cap sat on a barstool, devouring a breakfast bagel with the appetite of locusts.

He looked up at Jimmy, hopped off the stool, and went to pat him down.

"No need. Enzo's expecting me. Family business."

The man carefully placed his bagel back in the tinfoil and rested it on the stool. Without saying a word, he opened the cellar door and pointed downstairs. Jimmy walked down the creaky steps.

At the bottom, Enzo sat at a small table. He wore an immaculately tailored suit and sipped espresso.

"What the hell are you wearing, sunshine?" he barked at Jimmy.

Jimmy looked down at his gray sweatpants, black wifebeater, and red Jordan sneakers with a matching red Yankees cap. "You didn't say we were suiting up, *Zio*."

Enzo put his espresso down and placed his hands together, as if he were about to lead a prayer. "Kid, listen. All you little Brooklyn shits, you walk around this neighborhood, and you think you're the gods of hip-hop or some shit, with your sweatpants hanging off your asses and the elastic of your boxer briefs showing. You look like *cazzoni*. Meanwhile, you're so preoccupied with trying to be a rapper, you never stop to think that they're so desperate to be us, Jimmy. They want to be *you*. Why do you think they call themselves the Gottis and the Gambinos? They're playing at being tough guys. But their crime isn't organized like ours. You're a made man, now. You need to act like it, and I shouldn't need to say this: Dress like it. Clothes make the man."

Jimmy took off his hat and sat down.

"There," Enzo said. "That's a start at least."

A waiter came downstairs and brought Jimmy a Moka Drink.

"Your father always joked that this was your favorite," Enzo said.

Jimmy smiled. "Thank you, *Zio*." He went to bite off the cap as usual.

"*Che cazzo fai?*" Enzo yelled, handing him a bottle opener. "Kid, we gotta work on you."

Jimmy laughed and poured the drink like a gentleman into the glass that was provided. "So, you knew nothing about my uncle getting out of prison too, right?"

Enzo shook his head. "We all assumed Sale had a trick up his sleeve, but nothing like this, where he'd just unexpectedly pop out. Your father was always ready, though. He had plans in place to make sure Sale couldn't touch the business. That's one of the reasons he hurried up to have you made, so Sale couldn't try to jump in line at any point. Sale is so ignorant, he doesn't realize that's not how it works, but now that he's out, he's going to try and pull every stunt imaginable to get into this thing of ours. That ain't happening, no way, nohow, capisce?"

Jimmy nodded.

"First things first: Get him off the paperwork for Martello Construction."

Jimmy was confused. "How will I do that?"

Enzo pulled out a power of attorney, signed by his father and dated ages ago. "Your father had already made this power of attorney when Sale went to prison, giving you all of the rights to the business, just in case something was to occur. Now, sign this." It was a transfer of business, removing Salvatore indefinitely from the roster of the company, already notarized by their attorney.

"We've gotta tie his hands now, because who knows what that little shit is capable of with any power in the family's business," Enzo said. "I've alerted the families, because word has it that your uncle is deep into the drug cartels now, and that's not our route. We do a lot of things, but there's no honor in a business that leaves kids dead in ghettos, needles in their skin." It was old-school thinking, of course, and at least one family had begun to diversify. "There's only one who might welcome him into the fold, the Massinos. They're into some ugly business— you know, like trafficking hookers and pumping them with drugs—but that is a problem for another day. Today, we have one single piece of business on the books: to find out who killed your family."

A solid plan for avenging their deaths hadn't even crossed Jimmy's mind yet.

He immediately felt like less of a made man admitting that, even to himself, but the truth was, he had been so preoccupied over the last few weeks with trying to figure out business and planning the funeral, taking care of his mother and his aunt, that he hadn't wanted to indulge in any detailed revenge fantasies.

The waves of grief and anger reminded him, though, constantly.

"How will we get started?" Jimmy asked.

Enzo already had something in place. "You said you shot two of 'em, right?"

Jimmy nodded. "Yeah. One of them grabbed the wall with his bloody hand. The other one, I shot in the kneecap. He knelt on the marble floor with the bloody knee. So, two of them left plenty at the scene. The third guy, I dunno, maybe he touched nothing. We closed the door to the study and haven't opened it since. I assume we're getting Mulligan and the cops involved?"

Enzo laughed. "Only *our* cops. First thing we do is take those blood samples for DNA matches. If they're in the databases, we find them that way, and when we do, we'll do what we gotta to get answers out of them. You've got a piece, right?"

Jimmy nodded. "Yeah, it's at home."

Enzo shook his head. "What the fuck is it doing there, kid? Starting now, you carry it at all times. Even on the toilet, capisce? All times. Nothing more humiliating than getting capped on the crapper." He slid a license to carry across the table that read *James Joseph Martello* on it. "Keep the gun in your pants. There's enough room in there for three of them. While we're on the subject, here." He handed Jimmy a business card for a custom tailor named

Davide Santi. "Go to Davide, and get yourself a nice suit. Make it two, quality cut. Put them on my tab." He picked up Jimmy's hat and put it on sideways.

Jimmy started laughing.

"Starting today, MC Jimmy is done," Enzo said, folding his arms. "Word."

#

"Who the hell am I lookin' at right now?" Nicky yelled and slapped his knee as Jimmy walked up the short walk to Nicky's brownstone stoop, just a block away from his.

Jimmy was in a sharply tailored Armani suit.

His hair was still lined up straight on the sides, but he'd asked Johnny to keep the top longer, intending to start slicking it back.

Standing next to his cousin, who was dressed in basketball shorts and a hooded sweatshirt, their two-year age difference looked more like twenty.

"Listen, Nicky, we've gotta walk the walk. This business is ours now."

Nicky nodded in agreement. "I think I'm going to take some of my papa's suits and have them tailored for me."

Jimmy hadn't even thought of that. He nodded, even if there was something uncomfortable about wearing a dead man's clothes. "Good idea, *cugino*. I should do the same. Enzo fronted this one." He smoothed out the arms. "What do you think?"

Nicky chuckled. "You look like you own a used car lot in Queens."

Jimmy punched his cousin in the arm, and they both started laughing.

Enzo told Jimmy to head up to Arthur Avenue in the Bronx to meet with him a week later, to the minute, at the restaurant Dominic's. Pulling up, he saw Enzo outside with another man in an immaculately tailored suit, holding a manila envelope.

"There he is, the boy wonder, lookin' *sharp*!" Enzo shouted in his thick Brooklyn accent. "Louie Graziano, I want you to meet a friend of *ours*. This is Jimmy Martello, Italo's son."

Louie kissed both of Jimmy's cheeks. "My condolences to your family," Louie said solemnly. "We sent an arrangement to the funeral home. Sadly, we could not make the church as we were away when the news came. Tragic. Just tragic. Always had time for Italo. He was an honorable man."

Jimmy understood. "*Grazie*," Jimmy said.

"Shall we?" Enzo asked, showing everyone to the door.

Louie walked in; Jimmy followed with Enzo at his side. "You

might have noticed the introduction, a friend of *ours*?" Enzo asked.

"Yeah," Jimmy replied.

"That's because Louie's family is part of the Gambino crime family. When you're with a made man and another made man approaches, you introduce them as a friend of *ours*. If they're not made and you're with them, you introduce them as a friend of *yours*. So, you say, 'This is a friend of *mine*.' Capisce? This is important stuff to know. It's in the details. Always in the details. The little things."

Jimmy took note in his head. "I got it, *Zio*."

They approached the back of Dominic's, where a table was set with plates full of calamari, chicken cutlets, and gnocchi. Louie and Enzo sat down and tucked their cloth napkins into their shirt collars.

Jimmy sat down and did the same.

By the time they'd cleared half of the food from their plates and the waiters stopped serving, Enzo turned to Louie. "OK, Lou, what've we got?"

Louie cleaned his fingers off on the napkin under his chin. "The names you need are Raheim Perdomo and Franklin Casper. They're blood matches for the samples," Louie said, still chewing. "Which means the third guy is most likely Hector Castro. His uncle is the main guy of the Trinitario gang, Carlito

Fermin. They call him Lito. He's serving ten years at Rikers."

"Addresses? Should we want to go pay a visit?"

"Here." He pushed a folded piece of paper across the red and white checkered tablecloth. "These three, they live together in Castle Hill like animals. *Disgrazia!*" Louie ripped off his napkin and threw it on the table, as if he just realized he'd identified his goombahs' murderers.

Jimmy felt himself go very cold but very calm.

Enzo looked up and, with a flick of the wrist, beckoned to three more men. They were burly, dressed in the same uniform of turtlenecks with leather coats. The large neck on one of the men looked ripe to explode. "Louie, Jimmy, these are some friends of *mine*. This is Tommy, Stuey, and Gerald. They're coming with us to Castle Hill."

Jimmy's eyes widened. "What, *now*?"

"Yeah, *now*! No time to waste. We know who and where. It's only a matter of time before they get scared, so we move on them now. Why did you think we met in the Bronx? Guys, have some food while we splash some water on Jimmy's face and sort out fishing his balls from his belly. You got your piece on you, Jimmy?"

Jimmy patted his waist at the belt buckle. "I do."

Enzo smiled.

"OK, then. *Andiamo!*"

A little while later, the six men stood outside one of the largest of the Castle Hill housing projects buildings. They stood back, ten feet from the entrance, knowing that they were close enough to reach out and touch the Martellos' killers. They intended to do more than touch.

A kid dribbling a basketball approached the door.

Enzo inched near him, cracking a smile. "Hey, kid, that's a good dribble you got on you."

The little boy, no more than seven or eight, frowned. "Fuck you, stranger danger."

Enzo waved a hundred-dollar bill at the kid. "Ain't no danger here, sunshine. Look at Benjamin Franklin here, he look like a stranger to you too?"

The kid's eyes widened.

"You can have this, kid. You wanna earn it?"

The boy's brow furrowed, suspicion dark in his eyes.

"Nothing like that," Enzo promised. "All you gotta do is hold the door for us when your mom buzzes you in. Can you do that?"

The kid's mind raced through the gamut of mental calculations that always ended at one hundred bucks in his pocket, no matter how he counted things, and nodded eagerly. He dialed his unit code. As the loud buzzer rang throughout the housing development, he stepped back, holding the door for Enzo and the rest of the men with one hand while he held his other out expectantly, grinning like he'd just done a hard day's work.

Enzo handed him the hundred-dollar bill, then topped it off with a second bill. "And here's fifty more, kid," Enzo said. "Never talk to strangers again."

It took two elevator trips for all of them to reach the seventh floor, with Tommy, Stuey, and Gerald too big to fit in with the others, even if they were supposedly within the weight allowance. Better safe than getting stuck between floors when they should have been breaking some faces.

They walked up to apartment 7C, guns in hand, utterly silent.

Tommy backed up like he was about to pull a slingshot and flung himself at the door, knocking it right over.

Inside, Raheim, Franklin, and Hector were hunched over an Xbox, playing *Call of Duty* badly. Their digitized war zone was so loud that the gigantic crash and thud of the door falling over was half masked by the gunshots, grenades, and RPGs going off on the screen.

Tommy marched over, grabbed Raheim under the arms, and hauled him up, lifting the guy over his head. Stuey did the same with Franklin, and Gerald with Hector. It took all of two seconds.

"Man, what the fuck?" one of them yelled.

Enzo turned to Jimmy and said, "Consider it my offering. Take your pick: Which one you wanna torture? Make it count."

Jimmy looked at them. Raheim was the tallest. That made him the one who'd killed his father. "That one," he said, pointing at Raheim as he flailed and kicked and struggled, trying to wriggle free from Tommy's grasp.

Enzo nodded and pointed at Franklin to claim him, leaving Hector for Louie.

The three burly men muzzled the killers with their elbows to their necks.

Jimmy broke out his gun, walked up to Raheim, and pistol-whipped him across the face. He felt nothing, only deadly calm. "Hope it was worth it, whatever they paid you to kill my father." He backhanded the pistol grip across Raheim's nose, rupturing cartilage. "Who paid for the hit? Whose money bought it?" Inside his skull he was yelling, but the words that came out of Jimmy's mouth were icy cold and calm. He beat into Raheim's skull with the handle of the Smith & Wesson.

Louie drove punch after brutal punch into Hector's face. He wore an engraved pair of brass knuckles. The first punch fractured his nose. The rest only made the mess worse. "You gonna give us some names, *Disgrazia*?" Louie said, mirroring

Jimmy's calm. The juxtaposition of explosive violence being so well dressed was dizzying. The punches he hammered into Hector's ruined face sounded like meat being slapped by a tenderizer.

Enzo was different. He drove only a single punch into Franklin, hard enough, right between the eyes, that they started roll up into his skull.

He pulled out a switchblade, stepped in close, and stuck it into Franklin's mouth. "I paid one hundred fifty dollars to get into your apartment. You believe that? A Grant and a Ben Franklin. Now, I'm getting a buck fifty back in flesh." He inched the blade at the corner of Franklin's mouth and started dragging it.

Franklin shrieked in pain.

"*No más!*" Hector yelled. "We'll talk."

"You assume we want to listen, and don't just want to gut you like fish and leave you flapping about on the hardwood 'til you run out of breath."

"Please . . ."

Enzo gave the signal. The two other men stopped their beatdowns, but the musclemen didn't relinquish their choke holds.

"Who was it?" Jimmy said, his voice so quiet, it was terrifying. Tears were finally forming in his eyes, but none of his family's killers could see through their own blood.

"*Mi tio*, Lito, told us to do it. Word came from prison," Hector said, coughing and choking on his own blood. "He said if we got everyone, we could be Trinitarios. That was the payment. But when *you* started shooting . . ." He shook his head, pointed at Jimmy, and lifted the bottom of his basketball shorts, exposing a bandage on his knee. "We were done. We didn't want none of it. It wasn't for *Tio* Lito; he didn't order the hit. It was one of your own. And he told us nobody was meant to walk away from that room. No one."

"Who?"

"They call him *SB*."

Enzo turned toward Jimmy.

"Sale," Jimmy rasped. "He's got those letters tattooed on his hand. Prison tat. I saw them at the funeral. Motherfucker killed his own family, then pretended to grieve."

He felt sick to his stomach.

#

Jimmy pivoted back and forth in his office chair. He didn't always sit at the crown of Martello Construction's headquarters. Even though his father and grandfather hardly entered the building, their corporate thrones were fixed in one giant corner office. Nicky had his own tiny office to the side, and so did Jimmy. Yet now, here he was at the helm of both the business . . . and the *business*. It was more sobering than celebratory.

His mind drifted to the months following his graduation from Fordham. His father had stayed in the office that entire summer, showing Jimmy how to manage the operations. His grandfather reinforced the knack for numbers that they both shared. He vividly saw his father smiling at him and his grandfather—sans cannula at the time—both full of life and breath. He could hear Italo Jr.'s voice: "My boy! You have the spirit of a CEO with the heart of a Peace Corps volunteer. Never lose those qualities, even when life tells you otherwise."

Jimmy smiled to himself. He missed his father every minute of every day, but this memory hit him particularly hard as the void felt more prominent in that moment. A tear formed in his eye, but immediately it dried as the lanky figure of Sale sauntered right in front of him.

Sale walked over to Jimmy's office from his desk. He had a pen tucked behind his ear, like he was pretending to be a hard worker. "Hey, boss," Sale said, pulling the pen from his ear, "can you sign off on these blueprints?" Jimmy stiffened but tried not to make it obvious. He hadn't put Sale on the front desk; he didn't want this man being the first thing anyone saw of the company when they walked in. Instead, his desk was off to the side, like an intern given a space to work out of courtesy.

As Sale's hands came down to rest on Jimmy's desk, Jimmy saw those damned letters again, the prison ink *S* and *B*, and clenched his teeth, faking a smile. "Sure, *Zio*, sure."

Three weeks had passed since the Castle Hill incident.

They'd spared Hector, Franklin, and Raheim, which had surprised Jimmy. He'd wanted blood, but Enzo had bigger ideas. They were never to say a word to anyone—especially Lito—or they'd be dead within minutes, no second chances. They agreed to his terms. Enzo told Jimmy he needed to pretend nothing happened. They needed more information about Sale, to make sure it was lock-tight. There were circumstances, with Sale being in prison with Lito, and having those initials as a tattoo, that singled him out, but they weren't proof. They were circumstantial. For this, for what they were going to do, they needed to be sure they were destroying the right man.

Jimmy hated that they'd let the killers live. This was his family. His blood. And blood would have blood. But he was smart enough to know they were tools, and killing them was about as much a message as melting down a bullet. It didn't go all the way back to the finger that pulled the trigger—or the head of the man who'd called the hit.

That was the only death that would give him any sort of satisfaction.

#

When Salvatore walked into Martello Construction like the new boss, he had a rude awakening. One of the office managers emerged from the work hut and, smiling, informed him that his name wasn't part of the business these days.

He wanted to pitch a fit, but instead, he asked Jimmy for his front desk job back, feigning humility. When he was offered a smaller desk a few feet away, he was annoyed, yet it was closer to Jimmy's new office.

Sale figured he could keep an eye on his nephew.

They shared a mutual lack of trust, despite Sale feeling he had the upper hand. To him, even asking Jimmy to sign off on paperwork was a way to make Jimmy believe *he* was the empowered one. So, he did what he had to do.

Jimmy scribbled his initials at the bottom of the blueprint. "There you go, Sale," he said.

Enzo had given Jimmy more than just advice on how to deal with his turncoat uncle; he was given a device to bug the desk.

Enzo told Jimmy to paint it the same color as the desk and stick it to the inside corner of the desk, at an angle, so Sale wouldn't notice it.

On Sale's first day of work, Sale waited until everyone left, then turned on his phone's flashlight and used it to check for bugs on his desk.

His sweep of the light missed the camouflaged bug. He felt smug that he was dealing with an idiot who wouldn't last a week as don of the dead family. "Little shit ain't even smart enough to bug my desk," he told his reflection in the chipped phone screen. That misjudgment made him more careless than he might otherwise have been.

Every night, Salvatore stayed late, making up excuses that he either needed to finish his admin or to get a head start on the next morning.

His true purpose was prep work, yes, but not for anything as mundane as construction. It was all about the incoming drug shipments.

Jimmy didn't care. He and Nicky would sit in his room with a Zoom recorder, a notebook, and two bottles of Peroni, recording everything that came from the listening device attached to the desk as it happened in real time.

Within a week, they had everything: the exact coordinates

of where the heroin was going to arrive, as well as the cocaine, oxy, crystal meth, and fentanyl, along with the foot soldiers he was assembling to make his deliveries happen.

And in the midst of all of that, he put out a hit on Jimmy.

And Jimmy heard all of it and wrote it all down in his little black book.

There would be a reckoning.

"The little asshole gets his haircut on Fridays at two p.m.," Salvatore spoke on the recording. "Always the same place, same time. It's like he wants to get whacked. Knock him in his barbershop chair, Albert Anastasia style. I'll pay double if you get a video of him begging for his fucking life and making him piss himself in the process."

Jimmy knew that Albert Anastasia was one of the founding fathers of the American mafia. He was part of the legends of crime. Shot in a barbershop chair, through a hit ordered by the Genovese crime family.

The first thing Jimmy did was call and cancel his appointment with Johnny. He asked his barber to let him know if anyone suspicious showed up during his slot. Faces were good; names were better.

On Friday, 2:00 p.m. on the dot, Sale walked back into the office from his lunch break, whistling like he was on top of the world.

He damn near choked on his own air when he saw Jimmy standing next to the copy machine.

"Hey, uh, you good, Jimmy? Thought you'd be getting those luscious locks trimmed?"

"Decided to grow my hair out," Jimmy replied, like nothing was on his mind. "Plus, I bought these professional clippers to help me out if it gets a bit scruffy."

Salvatore slowly nodded in agreement, like it made sense, barely able to mask his frustration and anger. He shuffled over to his desk and picked up his phone to text. Walking out of the office, he sent the stand-down message: *The little shit never made it to the shop. Go home.*

Just then, Jimmy's pocket vibrated with a text from Johnny. He read the message:

Some weird, cracked-out-looking MF'ers were standing outside of the shop until one of them got a text, and they ran off.

Jimmy smirked.

He'd outplayed Sale this time, nice and easy.

But he wondered how Sale was paying for a hit. Even amateurs didn't come cheap. It was as big a mystery as how Sale had gone inside a loser and come out connected. He'd gotten himself all these contacts on the drug side and had a direct line to killers? He'd changed inside. And now, he was a lot more dangerous than before.

It became a game with them, even if Sale didn't know he was playing. Every time that his uncle ordered a hit, Jimmy found a way to ruin it—sometimes simply by not showing up; other times by having way more fun, making it impossible to pull the hit off. Meanwhile, Salvatore was too stupid to realize how Jimmy was always two steps ahead. He blamed the hit men. He called them incompetent. He raged and raved and eventually gave up, putting the hit on pause because it was distracting. He needed to focus his attentions on his burgeoning drug empire.

Of course, if Sale had realized just how much time and energy and effort went into eavesdropping on him, he could have set his nephews up some other way.

"We gotta wait on clipping my nephew," he told Angelo, not that he sounded happy about it. "Kid's whole schedule is upside-down. Probably grieving or whatever. He's weak-headed. Let him mourn. He can die another day."

"He's nothing," Angelo said. "Forget him. He's a waste of your time."

Angelo had no interest in personal feuds.

It was all about the money.

#

Jimmy brought Nicky to Zambetti's for a sit-down with Enzo.

As they approached the back, Alferio Genovese came walking out of the kitchen, all smiles.

"Alferio, this is a friend of *mine*, Nicky Martello." Jimmy saw Nicky look puzzled at the introduction. Since they were cousins, Nicky probably expected to be introduced as such; yet he didn't make a thing about it. That's why he loved his cousin. Nicky always rolled with the punches.

"Nice to meet you, Nicky. Jimmy, Enzo is downstairs. You can go on down."

Jimmy tapped the metal door open and high-fived the hulking doorman—Tino, the not so tiny—as they headed to the cellar.

Enzo was at the table finishing a *sfogliatella*. He looked up and smiled, "You have to try a *sfogliatella*," he said, chef's kissing the tips of his fingers. "I'm not a big fan of pastries from Campania, but damn it, these are genuinely amazing."

A waiter approached with two pastries for Jimmy and Nicky, along with two Moka Drinks.

"Two espressos too, *per favore*," Jimmy said to the waiter.

Enzo was impressed. "OK, *uomini*, what have we got?"

Jimmy motioned to Nicky, who laid down the notebook and

the Zoom recorder. "OK, so it's looking like Sale is trying to be the mayor of every city that has a Blood in it," Jimmy said. "He keeps name-dropping all these guys in prison, acting like he's the shit. If I've read his planning right, he's looking at heading out of town to Los Angeles to meet some more Bloods. And guess who is paying for his flights? Angelo Massino."

Enzo beat the table with the side of his fist, almost knocking over his demitasse full of espresso. "*Disgrazia!*" he said with a growl.

"There's more," Nicky added. "They're trying to recruit these young kids in Brooklyn to do their dirty work, luring them with vacations to Miami, promising them Spring Break fever, as long as they sell drugs while they're out there. They're even paying for Sprinters to drive them to North Florida, to sell where trailer park junkies live."

Enzo shook his head. "Unbelievable. Sale is one desperate psycho, but Angelo? He should know better." His face was full of disgust.

"Keep going." Jimmy motioned to his cousin.

Nicky presented a detailed log in a spiral notebook. "We saved the best for last. Here's every single time that rat ordered a hit on Jimmy, in detail, and here's how we ducked it."

Enzo rolled up his shirtsleeves. "From now on, Tommy is

going to be your bodyguard. No disagreements," Enzo ordered. "He will come with you everywhere you go. I thought these hits were trivial, but now, it's getting serious."

Jimmy and Nicky nodded.

"So, what do we do, now?" Jimmy asked.

"We beat him at his own game," Enzo responded. "This has gotten bigger than this disagreement of ours, Jimmy. As personal as that cuts, this is bigger. If we are going to get Sale where we want him, we've gotta get more muscle behind us. There's no way that man is doing all this on his own; that much is obvious. And with Massino paying his flights, you know he's bankrolling more."

"Makes no sense to me why anyone would want to work with him," Nicky said.

"Massino must be getting something out of it, or expecting to," Enzo said. "We're going to have to find out what, and make sure he doesn't get it."

Jimmy looked over at Nicky and smiled in return.

"I was really hoping you would say that, *Zio*. I have an idea . . ."

#

DUE

The bright lights from the DJ booth barely penetrated the filter of Jimmy's dark sunglasses.

He leaned back against the crushed velour sofa at Omnia, his eyes darting across every corner of the club.

The last year felt like one big blur, and Jimmy was exhausted—mentally and physically.

Every move he'd made in all that time was in service of this mission to prove Sale's culpability. Proof beyond doubt. So, when Nicky suggested that they attempt to find some joy in Las Vegas, to ring in Jimmy's twenty-sixth birthday, he made a promise to himself that they'd hit Omnia, where he knew that the Black Mafia Family, or BMF, would be.

Six months ago, it all seemed inconceivable, a plan of a thousand moving parts, and even now, Enzo still had doubts about it. But Jimmy's facts were facts, irrefutably so, and thought this was what they needed to really get a handle on the situation. More than once in the months following his father's death, Jimmy had felt like he was floundering, be it when he was forced to dodge every literal bullet Salvatore ordered his way, or the metaphorical ones that came with maintaining the legitimized business his family had built. It was a struggle. But as day turned to night turned to day, he survived.

Enzo had given Jimmy the formal blueprint to the other

aspects of the business: the money laundering, the funneling through casinos and strip clubs, along with the artillery of weapons that the family sold.

Before he knew it, a half of a year had gone by, and the closest Jimmy felt to grief were pangs of disappointment in himself that he still felt like he was learning the ropes. It was taking him too long for his own impatience.

He'd made an order to cease all illegal operations as part of his new plan, the goal to prove that his crime family was no longer double dipping. Let the other families run the industries. Outside of Enzo and Nicky, not a single soul knew about this plan. The other Italian families scoffed at his decision to pause illegal activity, like he was some kind of patron saint of the Mafia to be saying what was what and what wasn't. They saw weakness. Little did they know what he was planning, or how it would reshape the city in his image.

That kind of thinking took time to figure out, determine the best course of action, and act on it.

In the blink of an eye, time had gone by.

"I can't see this happening, Jimmy. I know you've invested heart and soul into it, but sometimes things just don't go the way we want them to, no matter how desperately we want them to," Enzo had said, struggling with sincere doubt. "You know, years back, the Italians and the Jews . . . we worked together: Meyer Lansky, Bugsy Siegel, Dutch Schultz. But organized crime is fractured now. I just don't see how you'll pull this off. Too many moving parts, too many things not under your control."

"I get your concerns, *Zio*, but trust me, I've had nothing but this to think about for almost a year now. I've mapped it all out. Every eventuality. Nothing can happen I haven't considered and built in contingencies for. We align with the top mobsters across organized crime," Jimmy said. "I'm talking about the Russian mob, the Latin Kings, the Yakuza, the Black Mafia Family. All of 'em!"

Enzo turned to his surrogate nephew as if *he* were the young man seeking counsel. "How do we do that?"

Jimmy gently patted Enzo's coffee table, tracing his finger along the glistening marble as though drawing a map that would join the dots with his fingertips. "We give them what they need. Every unit is suffering right now. It's a mess out there, with police, shithouse politics, all of it. The world is falling apart. At least, that's how it feels to everyone. Our job is to be the glue. I figure out what that need is, what will hold it together, and I supply it."

Enzo leaned forward to get a better hook into the plan, as Jimmy continued talking with a confidence that Enzo had never seen in him before. "I'll meet them everywhere they're at and provide them with the thing they're looking for. That's the only way to do it."

Enzo smiled. "You make it sound easy. But you know what, kid? The way your eyes light up when you talk about it, you look just like your father, God rest his soul, and I believe you might just pull this shit off."

Jimmy beamed with pride. "This is all about my father. It's all about getting justice for him. That's the big vision here."

"And you know I've got your back, every way I can," Enzo promised.

"I know, *Zio*. Always. Now it's time for me to get to work." Jimmy had done enough planning. At last, it was time for action.

#

Jimmy felt like Salvatore was too entrenched with the Bloods for it to be worth even attempting a sit-down with them. Better to foster his ties to those who had no regard for the Crips *or* the Bloods. My enemy's enemy is my friend. And with that in mind, Jimmy knew whom he had to speak with, and whom he really needed to get on his side.

With Salvatore attempting to penetrate the drug market, he

was going up against one of the biggest crime families outside of La Cosa Nostra. People who didn't take kindly to food being taken from their table. Jimmy knew that if he wanted real power behind him, he had to align with bosses who held their heads as high as he did, who believed in the same omertà, level of loyalty, and who fiercely defended one another.

What he still hadn't wrapped his head around was, who had picked Sale out of the crowd inside and decided he was someone to elevate?

The man had so little to offer, it just didn't make any sense.

But, for now at least, these next steps in his own plan had him cautiously optimistic.

On one hand, if successful, his plan could change everything. Then again, it *could* change *everything*. He needed his parents, one in the physical sense and the other in the spiritual. Jimmy walked into his father's closet and inhaled deeply, breathing in the essence of the old man. He didn't believe in ghosts, but the walk-in was haunted with the smell of Italo Jr., just like it had always been, with a combination of Creed cologne and Cohibas.

Jimmy started pulling some shirts and jackets from the hangers to pack for his flight.

He scanned his father's closet one last time.

He knew what he was looking for.

He pulled a black Gucci tie from the rack, along with a black Versace shirt.

"Your father always meant business when he dressed like that, black on black," his mother said from the bedroom doorway. "Be careful, my baby."

"Don't worry, Ma. I know it doesn't look like it, but what I'm doing isn't making war," Jimmy said. "I'm making peace."

He closed the closet door.

#

Jimmy snuck a smile on his face at Omnia, as he recalled that moment.

"You like this song, bro?" Nicky asked. "I didn't know you were an Avicii fan like that."

Jimmy turned his head toward Nicky. "I didn't even hear the song playing."

Nicky slumped into the velour sofa, extending his arms in doubt. "How? It's making my ears bleed right now!"

Jimmy motioned to a line of tall, Black gentlemen in dark suits, walking through the club like a monochromatic parade. "The BMF has arrived." As he went to gesture toward the cocktail waitress to send some more drinks, two trolls with spiky do's scurried up to the sofa.

"Ay aren't you Jimmy Martello? You're, like, the Mafia *don!*"

Jimmy rolled his eyes under his dark sunglasses as Nicky smirked.

Tommy appeared out of nowhere, ready to body-slam them into tomorrow.

Jimmy waved him off.

"Hey. Nice to meet you," Jimmy said flatly to the guys. "This is my cousin Nick, and that's Tommy."

The two quickly gave Nicky a pound with their fists.

They didn't dare try and touch Tommy.

They didn't even attempt to shake Jimmy's hand. It was as if they instinctively knew that you don't dare touch the hand of the crime boss, even in deference, though that's where their filter began and ended.

"So, uh, I know this is probably inappropriate, but I gotta ask . . . how do I get in the Mafia? I mean, if I wanted?" one asked inquisitively. "Everybody already thinks we're in, anyway. Ya know, one time I saw one of the Gotti boys while I was getting a taillight on my BMW fixed out in Jersey. And wouldn't ya know, Carmine Gotti was there getting his Phantom detailed! He complimented my Beamer! I have it tricked out so it looks like an Alpina, but it's not really one, ya know. I'll get there, though."

He was rambling, and he kept on rambling while Jimmy pretended to be invested in the conversation, though he stared to the left at the BMF through his dark lenses.

Across the room, Ronald and his brother Ricky sat with their armed guards observing the exchange. Ronald and Ricky were cousins of Big Meech and his brother Southwest T, the infamous Flenory brothers who founded the BMF.

"These guidos are gonna start pumping their fists soon to this wack-ass music."

Ronald turned to Ricky and said, "Ain't that one of the Italian Mafia boys, though?"

"The one with the blacked-out shades, looking like a pizzeria Ray Charles."

They both started howling with laughter.

The joke was on them, though.

Jimmy received word that Ricky was in town from Los Angeles and Ronald was in town from Atlanta. The two agreed to meet in Vegas to rendezvous with fellow BMF members out of Detroit, the purpose to figure out a game plan for the fall.

Salvatore's drug operations were gaining steam, but they were sloppy.

All of the unnecessary moves he was making were putting

the BMF under the watchful eye of people they didn't want digging into their business in Atlanta, where their record label was located.

The hip-hop task force was dying to throw RICO charges at them and have them all rapping from prison, making this entire ordeal very much nonbeneficial.

They knew they needed to bring Sale's operation in line, fast, before things got away from them.

Jimmy watched them laugh from across the room.

It was a delicate game, but it felt like now was the right time for the hunter to head over and embrace the good vibes with them.

The cocktail waitress walked over to Jimmy and flirtatiously cooed, "Hi, Jimmy, what do you need? Whatever and whenever, you only gotta whistle."

Nicky nudged the two other guys, who now made themselves comfortable on the sofa. The three of them smirked.

"Well, beautiful, you can start by getting me another Negroni, along with whatever else these guys want. But, before all of that, how about you send two bottles of Ace of Spades to those gentlemen over there?" He pointed to the BMF table with his chin. He slipped her another hundred-dollar bill. That was the fifth one this evening.

"She's into you, bro," Nicky said.

"I don't care, Nicky," Jimmy replied.

"Come on, man! You haven't dated a girl since Eliana, and when the hell was *that*? Like, a year and a half ago? People are gonna start calling you *the rainbow don* at this rate. You need to bust a nut so you can think straight."

The two wannabe Mafia guys cautiously chuckled, as Jimmy saw the two bottles of Ace of Spades placed on Ricky and Ronald's table.

They stared at the gold bottles with confusion.

Jimmy stood up and slowly walked over, taking off his sunglasses for the first time since he'd entered the club.

The lights made him squint, but he knew that there was respect in showing your eyes.

Tommy stood by a pillar nearby, ready to strike if need be.

"Ronald, Ricky, it's a pleasure to meet you both," Jimmy said as he approached the table, nodding his head to the bodyguards next to them in acknowledgment as well.

"Hey, Pauly D, you're wanted back in the DJ booth," Ronald quipped. "And how the hell do you know our names?"

Jimmy stood there calmly and smiled. "Oh, my bad. I should have introduced myself. The name's Jimmy. Jimmy Martello."

Ricky folded his arms and mouthed, "I told you!" to Ronald.

"I want us to have a little meeting while you're in town," Jimmy continued, like it was the most obvious thing in the world.

"For what? Are you gonna stop muscling in on our business?" Ronald jumped in reply.

"Only if you're gonna stop stealing our names for your rappers . . ." Jimmy remarked in return, cracking a grin.

Ronald shook his head. "This guy. This muthafuckin' guy." He turned back toward Jimmy. "Now look, Super Mario. I know you've been slipping fentanyl into your supply. Those white folks over in Orlando are dropping dead like Bambi's mother. We're in the business of money 'round here. Not massacre. Y'all are fucking with our supply lines and cutting our bottom line with your shit-stain business. Frankly, I'm about ready to dead this conversation before I dead you in the middle of this club."

His one bodyguard gripped the belt of his pants, acknowledging the piece he was concealing.

Jimmy remained calm.

He knew Tommy needed less than a second to take the pair down, two bullets between the eyes. "I understand your frustration," Jimmy said. "But right up front, you need to be aware, this isn't me or my people. We've got some family problems going on, and right now, my uncle is the one who has decided to fuck with your business."

"And we should care because?"

"Let's just say we don't see eye to eye."

Ricky shifted in his seat. "So, you're trying to tell us that you're not the one running around *my* city of LA in your little red Adidas tracksuit, out here begging the Bloods to be friends?"

Jimmy slid his fingers along the collar of his father's tailored suit he was wearing. "Do I look like I wear tracksuits?" He shook his head. "That definitely ain't me."

As much as Ronald and Ricky wanted to start blasting Jimmy, they were intrigued by his confidence and his charm. "So, you're like one of them bastard sons who turns on his family? OK, OK. Prove it. Go snap on one of your little brothers or cousins over there. Let me see you check one of your own."

Jimmy maintained his poker face.

On the inside, he was relieved by the assignment. He turned and walked away, rolling up his sleeves as he walked. He shot a whistle at Tommy, who emerged from behind the pillar, and the two approached Nicky and the two wannabe guys.

Jimmy whispered to Nicky, "I'm sorry, bro," and decked him in the cheek, using his fist to push him over the back of the sofa. "Stay down," he commanded.

He turned to the other two and started punching them in the stomach and the face, wailing on them. Tommy held back both of their sets of hands simultaneously as the one started spitting up the Negroni he guzzled in Jimmy's absence.

"Don't. You. Ever. Fucking. Ask. How. To. Get. Into. This. Thing. Of. *Mine*. Again," he punctuated each word with a punch harder than the last. "Now, fuck off and tell the Gotti boys that you just got the shit kicked out of you by a Martello."

The cocktail waitress leaned against the wall with her drink menu covering her skirt as she clenched her thighs together and bit her lower lip.

Even Pauly D looked up from the DJ booth and started watching, ignoring his own transition into the next song.

Ronald and Ricky watched the whole ordeal. "Well, that motherfucker fed his own family a two-piece," Ricky said to Ronald. "Those guys were with them when we got here."

Ronald nodded.

As Jimmy continued punching the guys, he felt a wave of guilt and then stopped.

He shook his bloody knuckles to signify that the only reason why he stopped was because *he* was injured.

He grabbed a black cloth napkin and wiped his hands, motioning back to the cocktail waitress, who ran over at the speed of light.

"I want you to comp these guys every time they come here, for the rest of their trip," he said to the waitress, who obediently nodded. "Also, get them a limo to the nearest twenty-four-hour Medicenter." He turned to the bloodied men. "Sorry I had to do that, but consider it a genuine lesson: You *never* ask about the family, not even joking. Tell the doctor at the Medicenter that you ran into a stripper pole, capisce?"

The two men slowly nodded. One spit out a tooth.

Jimmy stuffed $3,000 into one of their suit pockets. "For your dentist."

Nicky emerged from behind the sofa.

Jimmy had strategically hit his cousin's chubby cheek so that he wouldn't break anything in his face.

He wrapped the large ice cube from the Negroni in a clean cloth napkin and handed it to Nicky. "Put this on your face, bro. I'm so sorry, but I had to. You can pay me back later."

While Nicky iced his face, Ronald and Ricky approached the table. "Meet us in the Champagne Room at Scores in an hour."

"Got it," Jimmy replied.

#

Jimmy noticed Nicky was still a little rattled in the back of the Escalade.

The ride from Omnia to Scores was ten minutes, so Jimmy took the rest of the time to get Nicky's head back in the game.

"This is our first meeting with these guys, and they have zero reason to trust us or take anything at face value, so we have got to be smart," Jimmy explained. "I don't expect them to suddenly ride with us, but I'm hoping that with that little show back there I proved myself. Violence recognizes violence. And they bought the tourists were family."

Nicky smiled in laughter until a twinge of nerve pain hit his cheek muscle.

"Sorry again, man," Jimmy said sympathetically. "Crazy to think where we were at this time last year."

They both bowed their heads solemnly.

Nicky turned to Jimmy. "You've got a weak-ass right hook, bro. You've gotta work on that."

Jimmy started laughing. "Jackass! I didn't hit you properly. You want another round, kiddo?"

Nicky pushed Jimmy's fist back to his lap. "All good!"

They both started laughing.

#

"Well, I'll be damned, let's get this poor dude some ass and titties!" Ronald said to Nicky, as they entered the Champagne Room at Scores. "You got knocked *the fuck* out and are back on your feet. Outstanding!"

Jimmy put his hand on Nicky's shoulder. "Ronald, Ricky, this is my consigliere, Domenico. We call him *Nicky* for short."

Ronald shook Nicky's hand. "Let's get Nicky a quickie. He earned it for that beatdown you gave him. Where are your other two cousins?" Ricky inquired.

"They're in the hospital," Jimmy responded. "One day, they'll forgive me . . . I'll buy them cannoli or something." He cracked a grin.

Everyone sat down. Four strippers circled their chairs. Nicky's eyes looked like saucers as one of the dancers draped her leg along his left shoulder, affixing her clear stiletto to the edge of the cocktail table beside him.

The crotch of her lace panties was directly in his face.

"You havin' fun over there?" Jimmy hollered, as another stripper straddled him and ruffled his tie.

Ronald and Ricky entertained themselves by slapping either cheek of a dancer twerking between their two chairs. Both brothers pulled out a rack of bills; Ronald handed one to a dancer, Ricky feeding his to another.

Jimmy looked over to Nicky, who passed him a rack as he

pulled out another rack for himself.

They knew how to behave. It was a game to be played. They fed the bills to the remaining two dancers.

Ronald looked over at Ricky as they both smiled and nodded.

#

"I'm sick of *fuckin' counting!*" Sale yelled into his burner phone.

Sitting at the large oak desk in Jimmy's office made him feel a combination of power and embitterment. Jimmy hadn't been to the office in weeks, so it wasn't like he would come wandering in and find Sale playing boss, but knowing that his little nephew—the one he wanted crushed like a worm under his foot—ran the company that cut his biweekly check . . . it boiled his blood. Still, the little shit's office came in handy for all of the Zoom calls he was taking with potential "investors." He even did the air quotes in his mind when he thought about them.

Infiltrating the cocaine game had been easier than he'd expected. The problem was, now that he was on the inside, he was clueless. And he didn't like that one little bit. If people didn't come to him with ideas, he was flapping in the wind. Sometimes they did, and sometimes they didn't. It was a lottery where every other ticket left him feeling like he'd won the idiot draw. He connected with some Blixkys over in Crown Heights, getting in good with the gang territory, but he wanted much more. So, when another opportunity presented itself, he turned right around and went to Brownsville to shake hands with their rivals, the Woo gang, because why wouldn't he?

It never occurred to him once that someone could be pulling his strings.

"The fuck is you doin'?" Smugga yelled in Sale's face when he proudly told him his moves.

Smugga was the last of the Crips who paid attention to Sale since he started begging for the Bloods' attention, and only because it served him and his set. Smugga was smart enough to know a White-skinned dude could finagle his way into plenty of kilos, and would be trusted immediately by the guys looking to move bulk, more so than he ever could be. The problem was Sale. It was always Sale. It didn't matter whether he called himself *SB*, *Salvatore*, or any other damned name; he would always be the same old Sale. It was like he was blinded by the dollar bills the same way some fools were blinded by everything that the money brings. All he could think about was spreading the "wealth," and he was obsessed with trying to loop every gang into this operation. That wasn't sitting right with Smugga. He cautiously stayed for the ride, but when the time came to get off, he'd get off, no hesitation. And he'd willingly pull the trigger himself, because Sale pissed him off.

"No, see, Smuggs, big picture, huge picture! Just imagine it: We make a giant empire, link all the gangs to a single supply line, and we can have *all* the drugs to sell!" Sale assured him.

Smugga hated it when he called him *Smuggs*, but he kept listening, even if he knew that wasn't remotely how the real world worked. There was no single cartel, never had been and never would be, because there just weren't the foot soldiers to make it possible when it came to putting down the rivals. He said as much, and Sale just shook his head, like he was dealing with a child.

"No, no, see, think big. These gang leaders run their own show, sure, but they become our foot soldiers. It's a win-win."

That sounded about as likely as him winning on a slot machine when he didn't even put in a token. Sale didn't make good choices when it came to whom to trust. As soon as the supply hit his hands, he was the only one to weigh it out, repackage it into dime bags, and count the money coming in as the drugs went back out. Initially, Smugga had helped with the process, but now that Sale was doing the dance with other gangs, he wasn't prepared to handle the grunt work they would benefit from. So, Sale sat there, a victim of his own ambition, counting and counting grams at Jimmy's desk while he bitched at Smugga on the phone.

"Have ya li'l Blixky friends count that shit up," Smugga said with a laugh.

Sale slammed the phone down and kept counting.

He wasn't remotely fazed by the trouble he was causing across the country; he was actually enjoying it, being the eye of the hurricane for once. It made him feel powerful, and, most days, that was enough.

Most days.

But, with the weight of inevitability, once he started engaging with the Blixkys and the Woos, the hip-hop task force in New York City started hovering, like flies wanting in on his honey. Back in the '90s, there'd been the hip-hop cops with their fake Jordans and brassy chains, trying to pass with all the subtlety of a drag act, following rappers around at the clubs. They were a different beast now, twice as robust. They were the hammerhead to beat down on the gang activity happening in hip-hop, implementing RICO measures to collapse the crews. But, as there were so many Blixkys and Woos who were rappers, it made sense for the task force to follow the BMF around too. It didn't matter that they were completely different entities. The cops saw an opportunity to wipe everyone out, literally and figuratively.

Their world was all about connections, about dots being joined.

So, when Ronald and Ricky started noticing they were picking up tails, they started asking around, and their connection out in Bed-Stuy came back with an answer.

It was down to some mobbed-up Martello.

Which, of course, led to them mistakenly thinking it was Jimmy, rather than Sale, who was as far away from mobbed-up as Detroit was from Shanghai.

#

The King Cole Bar was one of the more luxurious joints in New York, and that luxury was matched by the ticket price. Jimmy wasn't drinking the kind of martini that had actual diamonds in it, just the ice, but for the dollar bills he was throwing back, he might as well have been. Business was going well—although not as well as drinking here would make people think. This was about being seen and noticed. It was all part of the plan.

"We're a long way from Moka Drink now, *cugino*," Nicky opined.

"No more pulling bottle caps off with our teeth," Jimmy

agreed with a smile.

He'd liked flying under the radar, but he had to admit, he was beginning to get a taste for the finer things now. He even enjoyed playing at being a gentleman. These days, he carried the dignity of the whole Martello family on his shoulders, and that was a burden he took seriously. So, he wore the sharpest suits and sipped Manhattans rather than chugging cheap Moka from a bottle, hoping the ghost of his old man would be proud of him. He started hanging around high-end bars and lounges, more for purpose over posh. He knew that the paparazzi would ultimately spot him, which was his own subtle signaling to Sale that he was out and about. To Jimmy, if Sale thought he was busy turning into a little scenester, then he couldn't possibly be plotting anything. It was all an act, but Jimmy enjoyed some of it.

"I have a question," Nicky said.

"Anything," Jimmy said, happy as ever to indulge his cousin.

He could count on Nicky to have his back, and he knew how important loyalty like that was.

He'd do anything for Nicky, and that went both ways.

"It's about Sale," Nicky said, hesitating before he pushed on. "I don't understand why he's still alive . . . after everything he's done to our family . . . after all the times he's tried to kill you.

Why not put him in a box?"

"In time. He's walking around now by our grace, not his cunning wit. There will be revenge for our fathers," Jimmy promised.

Nicky smiled. He'd needed to hear that. Waiting to settle the score was hard for him, but he was unquestioningly loyal. He trusted Jimmy.

"I've been putting together a plan," Jimmy confided. "It's a big plan. I mean, it's a lot, but believe me when I tell you there is no way we are avenging them with some shitty little back-street hit. It's not enough. It has to be a statement kill."

Nicky nodded thoughtfully. "This speaks to me."

"It's about honor," Jimmy said. "Martello honor. Our name, our dignity."

"You sound more like Enzo every day," Nicky said. There was no laugh.

"We've been talking. A lot. I like his thinking. Family, pride, reputation—we aren't just a bunch of no-account losers. We've got honor, and that's important. It sets us apart. We are better than that. Sale is doing damage to our honor and our name, and that is something I need to deal with before it causes irreparable damage. So, our situation, right now, it's not just revenge for those murders—as brutal a crime as that was against the family. It's about our standing in the world and the memory of our fathers. That's what this means to me."

"Killing him wouldn't be enough," Nicky agreed, glimpsing the bigger picture.

He got it, and Jimmy liked knowing that.

He knew he'd been slow putting things right—too slow for his own liking, but the kind of family restoration he was looking for took time. Respect wasn't easily earned within their kind.

"He will die," Jimmy promised. "He will die a hundred times over for betraying us the way he did. But before he dies, I want the world to know him, the real him, the pathetic, useless him we all know. We're going to expose him, humiliate him, and make sure everyone bears witness."

"Count me in," Nicky said. "Whatever you need, I'm with you all the way, *cugino*."

Jimmy slapped Nicky on the arm. "I know you are."

They sipped their drinks for a while, both lost in thought.

Jimmy knew Nicky wasn't the kind of guy to ask a lot of questions.

He didn't need to know the details.

He just needed to know there was a plan.

That was enough.

He trusted Jimmy to take care of things.

#

The BMF had their offices in a skyscraper so new, it was barely half-occupied, with tenants moving in every few weeks.

They liked to move around.

Their current head, Big Capo, had a real thing for new build.

He said it was all about the smell, same as with wheels. He liked to spend his time in places that had no history to them.

The Crime Lords imprint record label did the legal side of their business and raked in the dollars hand over fist with the rappers on their books. Jimmy knew most of their main acts, and he respected how well the BMF mixed its legit business with its other business. It was slick.

Or at least it had been, before Sale had gone off the rails and started making trouble for them.

Now there were rumblings and discontent.

Most of it aimed at his family, and he couldn't blame them.

Jimmy had shown up early for his meeting with Big Capo, partly out of respect, but mostly to allow him to scope the place out. He liked to know whom he was dealing with, and this building had a lot to tell him about how Big Capo wanted the world to see the Crime Lords.

Everything in here was modern and shiny, metal, glass,

chrome, and monochrome. It reeked of money, and just how much had been spent making it look just so. They probably had a golden toilet in the bathroom.

A few years ago, that sort of stuff would've impressed him, but his definition of cool had changed every bit as thoroughly as his clothing had.

Jimmy smiled indulgently at his younger self.

In his book, pouring a martini over diamonds and not just ice didn't cut it anymore, and neither did the Crime Lords offices. Perception was everything, and it looked like Big Capo was trying too hard. Understated oozed confidence. Jimmy wanted to be taken seriously in this world. No bling, black on black like his old man if he wanted to impress. Anyone taken in by a gold chain wasn't worth impressing.

There were plaques on the wall marking tunes that had gone gold and platinum, but it was as much about streams these days as sales. Jimmy scanned the names of the artists, the stars of the Crime Lords label: Gotti Bro, Li'l Gambino, and Uzi Bonanno. He had to fight not to laugh out loud. He'd bet any money that not one of those boys had an Italian ancestor in their bloodlines, all the way back to the missing link.

Not one originated from Sicily, the primary requisite to be made.

It was all a lie.

They wanted to sound like they were part of the family, because that conferred power. Whatever else, when it came to the war of the streets, no one would ever be as gangsta as the Mafia. And here they were, these musicians with their platinum plaques, all desperately wanting to bask in a little of the reflected fear and glory of La Cosa Nostra.

This whole setup was just boys wanting to be gangsters, the same way he and Nicky had played at being their dads when they were knee-high. This record label wanted to be him.

He found that funny.

He'd spent so much of his teens thinking rappers were cool and dreaming of being half as cool, but here he was, the real deal, and they were the fakes, the frauds, the wannabes. That was some irony. Jimmy knew in that moment he could walk into Big Capo's office like he owned the world. He didn't have to feel inferior. He didn't need to prove himself. He belonged to something ancient and deadly. It was in his blood in a way that they could never grasp. They wanted it and couldn't have it. He lived and breathed it.

"So, my man, dare I say it looks like we've got ourselves the same problem, just from different sides," Big Capo said once Jimmy had made himself comfortable.

"It brings shame to my family, and personal shame to me, that my uncle has acted against you in this way," Jimmy said. "That's why I have come to you, in your place of business, to apologize to your face and, I hope, clean up some of his mess."

Big Capo looked him up and down. It was obvious from his expression he didn't believe a word of it. And why should he? He had no reason to trust Jimmy. Not yet. Trust needed to be earned.

"I know he's brought a lot of negative attention to aspects of your business," Jimmy said, careful not to say more.

"Can't do nothing, thanks to the cops right now," Big Capo acknowledged. "Every-fucking-where. Costing me dollars, man. Wasting my time. I'm telling you, I'm washing this fucker's nuts down with a nice Chianti."

"I'll bring the bottle. It's the least I can do," Jimmy agreed. Truth be told, he had zero intention of handing Sale over to Big Capo to cut up, but it made sense to play along. "I have a plan for him."

"I'm sure you do, but what are we talking about in terms of exposure for me?" Big Capo wanted to know.

"Some," said Jimmy, not wanting to front it in a lie. "But not as much as it could be if you've got some smart foot soldiers on the payroll."

Big Capo grinned. "Goes without saying. You don't live long in this life without a good crew around you."

"Good. Then here's how we turn this around, get the cops off your case, and focused on Sale," Jimmy said, laying it out. He had the insights into Sale's plans, thanks to the office bug, meaning he was caught up before an idea was half out of Sale's mouth and two steps ahead before the phone was back in his pocket. Sale wouldn't know who, or what, had hit him. And that ignorance meant there was no obvious way of tracing it back to Jimmy.

Big Capo nodded along as Jimmy walked him through it all. Then it got to the million-dollar question. "And we take the cash?"

"Recompense," said Jimmy.

He nodded, as if to say, "Of course." That was the only way. "You've shown me respect, Jimmy. I appreciate that," Big Capo said. "So, in return, I'm not gonna toss you out of here on your ass. I'm going to give you and your plan a chance. Don't make me regret my trustful nature."

"Wouldn't dream of it."

\#

Alessandro Massino recognized Jimmy Martello the moment he walked into the bar.

How could he not?

It wasn't an accident that he was there that night.

He'd put out feelers weeks ago. He was curious. His father, Angelo, had spent too much time talking about this man recently, and Alessandro was uncomfortable with the seeming obsession. Like most boys, growing up, Alessandro had thought his father to be a god among men. That process of growing up—and learning flaw by flaw that the man he adored wasn't so very special after all—had been painful. The truth was Angelo Massino was clever enough for the cut and thrust of everyday business, but being clever didn't mean he made good choices when it came to who to trust, and who to steer well away from.

And like it or not, the truth was, he had made appalling choices when it came to who needed to be put six feet under.

At twenty-four, still wet behind the ears in his father's eyes, Alessandro knew he was savvier than his father. He was unsentimental where his father had heart strings to be played. He was ruthless where his father might have erred on the side of caution. He was merciless where his father might have offered a second chance. However he looked at them, those things that he had admired as a child were weaknesses when seen as a man.

And now, those weaknesses had led him into a hot mess with the Martello family.

Three murders and no one called to account didn't look good.

From the outside, he could have read it a couple of ways. One, that Jimmy Martello was too weak to get vengeance; the other, that he'd pulled the trigger himself.

Those alternatives had implications.

To put it bluntly, with Sale Martello trying to work Angelo, Alessandro needed to know if he was dealing with a killer or a coward, so that he could treat the man accordingly.

So, he did the smart thing. He sounded out the word on the street.

It was easy enough to read Jimmy, and he wasn't making it hard, fronting up in the kind of scenester bars where rich idiots hung around outside, wanting to get their faces in the paparazzi shots of whomever was hot among the internet's celeb and gossip sites. Clout by subliminal association. That was fine for some, but Alessandro preferred a low-profile approach to life.

Jimmy Martello dressed in understated elegance, so maybe he had *some* taste through his newly inherited wealth. The two weren't mutually exclusive in Alessandro's world. The thing was, watching him, he didn't move like a man suited to those clothes. There was still the swagger of a player about him, meaning

Jimmy stood out even when he was trying to blend in. Alessandro veered to the other extreme and dressed to be forgotten. His own clothes suggested money, but not extravagance. Style, but not flamboyance. He looked like someone deserving respect, not like someone you'd kidnap.

Like everything else in his life, this was intentional.

"Let me buy you a drink, my friend," he said, approaching Jimmy at the bar.

Jimmy shot him a questioning look.

"I wouldn't expect you to remember me, Jimmy. It's been half a lifetime. My father, he was friends with Italo. I'll spare us both the embarrassment of you forgetting my name. It's Alessandro Massino."

Jimmy gave him a slow up-and-down appraisal as he shook his hand.

"*Come stai?*" Alessandro asked. It was a nothing question, followed with a string of similarly dull, polite, and unthreatening questions, which Jimmy answered without really seeming fully engaged in the conversation. Despite the simplicity of the interrogation, Alessandro gleaned plenty.

Not a man who killed his own father, Alessandro concluded.

But not the weak man he'd thought, either. He was a man with some spine, some sense of honor, and therefore, a man who might be working on his revenge. Interesting. One to keep an eye on, certainly.

By the end of the evening, Jimmy had come to the conclusion that Alessandro was a charming young man, and most likely a useful new ally. He wouldn't have called them friends, but he was undeniably a gentleman—very gentle, in fact, leading Jimmy to surmise his low profile was down to an affinity for the business side of the business as opposed to a life of the knife or the gun.

That was good too.

#

After the sit-down with Big Capo, Jimmy began to feel like his plan could actually work.

Jimmy was a talker; he always had been. Silver-tongued. Good with people. Good at making connections. Building up his networks came easily. It didn't hurt that he was easy on the eyes, so he often found himself welcome simply because he looked the part, especially in a sharp suit. Nicky was a solid partner in crime as well, charming enough and stylish. Word spread they were ready-made money, which meant they were the faces people wanted to be seen with.

"The rumor mill is running hot." Enzo sounded proud. They

were on the phone. "Everybody knows you're making moves, but the beauty is, no one knows what you're aiming for. I tell you, kid, if I had a dollar for every crazy theory I've heard about you this last week alone, I could go finance a new Rolls-Royce."

Jimmy grinned, even though the other man couldn't see it. "Let's keep them guessing."

"Like I told you, kid, dangle yourself like bait, someone will bite simply because they can't bear not knowing," Enzo said. "Some of those old dons, they can't resist a bit of intrigue. Boils their blood."

"Just keep telling them there's no secrets, and keep saying it so they are sure we're protesting too much," Jimmy said. "Let their own cleverness play our way."

Keep them all guessing, watching, and wondering.

More than anything, that made sure word got back to Sale and gave that idiot something to think about.

Did he wake up in the night, sweating with fear, haunted by bad dreams? Did he regret calling the hit on his kin? Was he jumping at shadows, convincing himself Jimmy was coming for him because he knew—or was he blissfully ignorant, thinking he'd gotten away with capping his family, no retribution, no price to be paid? And now, was his nephew drowning his tears in vodka at an overpriced bar? Could be any or all of the above, in Sale's empty mind.

Word trickled back to Jimmy slowly that family heads, lieutenants, red right hands, and the dons themselves—all the crime lords were paying attention. For every player he was seen with, three more seemed to think they needed to get in on the action. He was on tour for a month, taking meetings with every figure imaginable. And they'd ask for more context—how could they not?—but Jimmy wasn't talking. They didn't need to know what he had in mind. Yet.

"I want to do you a favor," he told each of them, making it sound like he absolutely was, and that doing so was the only way his heart could find peace. "I want to help you with something." It was always a different something, always tailored to the man across the table, and always worth more than any price it might cost, or so it felt to them in that moment. He did his research. "Gratis. No hidden fees. No tricks. All I ask is that in a little while, if I need a favor, I can trust you to be there for me."

The answer was always the same: "What kind of favor?"

To which he'd answer with a smile, "Nothing that costs you; you have my word. It isn't about money for me. If you'd rather repay your debt that way, we can make arrangements, but I'm a big believer in the old ways of doing things, you feel me?"

That throwback to the old ways always made it an

intriguing proposition, and Enzo was right—most of them couldn't resist it.

Jimmy had a way of making it seem almost inconsequential, such a small thing, and yet the ask was always tempting because they had nothing to lose.

One by one, they came back to him, agreeing to the favors he'd dangled, impressed that he'd known their business so well. A few came back with counters, and from the scale of those, Jimmy had a better than decent idea what they were willing to offer in return.

Then there was Sazuki Haruto, one of the founding fathers of the Kasen Yakuza in New York City. Most of the Sazukis had relocated to Hawaii, but not Haruto.

Nicky did the ground work, and found the need, but it was a need unlike any other. Beyond a big ask. Haruto's father had a fast-failing liver and a precious few days left before he shuffled off this mortal coil.

There were favors, and there were *favors*.

All he had to do was source a liver for the old man.

#

"Hey, *cugino*," Nicky said. "How much do you love me?"

"I don't know. How much do I love you?" Jimmy said, like it was the setup to a joke, though he loved the punch line.

"You tell me. I think I've got *exactly* what you need."

"Then I love you long time." Jimmy cracked a smile.

"Our beloved murderous uncle's gotten into bed with a chemist who's making this new party drug, the ultimate high, sex enhancer, dance 'til you drop. Like MDMA, only without the worst of the side effects."

"OK, so, Sale's getting in on the club scene?"

"Setting up distribution."

"This is where you tell me you have deets?"

"Dates, times, and locations. Names and numbers. I'm a walking black fucking book. Only thing I don't have is their dick size," Nicky finished with a laugh.

"Which we can live without. Now, we get to have some fun."

"Fun, fun, fun."

He had Nicky send the details to Big Capo, then sat back and waited to see how the BMF would play it.

And play it they did.

Outstandingly.

The operation was a fusion of intelligence, tipping off the cops, and stealing the merch. The upshot was the law knew there was a new drug in town, and that gave them a boner. Nothing like a whole new epidemic to get the blue bloods hard.

Some of the thefts were subtle, with solid cleanup, no trace left behind. Some, though, were deliberately messy, with paperwork planted for the sole purpose of discovery, to feed the cops. Notes in the pockets of corpses, prepaid burner phones full of numbers, each primed, a breadcrumb trail that worked its way across the city to Sale.

Meanwhile, Big Capo's crew had a huge haul of the hot new thing on their hands and a city of clubgoers eager to buy.

It eased recent financial burdens.

It also sent a clear message: Fucking with their operations was not tolerated.

That message filtered out to the street sellers and corner boys. No one wanted to work for Sale if it painted a target on their foreheads.

Job done.

The BMF were content, and now they owed Jimmy a favor.

#

"Jimmy, my boy, it's so good to see you," Sale said, ambushing Jimmy as he walked into the office.

"It's good to be seen," Jimmy said, wearing a mask of

indifference. He wasn't about to let his face betray how much he hated his uncle. But some days, those ending in a *y*, it was difficult to resist the urge to punch him into a coma.

"A word from a wise old head, my boy. I know you think the world is against you and that this is a grind, but I reckon you're trying too hard, wanting it all right now. Naples wasn't built in a week. Remember that."

"Wisdom appreciated, as always, *Zio*. Don't mean to be rude, but if there's nothing pressing, I've got places I need to be." It was hard to keep the edge of out his voice, but he had to, even though the sum of his ambitions in that second could be summed up as getting the hell away from him. No more, no less.

"Ah, I was hoping to have a proper word, I'm afraid. See, I've been hearing things, and they're not necessarily great things, but people out there respect and trust me, so they tell me things. And I've amassed a world full of connects over the years, in other families and beyond."

Jimmy nodded, knowing Sale needed to say this, even if he didn't necessarily need to hear it. Maybe it would offer an angle into Sale's thoughts, and beyond that, how he intended to react. It was always better to be in possession of all the facts.

"You're a good son," Sale said. "You really are, and Italo would be proud if he was here to see how you've held his empire together. But the truth is, you're young, and as well as you are comporting yourself, you're unproven. Friends of the families are finding it hard to take you seriously, especially big men, the ones that matter." He was avoiding naming the dons, talking in euphemisms, and trying to make it seem like he was more connected than he was. "They want to like you. I'm one hundred percent sure of that, for your father's sake, if nothing else. But it's hard for them. You're not him, no matter how much you look like him sometimes—and believe me, it's spooky seeing you walking around in his old suits. Just between us, whispers I'm hearing through the grapevine, there are a few families who feel that the Martellos have made some bad choices as of late, and they're beginning to wonder if you were ready for this."

Jimmy thought about what his uncle was saying, and the not-so-subtle way in which he was trying to plant the idea: They think you should've died.

Sale continued. "There are people saying that you've benefited a lot from all the deaths in your family. I hate to be the one to tell you this, but it's true: You've done very well for yourself. People don't trust you, Jimmy."

It was an obvious gamble, and part of him had actually expected more from Sale, given the way he seemed to have amassed a certain amount of influence within the families. But he was cheap. His methods were shallow. He was not a serious individual.

With that realization, Jimmy took a deep breath and managed not to punch his uncle in the throat, as much as he wanted to. The memory of his father collapsing into his arms was never too far away. Everything he was doing was about justice for his father. And as easy as it would be to beat the miserable little shit to a pulp, fashion a nice pair of concrete shoes, and dump him in the Hudson, real justice meant doing more than merely putting Sale down.

He wanted real justice.

More than anything.

Real justice.

So, he could wait.

Of course, he'd always known this was a possibility, and that there would be backlash where he was doubted or considered weak for not putting Sale down. More than a possibility—a probability. It had never been a stretch to consider Sale trying to use that for his own ends. He was curious to see how his uncle would play it from here, so he simply nodded. It was the slightest of moments, like he was inviting him to go on.

Sale obliged. "You want my advice? You're talking too much. People get nervous around so much chatter. It isn't the family way. They're old-fashioned. There's a way of doing things. In your shoes, I think I'd look to slow it down, focus on the legit side of the business. Give it a couple of years. You're still young. Let people get to know you, before you look to expand the influence."

Again, he nodded, like Sale was dropping some serious wisdom on him. He was getting alarmingly good at lying. "Well, you know I honor and trust you above all others, *Zio*. If you want to offer me advice on expansion, on the legit business as well as the other matters, I would appreciate that. It is a fool who doesn't listen to the wisdom of his elders," Jimmy said. He particularly enjoyed Sale's wincing, mainly because he knew just how horribly Sale's latest power grab had gone only days ago. It was all the sweeter because Sale was clueless.

"OK, honest talk, and these aren't my words, they're from the mouths of other crime families. I'm only the monkey here, not the organ grinder—"

"You can speak plainly, *Zio*, I won't hold anything against you."

"They are concerned there's a lot of bad feelings around, and you're fucking up by not making friends inside the family before you go whoring your ass to every gangbanger and lowlife you can find," Sale said, relishing the words as he put them out there. "Like I said, their words, not mine. Me, I'm sure you've got a good reason for what you're doing. I have total faith in you. I just wish I could do more to help, but I'm on the outside these days." Sale paused, like an idea was just beginning to ferment in his twisted little mind. "You know, if you really do value your old uncle, you might want to fill me in on what all of this is about, bring me into the inner circle as your consigliere . . . show the outside world there's continuity and honor in the family . . . and take advantage of what's in here." He tapped his temple. "I'm sure I could be of far more use to you. Think of it this way: bringing me in from the cold sends a message to my connects in the other families, doesn't it? It says we are Martellos, blood is blood, now everyone can calm the fuck down. We've got it."

Jimmy smiled and nodded. "That's certainly something to chew over, *Zio*. And yeah, there's merit to it. Let me ponder. The messaging needs to be just right on any sort of move we make."

So, that was it.

Sale was trying to worm his way into the inner circle so he could get close and stick the knife in when they least expected it. It was old school. And so was the logical response. But was there any truth to the stuff he'd come out with? La Cosa Nostra had been gracious enough to him whenever he'd met with any of them. But graciousness, civility, cold charm—that was just the way. There was no knowing what was surface level, purely for show, and what any of them really thought beneath the surface. That inscrutability was paramount to how they operated. Always had been. You didn't sit down at a poker table with those old men unless you expected to walk away with your pockets turned out, the lint inside the only prize. It was easy enough to imagine the older dons were the same when giving a kill order as they were when they sent a boy to bring back cannoli from the bakery around the corner, like the two were of similar proportion and importance.

"I met Alessandro a few weeks ago," Jimmy said, to see Sale's reaction. "Angelo Massino's son, yes? Not like his father at all."

"True, true," Sale said. "He's also been speaking about your shortcomings around town, I'm afraid. His father is a great man, though, one of the best. Have to say, I don't harbor any great hopes for young Alessandro. Too wet behind the ears. No real style."

"But it worried you that he thought ill of me?" Jimmy reasoned.

"What can I say, nephew? I'm very protective of you. You're my blood. Last link to my family, my father, my brother. You are the world to me. I won't hear a word said against you."

"I'm touched, Unc. You have no idea how much that means to me," said Jimmy, nodding. "And you know it goes both ways. You are the closest thing I have to a father now . . . When I look at you sometimes, I see him in there, you know, like a ghost just beneath the skin. It's nice to think about him sometimes."

Sale had a tendency to let his tongue run away with him, without really thinking about what the unsaid things in those conversations gave away, like the fact he was admitting to spending a lot of time with the Massino family without actually admitting it. He could have named any family, any heir, but he didn't. He named Alessandro Massino, and that meant something. So, why them? Was Sale looking for influence, or help?

Did it matter? Either way, it would be a problem.

#

Angelo and Sale sat beneath the pergola in Angelo's garden.

The air was still uncomfortably warm, although the sun was close to setting.

"Close your eyes, breathe deep, and you could almost believe we were back in the old country," Sale said, playing the part. It was whom he had become. He was a reflection of the person he was with, presenting them with the face they wanted to see, the person they wanted him to be. He'd never been remotely interested in gardens, but Angelo was green-thumbed, and this was his pride and joy.

"Well, for the illusion to be complete, you'll want a glass of limoncello to go with that thought," Angelo said. "Or perhaps some *anisetta* if that is more to your taste?"

"Oh, whatever you're having, whatever you recommend," Sale said. "I trust your taste."

Angelo smiled. "Any news of your wayward nephew?"

"I don't know what to do about that boy." He shook his head. "Sometimes I don't know where his head is. Or what he's thinking. He'll be the death of me."

"How so?"

"Ambition. It's the bane of lesser men. He's too ambitious. Too keen to make his mark. Feels like he has so much to prove. He's living with those ghosts of better men, painfully aware that he did nothing. He just stood there while his family was massacred. And he's not found the perpetrators. It's not a good look."

"You think he's going to do something ill-advised?"

"I'm sadly sure of it, and I know people," Sale said, knocking back the limoncello without savoring it at all. "Not that he's confided any specific plans, but yes, I worry. And I can't help but think there's bad feelings between him and your boy . . ." He let that hang for a moment, knowing the gangster would draw his own conclusions from that simple sentence, before he drove the point home. "You know what these young bloods are like with their *testicoli* driving their brains half the time."

"*Coglione*," Angelo said. "You wouldn't think it to look at him, but my Alessandro has the fire burning in him. I'd pity young Jimmy if he was foolish enough to lock horns with him. It ends only one way."

"You know me, Angelo, and the utmost respect I have for you. You're like kin to me. The last thing I want is blood spilled between our families," Sale said, shaking his head. "I think we need to keep an eye on those boys. Make sure things don't take a turn into tragedy."

Angelo nodded thoughtfully. "It would have been easier if you'd put him down like you said you wanted to."

Sale sighed. "Weakness, I know. Sentimentality, him being my brother's boy, but you're right, as ever. But he's proved a hard man to kill, and I worry for your boy."

Of course, what he absolutely wanted was to see blood spilled, the bloodier it was, the better. These few words had a simple purpose. He was planting a seed. Let Angelo stew until he came to the conclusion that Jimmy posed a genuine threat.

What he didn't know was that Alessandro had heard everything through a window above the pergola. He'd been spying on his father from that same window for years.

Alessandro was no fool. He heard the undertow of those words and knew Sale was looking to stir up trouble for Jimmy. Why, though? That was something he couldn't figure out. How did Sale benefit from conflict between their families? Surely, it wasn't just bitterness at Jimmy's inheritance. Or maybe it was. Sale had been cut out, and greed was anything but good. Was it enough to make him turn on his nephew? Maybe.

So, then the question had to be, how could Alessandro make use of his newly acquired knowledge and turn Sale into the kind of useful idiot that served him well?

#

Rosaria and Anna maintained the tradition of Sunday afternoon dinners for the family.

It had been difficult at first, with the echoes of gunfire still an audible memory in the house, and the smell of blood that had seeped into the floorboards, but there came a time when the house needed life, and life was family.

It was good to make time to get together.

While everyone wanted to show their care for the two widows, it allowed them to show theirs in return, allowing them to comfort and be comforted by family.

Sale had enough good grace not to turn up most weeks, but most wasn't all. Jimmy's heart sank when he came through the door and heard his uncle's self-important drone coming from the dining room.

Anna hit him with questions as soon as he set foot in the kitchen. "What's this about you having a feud with Alessandro Massino?" He hadn't even had time to wash his hands, never mind sit down at the table. "And you're late."

"I'm sorry, Mamma," he said. "Traffic. And trust me, there is no feud. You have my word."

"That's not what I've been hearing," Sale said, appearing in the doorway. "Alessandro's talking about taking you down. He's not playing, kid. I've heard it with my own ears. He wants to humble you. Show you that you can't just make moves to take over the top table."

"That's . . ." Jimmy caught himself before he swore in front of his mother. "That's not what I'm doing."

"Doesn't matter if it's true or not; it's all about perception," Sale pointed out. "And if Alessandro thinks that's what you're doing, then it's true enough for him to make sure you've got a problem. That's this life, Jimmy. We've had this talk."

"I don't like this at all," Anna said. "Look at me, son. Whatever this is, you have to make it right. I'm serious. Do it for me."

"Promise," he said, thinking about one of the last things his father had ever said to him. *You live and die by the knife now.* He could say the word, because it was just a word and it didn't change anything in the real world, but it couldn't guarantee his safety. This was the life of the knife now.

Some of his *cugini* started adding their thoughts as they sat around the family table, breaking bread. There was nothing particularly revelatory about their commentary, most saying that Alessandro was a mouth with a limp dick, no real threat to anyone. Jimmy knew it was what his mother needed to hear, so he let them carry on with their grandstanding for her sake.

They got through the main course and were clearing the table when Sale picked up the topic again. The idiot just couldn't let it go. He was like a dog with a bone.

"Don't you go listening to the cousins, boy. You don't want to underestimate Alessandro," he said. And then, like it had just occurred to him, "Or his father, for that matter. Angelo is a piece of work. A viper. And when he turns against someone, his kind of poison kills. Not that the law can ever pin anything on him. He's too clever by far. Hell, even when I know where the bodies are buried, I still can't find the proof."

"What exactly are you implying, Salvatore?" Anna asked, her whole body tense as though she might fly apart at any moment.

Sale raised his hands as though there was nothing he could do. "I've said way more than I should . . . Sorry, dear heart. It was only ever a rumor . . ." But instead of letting it drop, he dangled another tasty morsel. "You hear things in prison all the time. Half of it isn't true. Half of it is exaggerated. But half of it has its footing in reality . . ."

Jimmy resisted the temptation to remark that was a lot of halves.

"Before I came out, some of the boys were talking. The gist of it was how Angelo Massino felt he'd been wronged by a family. No name mentioned, of course, but a reckoning was coming . . . And then, of course . . . well, the rest you know . . . But I can't prove anything."

"And here was me thinking you and him were real tight," Jimmy said.

"Ever heard the phrase, 'Keep your friends close, and your enemies closer'?" Sale said, without missing a beat. "What, pray tell, did you think I was doing hanging around with that scum? I told you, kiddo. I've got your back. I'm putting my *testicoli* on the chopping block trying to get the proof we need. The ladies need closure. You do, too, even if you won't admit it to yourself. You need to know what happened to our family."

Rosaria reached across the table and put her hand over his. "Thank you," she said. "From the bottom of my heart, Salvatore. Thank you. It means so much. I can't rest without answers."

"None of us can," Sale told her. "*Giuro su dio*, I'll never stop trying to find the truth of what happened that day. And there isn't a day that goes by where I don't thank the gods of the old country that young Nicky and Jimmy didn't join their fathers . . . but that is what frightens me too. It doesn't make sense for them to have left our boys alive. And it's definitely not Angelo's style. Remember what he did to those Triads?"

Jimmy had been young when that happened, but he'd heard the stories. He glanced over at Nicky and made brief eye contact.

"You think he's coming back for them?" Anna said.

"Part of me is," Sale admitted, reluctantly. "I don't know if it's all talk, but I know there have been a couple of attempted hits on our boys. That business with the car brakes last year, the knife attack back in the spring. I think we all need to be a lot more careful going forward."

Giovanni, one of the *cugini*, made the obvious suggestion:

"We should strike first."

Playing to the table, Sale protested that would be a terrible idea, that a war with the Massinos would be a disaster for everyone, and again, half whispered that he couldn't be entirely sure the Massinos hadn't wiped out three of their own. He was good at this, being a traitorous little weasel, Jimmy thought, seeing the seeds planted.

Likewise, Sale felt good about the meal.

Violence would follow.

It didn't really matter to him who won—Alessandro Massino was rapidly becoming a pain in the ass, and Jimmy was a thorn in his side. He could afford to lose a few of these young men in the name of advancing his cause.

#

The garage didn't look like much, but that was the point.

It was where the Massinos dealt with stolen and smuggled cars.

They weren't small-time crooks hot-wiring whatever they found on the side of the road. They stole to order, only the very best, and within six hours had them stripped of any identifiers, repurposed for sale, and shipped out. Legit. Almost.

Alessandro enjoyed stealing cars that had already been stolen, especially from the Russian mob. It made him feel like he was doing God's work annoying Putin's boys. Sometimes he called it his war effort and joked that every car he jacked from them was sent back to the Ukraine and Crimea to piss off Putin some more.

When a battered old van pulled in, he didn't think anything of it.

Why would he?

He pushed himself up from the desk and walked toward the office door, ready to tell them they'd picked the wrong garage when the back door swung open, and gunfire cut through the afternoon quiet.

Alessandro didn't think. Everything was instinctive in that moment. He threw himself to the floor, pulled out his gun, then scrambled the few feet more to the doorway on his hands and knees, not taking his eyes off the battered old van that had driven into the heart of his kingdom and unloaded lead.

His first shot grazed a shooter in the upper arm.

He got off a few more, not aiming as he memorized the van's plate.

Shots from around the garage told their own story. His people were fighting back. He knew they would. Alessandro changed tactics, aiming for the tires instead. In those hot seconds, it was hard to read any real strategy behind the attack.

Someone screamed.

In that moment, the silence between shots, Alessandro pulled the trigger, hitting a tire. The van leaned hard. That had the desired effect. Panic ripped through the shooters. They scrambled to reverse out of the garage before Alessandro could put them down. The good tire screamed as rubber burned, the driver nearly losing control in his desperation to get out of there. The rubber strip of a tire flew off, spinning away to slap the hardstand of the workshop floor. That didn't stop them. Before Alessandro reached the concrete they were gone, burning black up the road.

Alessandro walked through his garage, doing a head count.

Anger burned inside.

They had come for him, in his house.

They had driven into his place of work and unloaded.

They had messed with the wrong man.

And now, they were going to take a trip to hell in return.

It wasn't the Russians, looking to rough him up over a couple of stolen cars. If they'd even known it was him, they had no idea where to start looking, and these four walls were a front. Only someone who knew him personally would have known to look for him there. Which made it personal. Which made Sale right.

Jimmy Martello was gunning for him . . . or so Alessandro was led to believe.

TRE

A lot of people in Japan don't have tattoos.

If you wanted any sort of ordinary life without shame—going to the baths and hot springs, places like that—you couldn't get a tattoo. People might draw the wrong conclusions and think you were there to meet with other tattooed people. Yakuza. They weren't the only ones who marked their skin, but the meaning and reason for their ink was layered. New Yorkers had all sorts of tattoos for all kinds of reasons, few with any links back to organized crime, gangs, or families. But there was gang ink, symbols that marked the wearer as part of this crew or that crew, some chalked up to kills. Others were works of macabre art.

Sazuki Kazu was probably the only man in the city with a Yakuza tattoo.

These were more than ornamentation. More, too, than badges of belonging. Only a tattoo master could decide if you were worthy of Yakuza ink.

And he was.

Sazuki Kazu had fought many battles in his long life, even before he'd been inked. But when his younger brother died in his arms, his guts torn to shreds with bullets, Kazu had known he had to earn his ink. He already had tattoos across his back, but nothing like this. This one symbol would change the path of his life forever.

He avenged his brother first.

He was ruthless in taking out the dirty cop who had double-crossed them. There was no moment of mercy, only a message to take with him into the fiery pits of hell. This was for the Sazuki clan.

Then, with the blood still on his hands, he went to the tattoo master and recounted his vengeance.

He needed something special to mark what had happened with his brother, and after talking with the master, he decided to have the rest of his skin tattooed with a crust of black snake scales.

It was a powerful tattoo, but putting that much black ink into his body in one go placed a terrible strain on Kazu's liver, and he grew sick. So sick, indeed, the doctors thought he must have been ill before the tattoo, and the extra toxins had been a tipping point. They should have killed him. In just a few months, he went from being a strong and dangerous man to a fragile bodied fool who needed to spend his waking hours resting in bed.

And he hated it.

Revealing his truth to the community was not easy, especially because the Japanese Yakuza families were incredibly introverted and shared nothing of their lives. However, a family like the Sazukis attracted a lot of interest. And a big man like Sazuki Kazu going quiet was cause for the curious to wonder what had happened with him.

Nicky picked up some of the rumors from one of the Japanese bathhouses he enjoyed. The bathhouses were fronts for brothels, and it wasn't steam that he enjoyed. Nicky had been going to the baths for months now, gathering what gossip he could. Anything that might help Jimmy. That's where he first heard someone say the immortal line, "Sazuki Kazu is out of the game." He wasn't sure if he could believe it, but the word was Kazu's son, Haruto, had taken over running the family business. Haruto was quickly developing a reputation for taking care of his people, meaning Nicky heard good things. While no one wanted to talk about Kazu, they rhapsodized Haruto.

"So, all we have to do is figure out how to get our hands on a black-market liver," Nicky explained to Jimmy over gelato at Amorino's like it was the easiest ask in the world. "How hard can that be?"

"Don't the Chinese sell body parts?" Jimmy mused.

He wasn't sure, but he was pretty certain he'd heard some stories about it. Most were horrific, of course, tales of organ theft, tourists being drugged and waking up missing a kidney.

"It's a way of handling their political rivals, is what I heard," Nicky said. "Of course, the Yakuza would never deal directly with them. They hate each other on principle."

Jimmy nodded. "Of course, they do." This was exactly the kind of problem he'd been hoping for—something he could solve for someone that they couldn't solve for themselves. "Do we, by any chance, have a Chinese contact we can trust?"

"Not so much, but I suspect this is more of a dark-web shopping trip than asking around for a friend to grease the wheels . . . or the organs."

"We all have to move with the times," Jimmy noted. "No matter how distasteful we find it. Some of the guys I studied math with were heading toward computing and codes and all that, rather than business. I'll put some feelers out and see if I know anyone with that particular skill set. How long has the old guy got?"

"Couple of months, maybe?" Nicky said. "Lots of rumors and no facts, so far. Could be a lot less."

"OK, keep working on getting in with the Sazukis. Facilitate a meeting with Haruto, and I'll find a way to get that liver for him."

#

The Yakuza weren't the only organized crime mobs who favored tattoos as a way of showing respect for the kills. The Russians, though, had a different take on ink. In prisons, Russian men often inked everything from stars to architecture to represent their time served or the nature of their crimes. The more stars or more points on a building, the better. Inked badges of honor for pure chaos. It was more common, though, for their victims to have their stories inked into their skin. Girls who ended up as prostitutes saw butterflies tattooed onto their bodies, and beneath the butterfly, they'd have the word *mother* or maybe *forgive me* or some other word that represented their fall from grace. Some even had their owners' names inked onto them like they were cattle that had been branded. Too many Balkan girls ended up trapped in that life of prostitution, snared by what amounted to human trafficking. That ink might have appeared like a small rebellion to someone on the outside, but it was the only autonomy they had over their own bodies.

Ivan Popov had made a terrible mistake.

Scratch that, he'd made a whole run of terrible mistakes, fueled at first by pride and vodka and a chronic need to impress Lev Volkov, and they had only gotten worse.

It had started with a business trip to Novosibirsk that should have been the making of him; he'd been tasked with setting up a Laundromat for the infamous man. A Laundromat. That was Russian humor. They never washed clothes. It was all about money. Cleaning dirty money so it could go back into circulation without leading back to them.

Volkov handled a lot of government contracts, notably for prisons and detention centers, which mostly meant that the state gave him money and then turned a blind eye to his more unsavory proclivities, pretending he was doing only what they wanted him to do. It amounted to complicated networks of bribes and deals that kept the money flowing away from regular Russian people and into the pockets of the superrich, the oligarchs with their yachts that cost more than an island state. Rumor had it Volkov was looking to establish a foothold in the States, and people in positions to do him favors would find him a most generous friend.

Popov was well established in America.

His parents had made the move as defectors but were in fact KGB plants working to gather intel during the Cold War. He'd never been sure whom they had crossed and double-crossed to build their own empire, but there was no mistaking the determination or efficacy of their transition to this new way of life. Did it matter that his mother slept with a gun under her pillow her whole life? How did that stack up against the wealth she had amassed by the time she died? Were the zeroes in the bank balance victory enough? What about the fact she had no friends or enemies left because she had burned everyone who had ever tried to control her?

Ivan had inherited her ambition, but alas, not her ruthless shrewdness.

That was how he ended up across a poker table late into the night with Lev Volkov and a few of Volkov's inner circle. He was desperate to make a good impression. Chances like this didn't come around often, so when the stars aligned, that meant betting large and slugging vodka. Pride and vodka, and stakes that kept rising with each hand. He won some, he lost more, but he didn't care because Volkov kept saying they would become the best of friends.

He made mistakes.

The next morning, with a pounding skull and a gut full of fear, he found out exactly what he'd lost.

It was far more than he could actually cover.

Yes, in theory he had a lot of money, but it wasn't liquid. Most of his wealth was tied up in businesses, properties, and other assets. He couldn't free it up overnight. And that meant all of those promises of friendship were worth nothing.

"It seems you have amassed quite a substantial debt, my

friend!" said Volkov. "I think you got a little carried away."

Popov smiled and tried to look calm. "I would say it's only money."

"You could, but from my side of the table, it looks to me like you gambled your entire life away and lost," Volkov said, smiling. "So, it comes to this, a question for the ages, one that will define every day from here on out. How shall we proceed?"

"I'll get you the money," Popov said.

"Admirable sentiment, but we both know you won't," Volkov replied. "And trust me when I say that. I know exactly what you're worth, and how desperate you are, but the combination is not a good one. So, trust me when I tell you I have seen this before, too many times to count, sadly. I know it can't be done. You bet beyond your means. Now, in the spirit of friendship, I should remind you that I don't like it when people try to cheat me."

Popov knew with grim certainty he would be dead soon.

He had had a good life. Not spectacular, but he had enjoyed some of the finer things, if not the finest. There were worse ways to spend your days on this earth. But all the fight went out of his body. He waited for the bullet, literal or metaphorical.

"But perhaps there is an alternative," Volkov said.

Popov realized in that moment he would to say yes to

anything that would keep him alive. You learn a great deal about yourself in times of extremes, and in all his days, he could think of none more extreme than this seemingly innocent conversation between friends.

"There might be an asset I'd accept and consider all debts repaid in full."

Popov nodded. "Anything, name it."

"Your daughter is a fine-looking specimen. My proposal is this: You give me her passport, and I'll put her to work. And I'll keep her, as a . . . token of your good intentions. Think of it this way. You'll work for me, your daughter will work for me, and best for both of you, everyone gets to live. I am a generous man, but everything you have heard about me is almost certainly true. Believe me, I have earned my reputation."

Popov knew exactly what he meant with that seemingly bland offer to work off his debt.

"Most generous," Popov said, sick to the core. "I'm grateful."

His beautiful girl, his beautiful Chiara, light of his soul, beacon of his heart, would be taken from him, and he'd never see her again.

Volkov would put her into some high-class escort agency, somewhere in Europe, Vilnius, perhaps, or most likely Riga. He'd sell her body to the highest bidder, by the night at first, offering her up as a courtesan, then by the hour as she slowly broke down. Then she'd find herself in a downward spiral of ever cheaper and nastier brothels, the luxury hotels and fine dining a thing of the past, until she was worthless and her face appeared in various torture-porn videos and other ultimate humiliations for perverts with money. Assuming she survived that, there was a direct correlation between the shit she put into her veins to stay sane, how long she stayed physically desirable, and the number of days she had left on this planet.

Ultimately, in taking the deal, he was signing her death warrant. But he told himself that the alternative was refusing the deal and living long enough to see her murdered, anyway. Was it better or worse to condemn his daughter to a living death?

Plus, if Volkov wanted her, he'd take her, regardless of whatever "deal" Popov struck, wouldn't he?

So, hadn't he condemned her the moment he'd sat down at that card table?

He couldn't protect Chiara from this man.

The thought of his beautiful daughter being used by countless men made him sick and sad, but he knew in that moment, he was powerless and she was damned.

Would she ever find out that it was his fault? That he had robbed her of every joy of life in a hand of cards?

Would she get her own butterfly tattoo?

Popov had done things to other men's beautiful daughters—too many for him not to be terrified for his Chiara. This was karma restoring the balance.

#

"We need to talk," was all the message from Alessandro said, but it was enough to make Sale smile.

The boy had taken the bait.

That was all he needed to move forward with his plans.

Sale's thought process was simple: The more chaos he could cause, the more scope he had to play the consigliere, and the better the outcome for him.

He was well on his way to persuading the rest of the Martellos that he had the smarts to be running the show, not that runt, Jimmy. The boy was weak. He had done nothing to honor the fallen fathers. No one respected him. It was different for Sale. The dons knew him, and in the long months since his release, they had come to see him as a changed man, one worthy of respect. They saw SB, not Sale. That loser was a thing of the past. Soon, he would take up his rightful place in the world.

They met at a Jewish bookshop and café, deliberately

chosen, as it was somewhere neither of them would normally frequent. The location had taken some figuring out, because of the demands of propriety. It had to be neutral territory. It had to be somewhere no one would see them. Both men were cautious. And rightly so. Caution kept you alive in their game. It was a bright day, and they sat at a quiet table in the shade under an awning in a street that was almost empty and talked for more than an hour.

"I doubted you at first, SB, but I have come to the realization you were right to warn my father," Alessandro said.

"I'm glad to hear that and sorry to hear it as well, if that makes sense," Sale replied. "Has something happened to change your heart?"

The young mobster nodded. "Something happened. Blood was spilled. They drove a van into our place of work and gunned down some of my people. A license plate was seen. It has been traced to some of your kin."

"I have only regrets," Sale said. "I cannot control them, and they need a steady hand. This is the worst of all worlds. None of us need troubled blood. Especially not you, the son of my dearest friend."

"Appreciated, Salvatore, and that sentiment put me to thinking . . . if only you were head of the Martello family,"

Alessandro said. "Then there would be peace between the families. Long-standing peace. A bond beyond blood."

Sale smiled slightly, "I appreciate your confidence, but I am not sure I am the man for the task."

"He who seeks power is the last who should ever wield it," Alessandro said. "You're like me, Salvatore, a man of dignity, a man of business. You don't like wasted lives any more than I do. You want the good things in this life. You do not crave power for the sake of it."

"You are speaking my language," Sale said. Although he would have agreed with pretty much anything Alessandro said right then.

"Your nephew worries me," Alessandro continued. "I've been watching him for a while, where he goes, who he talks to, and I don't like it."

"Neither do I," said Sale.

"It feels like he is making moves . . . and that makes me wonder, and fear, is he not satisfied with running the Martello family?"

Sale sighed heavily. "And as you so wisely said, he who seeks power is the last who should wield it. Aye, the lad is painfully ambitious, and too much ambition is never a good thing. Couple that with a need to be more of a man than his father, to emerge from his long shadow . . ."

"I've heard whispers the Martellos are muscling in on the drug trade, treading on other people's toes. It is not wise."

"I've heard that too," Sale said. There was a delicious irony in his own schemes making Jimmy look like the cancer eating away at the peace of the city.

"All these meetings, constantly cozying up to the powerful people, it's got me to thinking there has to be a pattern to it, a thought process behind it, and now I am sure I know his intention . . . He's trying to take over the whole business. He wants to seize control of La Cosa Nostra, to wear the crown. King of New York," Alessandro said.

"Which would mean the boy doesn't know his own limits," Sale agreed. "And that way lies tragedy for one and all."

Alessandro nodded.

"The families have been patient with him, on account of his personal tragedies and out of the love and respect they had for his father. But there are limitations. Always. I need you to help me, Salvatore. I need you to help me persuade my father not to put his faith in Jimmy Martello."

"I think your father trusts me, and that I want what is best for him," Sale said.

"Good. This pleases me, Salvatore. I am content that we have similar aspirations. Similar values. I look forward to the day I can call you Don Martello."

Sale couldn't help but smile at that.

It was the first time anyone had addressed him that way, and it felt good.

"Your father will be proud of you," he said in return.

#

Jimmy and Enzo spent the first part of their sit-down going over the figures.

The legitimate aspects of the family business were in good shape—better, in truth, than they had any right to be, all things considered. Over the last year and a half, they'd explored new revenue streams. Online gambling had been one of the more tantalizing ones to catch Jimmy's interests. There were no territories to think about on the internet, no syndicates who were eager to keep you off their turf, no one owning that landscape simply because no one could. It was like the Wild West out there, meaning money was to be made by the right kinds of prospects.

"The more I look, the more I think the cops are far, far behind when it comes to policing digital fraud," Enzo said.

"It doesn't hold the same romance as an underground gambling den or the glamor of a casino, but it makes business sense. If you can build the right infrastructure—keep the system's integrity, reduce risk against reward—you watch the money roll in. Because there is no fool like an addicted one, and this stuff, it's black tar heroin in their veins."

"True, true . . . but if we're getting back into gambling, we need an edge. There are so many big companies out there offering casino games or odds on the next title fight, that sort of thing. We need a reason for people to come to us with their bets. An angle," Enzo said.

"What are you thinking?"

"Fighting," Enzo said. "People love blood. They always have. So, I'm thinking venue: an old warehouse in the shipyard, somewhere out of earshot of the blue bloods, where no one bats an eye if we've got dogs fighting in the pit on the same bill as some bare-knuckle boxing. Proper street fighting. Bring your champion in. Have him fight night after night. Risk and reward. More than just taking up odds on the over and under, it gives you something you can smell. It's all about the experience industry. That's what we'd be selling. The thrill. The punishment. The blood. Visceral sport. Seeing it all happen right in front of you, not sanitized on the flat-screen TV at home."

"High risk," Jimmy said.

"People like risk," said Enzo. "It only adds to the experience. It's all about calculating how much risk you can take. Get that wrong, you go down. That's the thrill. The more risk, the more thrill, and the more money we lift from their wallets."

Jimmy nodded. "And less risk than armed robbery," he said with a smile.

Enzo nodded. "That's a young man's game, and I'm not as young as I used to be."

"I used to try very hard not to know about that side of the business," Jimmy said. "I was a child, I know, idealistic, full of right and wrong morals, and dumb as a doornail. It was disrespectful to my father and grandfather not to want to understand the genius of what they did. I see that now. I mean to look after this family."

"You were always a good boy, Jimmy. And in a family business like ours, that isn't necessarily for the best, but I love you for it, anyway, just as your father and grandfather did."

"The Latin Kings are significant players around here, aren't they?" Jimmy asked, changing the topic slightly.

"Their fronts are mostly dives, full of street kids, but when it comes to weapons, they rule. Everyone buys from them."

"That's interesting to know," Jimmy said.

"I'm not sure I want to know what you are thinking." Enzo smiled softly. "Are they the next in line for your generosity?"

"I think so," said Jimmy. "It's like spinning plates. I've got a few little favors I'm doing here and there, keeping them all going, but it's not enough. I'm going to need something more dramatic to convince the Latin Kings I'm someone worth talking to."

"Hard to imagine what kind of favor they'd want that they couldn't do for themselves," Enzo said after a few moments of thought. He scratched at his jaw. "They have a lot of weapons, and like I said, we all buy from them. No one's trying to mess with that market."

"Everyone needs something," Jimmy replied. "Or wants something bad enough it might as well be a need. All we've got to do is work out what it is."

"Easy as that, eh?"

"Doesn't need to be any more complicated," Jimmy agreed.

#

Jimmy's old college friend Daniel Schmidt came through for him in a matter of days.

"I never had you pegged as a guy who'd need to use the dark

web, Jimbo," he said over the phone. "You always seemed so squeaky-clean." The inference being, not like the rest of your kin.

"And I'd never have guessed you were an expert on all things nefarious, my friend. You always seemed like such a nerd," Jimmy replied. The other man could hear the grin in his voice.

"I guess we all have secrets, and you've got some impressive ones floating about in your gene pool, Jimbo. Although, I'll be honest, I can't for the life of me figure out what the fuck you want a liver for. Doesn't mean I'm not intrigued, though. It's rare I can't get an answer to something that's puzzling me."

"I'm doing a favor for a friend," Jimmy said.

"Not the sort of friend you'd find me connected to on Facebook, I assume? Well, there are a couple of ways of doing this. First up, if you've got the time, you advertise for a willing donor, and then you pay whatever they want. You get a chunk of their liver, they get a chunk of your cash, everyone lives happily ever after."

"And if you haven't got time?" Jimmy pressed.

"You get an organ farmer. They rear kids as donors, sell their body parts. Usually try and take a few of the spares first, you know: a kidney, a liver segment, just the one lung. Keep them alive as long as they can. You can't store organs for long, not outside of the body. So, you have to move fast. Get a specialist medical courier, and get your friend under the knife as fast as possible."

"Understood," said Jimmy. "I think I might handle the delivery myself, all things considered." The idea of an organ farmer made him uncomfortable, but at the same time, it was none of his business how other families made their dime.

Kids conceived simply to be harvested—that was some dark shit.

But it didn't change the fact he needed a young, healthy matching liver fast.

#

Chiara had just gotten out of her car, having come home from the gym, when they grabbed her.

Right up until that moment, it had been a normal day. Boring, even. Her kickboxing class hadn't really stretched her, but that was down to her not pushing herself as much because it was a different instructor. Afterward, she'd been thinking about meeting up with her best friend, Maryum, and a few others. Normal stuff. Her long brown hair fell to her waist when it was untied, only accentuating her deep brown eyes that somehow reflected gray hints in the sun. Chiara was beautiful—gorgeous, even—and statuesque. Her blood was from Italy, more specifically Sicily; yet she stood tall like a Russian, thanks to her father's home training. She pulled down her hair, bunching it back up again to place it in a new ponytail as she kept her hair tie in her mouth.

Hands grabbed her from behind. Brutal. Snatching her wrists behind her back before she knew what was happening. Her hair tie fell out of her mouth and onto the ground as her hair dropped in unison. But she wasn't some helpless princess. She was a fighter. She kicked out hard, lashed, used her elbows, tried to reach around and claw at his eyes with her fingers like she'd been taught, but the man who'd grabbed her was built from brick and steel.

A second man clamped a cloth to her nose and mouth, choking her. She couldn't breathe through the rag, the chemicals getting into her lungs, searing her airways.

She felt the world slipping away.

When she woke, she couldn't move.

There was only darkness.

Panic flooded her system.

Her mind raced.

The only thing she could think was that she was in some sort of coffin, buried alive. There was no room to move. She bit back on the urge to scream. She needed to get a grip. Think. Use her mind. The alternative was to lose. She was not a loser. She was her father's daughter. Even though he'd adopted her from Sicily when she was just a child, she felt as though they shared the same genes. She, too, was a fighter. Even as a young girl, her father taught her how to escape any situation, how to fire a gun, and how to fatally stab. She knew she could instinctively destroy anyone in her path, though how could she get to them if she were locked away?

It took minutes, but slowly and steadily, she felt her heartbeat slow, her breathing settle, and she was thinking clearly. The air was fresh. She wasn't going to suffocate. That meant they wanted her alive, not buried alive.

She stretched, testing the limits of her confinement, and understood that the reality of her "coffin" was actually bonds— she'd been tied up, which stopped her from exploring the space around her, but there was more than she'd have in any sort of barrel or coffin.

With every minute that passed, she grew surer of herself and more determined that whatever else happened, whoever these people were, she was going to survive this.

She tried to piece her new world together from the sounds

around her.

She was in some kind of small vehicle, but not a car. The engine sounds were different. Bigger.

Best guess, more from the way it moved, and the sick feeling that motion stirred, some sort of small private jet.

That realization had its own implications. Whoever had snatched her was powerful. This wasn't kidnap for ransom.

Her father was rich, but not private-jet rich.

Chiara had an idea of what her father did to amass his wealth.

He wasn't so innocent in his business affairs.

He'd worked hard to keep the details from her.

Mostly, they revolved around construction contracts and fraud, but she didn't have to dig too deeply into the concrete and rebar foundations to find the extortion and money laundering that underpinned every building he constructed.

But there were a whole lot of other things she didn't know about.

Guaranteed.

So, if someone with more money than he had snatched her off the street, it wasn't some low-grade beef. He'd fucked over someone *important*.

She was smart enough to know that made her one of three things: a hostage, a payment, or worst case, both.

He wouldn't have sold her if he'd had a choice. That kind of callousness took a special kind of bastard. But there wasn't much comfort in the thought because there was a second side to all of this. Saving herself would put his life at risk.

In that moment, in the dark, somewhere over the world, she knew that she'd do it, whatever it took, because he'd expect her to.

He'd be counting on it, because he'd raised her to be a survivor.

#

"I would like to do you a favor, Sazuki-san," Jimmy said.

Enzo had coached him through the various protocols and honor, perception, and slights that were the landmine-strewn field that was the art of talking politely to Japanese people.

"I am in no need of favors, and I am confused as to why you would want to come to my house looking to help me with something I do not need help with, Mr. Martello," Haruto said.

"In truth, because I do not believe a relationship can be built upon lies. I would very much like for you to owe me a favor."

"Would you now?"

"You'd be free not to repay it, of course. A favor is not an obligation, but I would hope that when the time came, it would be a small thing that I ask, not something of importance to you," Jimmy said.

"Interesting," Haruto said. "You have obviously given this some thought, but still are at a loss. I have no need of favors, so what did you have in mind?"

"A liver," Jimmy said.

On the other end of the phone, silence.

Not even the in-out, inhale-exhale of breathing.

Haruto remained silent and still for some time.

Jimmy knew better than to try and fill the silence.

He kept his nerve and waited.

Haruto would speak.

When he did, it was to say, "I hope you are being serious with me, Mr. Martello. This is not a good topic for a joke."

"I can assure you, I am most serious in my offer," Jimmy said. "I would never make light of your circumstances, Sazuki-san. I know of your family's need. I am in a position to help you. I can bring you a liver. All I need to know is where and when, and I will make sure it arrives at the surgery in perfect condition to enable your father to have his operation. That is my offer to you."

"Why would you do this?" Haruto pressed.

"As I said, aside from the goodwill of your family," Jimmy said, "I may have a small, very small, favor to ask down the line."

"I am suspicious of the size of this favor for you to do something of such importance for my family, but we are in no position to refuse, so let us make arrangements together," Haruto said.

"I trust this is the beginning of a beautiful friendship," Jimmy told him.

#

Alessandro had taken to going out with Sale like he was a man trying to bone a beauty way out of his league, pumping him with fine wines in expensive restaurants, sampling the delicacies of artisanal patisseries, being seen in the most fashionable bars. One time, they even went around an art gallery. Alessandro had zero interest in the exhibits. He was trying to get the measure of Sale. The man was . . . not exactly an enigma, but getting to the root of what made him tick was decidedly more complex than it was with most people. Of course, he liked money; that was obvious. But he only saw the price tags, not the quality. Like his father would say, Sale was a man who knew the price of everything and the value of nothing. You could impress him with a sticker as long as the numbers on it were high enough; yet he showed no signs of having the class or culture to appreciate the quality. Whether they were looking at guns or girls, every single time the price tag fired him up.

Alessandro wasn't a fan.

The more time they spent talking, the more he came to realize the man had not-so-hidden shallows. He was vain and foolish. Not a good combination. He was beginning to understand why the elder statesmen of the Martello family hadn't wanted him to take over. In his own head, Alessandro could see how Jimmy was the better choice, and that was despite the fact he'd begun to genuinely hate Jimmy.

A tortoise would have been a better choice to head the Martello family than Salvatore.

Or a rat.

Sale's urges were simplistic—he craved respect and admiration. His problem was that he had no real way of amassing those things.

He wasn't clever. He had very little in the way of charisma, and after any sort of prolonged exposure, his personality began to grate on people.

In no small part, it was because he so desperately wanted to be important.

But Alessandro had long since seen through that paper-thin facade. Most ventures he undertook failed, and he was the cause of their failure. Refusing to see the truth for himself, Sale blamed all the woes of his world on Jimmy.

On the flip side, if Jimmy *was* actually wrecking Sale's plots in the way that he obsessed, then Jimmy was worthy of respect. That kind of all-seeing, all-knowing interception took 3D chess levels of scheming.

Sale wanted attention.

No, it went beyond want. He needed it like a junkie craved his next hit.

All Alessandro had to do was call him *Don Martello*, like that was how he really saw the man. After that, anything that came out of his mouth was like he was dropping truth bombs left and right for Sale. He was all over it, lapping it up. It shouldn't be too difficult to enlist Sale to take out Jimmy. The trick was to do it without putting Sale into power.

That way, Jimmy would be denied his ruthless climb to King of New York, and no one would notice Alessandro moving about in the background.

Alessandro had his ideas about what the future might hold and who, ultimately, would wear the crown.

The difference was, he had no interest in drawing attention

to himself.

Life had already shown him that he could get a lot done very quietly. More than he could ever have accomplished by jumping up and down and making noise.

Leave it to men like Jimmy to draw all the attention.

Real power didn't work like that, and real power was what Alessandro wanted.

"Jimmy would be nothing without the support of your family," Alessandro pointed out. "That's the foundation to everything he does, the matriarchs."

"True enough," Sale said.

"So, the question is, what do we do about that?"

"It's all about those murders," Sale said. "Jimmy never found out who was behind the shooters. There has been no justice, no revenge, for the wives and mothers, and that leaves a bad taste in the mouth."

"Understandable," Alessandro acknowledged.

"The thing is, the more I think about it, the more I'm coming around to a pretty ugly line of thinking."

"Speak freely. We are friends, Don Martello."

"Honestly, I'm beginning to think Jimmy might have ordered the hit himself." He let that hang in the air between them for a while. "Think about it. He and Nicky magically survive a shooting in that small study, but three other, better, more experienced men die, and the shooters run without putting the youngest generation in the ground. Does that seem likely to you? 'Cause it sure as hell doesn't pass the sniff test to me."

"It does not," Alessandro agreed, but in truth, he wasn't sure what he believed. It was a good story, though. It had credibility to it, and just the right amount of backstabbing for it to work for him, so he'd share it. It wouldn't hurt him for people to start wondering if Jimmy might have whacked his own family. It made it hard to trust someone like that. And if you can't trust them, you aren't so quick to get into bed with them. It was the kind of rumor that, true or not, didn't matter; it would slow Jimmy down. "You need to work on the widows, Salvatore. A boy who doesn't have his mother's love doesn't last long in a family."

Alessandro saw Sale wince at his suggestion; it was a tell. His body betraying his truth. That was exactly what had happened to him. Without knowing for sure, he suspected there was bad blood between him and his brothers that went all the way back. That would explain a lot.

So, for now, at least, the extent of his ambitions was to keep Sale focused on the Martellos.

#

The buildings housing Martello Construction had always been bigger than necessary. The idea was to have room to expand, future-proofing the bricks and mortar. Jimmy's father and uncle had plans for developing the family interests without question, but nothing was ever set in stone, and they hadn't talked plans in front of him, so this new future was one of his own imagining. He hoped they would approve.

Right now, Jimmy needed his new team for personal reasons, but he could see a lot of ways in which they might help him down the line. There were five of them—Daniel Schmidt, whom he knew from college. Jennifer Spinelli, whom Daniel had brought in because she could break into anything digital, along with Janice Wilkins, who could crack the most impossible of passwords. Together, the two were known as *J&J*, the ultimate duo for digital breaking and entering. Travis Tate, the fourth member of the team, specialized in cryptocurrencies and the dark web. And then there was Indie, a curious little person who seemed to be mostly hair and dark glasses. Jimmy had never heard them speak. Indie, though, apparently knew everything there was to know about internet security and proofing any virtual casino operation against the likes of Jennifer. Indie was the only one of the crew he'd never met before; the rest, he at least knew in passing from those glory days of college.

In the short term, what he needed to do was gather information.

So, he picked out a nice, quiet space toward the rear of the building and set them up, buying everything they'd asked for on the inventory.

"I'm calling you *Research and Development* for the tax man," he said. "As far as the IRS is concerned, I guess research is a fair description of what you're doing."

He explained to them who exactly he wanted them to research and what kind of information he needed them to dig up.

"Development we can get around to, but if you are suddenly struck with a lightning idea that will make us all very rich, don't keep it to yourselves." He grinned at that.

Later, Sale caught up with him in his office. "Research and Development? You sure we're big enough an operation to warrant that? Seems like an unnecessary expense," his uncle asked, the questions fusing together.

"I thought we might need some fresh ideas," Jimmy said.

Sale nodded. "I can see that. Tried to have a chat with them. Unfriendly bunch, especially that long-haired one . . ."

Jimmy wasn't surprised. He'd given them clear instructions to avoid talking to Sale about anything pertaining to their work, what he'd asked them to do, and anything they unearthed, as he'd set them on Project Salvatore Martello. He wanted whatever information they could gather on his moves and plans. Listening to the bugs in his office took up too much of Nicky's time. He had better things for his cousin to be doing.

Later, he got a message from Daniel to say that Jennifer had picked Sale's pocket when he'd come over to annoy them, stealing his phone. She'd installed an app of her own making onto it.

They'd bring it over to him, and he could tell Sale it must have been dropped it in the office. The home-brewed app would do everything Nicky's bug had done and more, as well as being mobile. Sale would carry it with him everywhere. They'd be able to track him wherever that phone went. Whatever he typed, they'd read. What he saw on his six-inch screen, they would see on theirs, and when he phoned anyone, it would both play and record his conversations.

Sale wouldn't be able to take a leak without them knowing he was unzipping.

It served to make Jimmy feel considerably safer.

Trying to constantly outwit the man had been exhausting,

but at least now, he wouldn't have to worry so much about trying to stay two steps ahead of his uncle.

As far as he was concerned, his new crew had more than earned their paychecks just for that.

And this was barely scratching the surface. He'd get a lot more help from them over the coming weeks.

All he had to do was wait.

They would dig, and somewhere in their excavations, they'd find what he needed to move forward with his plans.

#

Being predictable was a safety risk, but whenever Jimmy was in town, he made a point of drinking at the same cocktail lounge, always on a Wednesday. He was taunting the rest of the families. He wanted to be found. If someone came looking, there was a lot to be said for approachability. He kept one bodyguard with him, but there was always a second one lurking inconspicuously somewhere within the venue. Backup in case things turned ugly.

So far, the worst they'd been involved in was throwing a couple of wannabe thugs out of the building.

Anyone who wanted to talk to him could walk up and

introduce themselves.

Most weeks, someone did just that.

Often, it was more than just the one. It became a pilgrimage for them. They wanted to check him out, or make sure they were on his radar. Some came looking to sell him something, often information, and more often than not, he bought it. Even if it wasn't relevant to his interests, it was about fostering a reputation for paying well for good information. Knowledge was power in this world. It gave him a steady supply of people who wanted to get bed with him, some more literally than others, and some of them, he ended up obliging.

There was no one in life worth a return visit, but he had nothing against a little fun. He'd take photos too—not as souvenirs or trophies, but again in the name of information gathering. He'd send the images to his research and development team, who would work their magic. They never slept. There was always someone at the other end of the message, whatever time he sent it.

Maybe he wasn't the only vampire in the world after all.

This time the girl who sashayed across the lounge was quite obviously looking for something. She was blonde and sun-kissed bronze. He liked how she moved.

From the way she scanned the room, it was clear she was

looking for him.

When she finally spotted him, there was a moment's hesitation. She bit her lip, unsure, then committed to the moment and walked over.

"Are you Jimmy Martello?"

"I am," he admitted, signaling for a drink to be brought over. "Sit, please." He could tell she was nervous.

"My name is Stephanie Kaminski," she said. "Not that it should mean anything to you . . . I heard that you like to be helpful."

"I do. So, tell me, how can I help you, Stephanie?"

"My friend has gone missing. I'm worried about her."

"I'm sorry to hear that."

"I think this might be of interest to you because of who her father is."

"I'm listening," Jimmy said, leaning forward attentively. There was a gentle smile on his face, filled with warmth. It always worked with people starved of human contact and kindness. Such a simple thing, a little smile.

"Her father is Ivan Popov."

Stephanie watched his face, waiting to see if he knew the name.

Of course, he did. Working in construction himself, it was impossible not to run into Ivan Popov. The man had sway. He had the political power to make or break projects.

If you wanted to break ground in certain areas, Popov would need his palm greased to facilitate it, or your shovel would never dig up that first bucket of soil and clay. For all intents and purposes, Popov ran a fairly simple extortion racket and made good bank from it. Mostly, the Martellos tried to keep out of his way. It was impossible not to cross paths eventually, and when they did, they'd see he got whatever he wanted, just to keep things smooth.

"Tell me about your friend," Jimmy said.

He'd been looking to find a way to add a Russian favor to his slowly growing list of names he could call upon. A gift horse had just walked into his club.

"She's been gone a week. No one has heard from her, not her friends, people she spent time with, no one. And before you say she's young, maybe bored and looking for a thrill, having run away with some guy and to hell with everyone else . . . this isn't like her. She doesn't do this. Ever. She's a part of the modern world, the social media age. Sure, she jets off all over the place, but she's always posting photos, posing for selfies, and living her best life very publicly. And she's never alone. There's always someone along for the ride. She was supposed to be meeting with our friend Maryum, but she never showed up. This isn't like her. I'm worried. When Maryum told me, I thought of you."

Jimmy hid a smile. He liked feeling reliable, even given the circumstances. "Have you talked to her father?" Jimmy asked.

Stephanie sighed, like she'd known she was going to have to say this—and didn't want to say it—but knew he needed to hear it. Yet she wasn't sure it painted her friend's father in a good light. "I've talked to his personal assistant, who says Chiara is going to be away for a while and not to bother them again," said Stephanie. "Those were her exact words. Not exactly the anxious father, you know. So I kept calling her, and her phone rang and rang the first few days, but she didn't answer it or reply to texts. Now it goes straight to her voice mail. Number isn't answering, leave a message. That freaked me out. That's not like her. I've been around to her apartment, and she wasn't there. I've banged on neighbors' doors. I've made a nuisance of myself. Last time anyone saw her was when she was at her kickboxing class, and that was a week ago. Look, I know what you're going to say, but she's not the sort of person to do this. Something has happened to her."

"When you say *something*, you think she's been kidnapped?" Jimmy asked.

She nodded. "It's not the only thing that makes sense, but . . . the way her father's PA acted, cutting me off dead, the man he is . . . It just seems like they are lying, so yes."

"Any idea who might do that? You're her friend. You know the family circle." It was a long shot, he knew.

Stephanie shook her head. "Her father's terrifying. I don't think anyone who knows who she is, who *he* is, would risk making him angry."

"Unless he offended someone considerably more connected than he is. Someone who wields true power in this city," Jimmy speculated. "Someone who really doesn't need to care about consequences because there are none in their world."

"Can you help?"

"I can try," Jimmy said. "Trying and actually helping are two very different animals. But you have my word, I will do everything I can."

He gave her the contacts for his research and development team, and told her to send them everything she could about Chiara and her father, anything she thought might help them, no matter how insignificant or if she'd already run down that avenue. It was a daunting task, way beyond a needle-in-a-haystack level of improbability. The young woman could be anywhere in America—actually, anywhere in the world. Pull this off, and he might want more than one favor from Popov. A little goodwill on the construction front would be welcome.

Assuming, of course, that it wasn't a family problem akin to his own, and that Popov wasn't behind his daughter's disappearance. Which, given the world they lived in, was far from an impossibility.

Still, the idea of rescuing a lady appealed to him.

There was something noble about it.

Old school.

#

"For a man who has nothing good to say about Salvatore Martello, you seem to be spending an awful lot of time with him," Angelo pointed out with a wry smile over a plate of linguine.

"What can I say, Papa? I was swayed by your obvious fondness for him," Alessandro said.

Angelo laughed at this. "You little dick. You know me better than that."

Alessandro nodded. "I do. You're enjoying the chaos he is causing, aren't you?"

"It really is quite delicious," Angelo conceded. "For an idiot, he has a lot of schemes, and some of them aren't actually pipe dreams. He amuses me, for now. I am not foolish enough to believe he is the man capable of turning those half-decent ideas into very decent realities. But you have to admit, it is amusing watching the rest of the families scramble around trying to work out what the fuck he is actually doing."

The conversation drifted to different topics, most tangential but all of family interest, before Angelo gently came back around to grilling his son. "So, are you going confide in your old man? I want to know what you're up to."

Alessandro smiled at that. "Ah, Papa, you know me better than that," he echoed, enjoying himself.

His mother, Maria Luisa, chuckled at the turnabout. "Oh, Angelo, you really haven't been paying attention, have you?" She shook her head even as she turned the fork through the noodles and lifted dripping linguine to her lips. She didn't put them in her mouth for a moment. Instead, she asked. "Do you even know where your boy spends most of his evenings?"

"What, aside from associating with Martello? There's somewhere else? Dare I even ask?" He peered at his boy, waiting for him to fill the silence.

"Ah, well, I admit I've been dabbling in a little local politics. Nothing too serious, just sounding people out," Alessandro admitted.

"Politicians are expensive, boy, and in my experience, rarely worth the investment," Angelo said.

Alessandro nodded. "Yes. Which is precisely why I was thinking it might be more interesting to *be* one than trying to pocket one."

"You want to run for election?" He thought about it for a moment. "Well . . . it isn't a horrifying idea. It might even be an interesting one. Tell me, do you really think you have the stomach for it, my boy? The sheer levels of boredom, all those endless meetings with pen pushers and scheming, conniving, little bastards trying to get something to line their pockets? You do know you can't shoot them if they piss you off." Angelo laughed, clearly having amused himself.

"You know I never much liked violence," Alessandro said. "At least not overt confrontation. There are much more satisfying ways to destroy a person."

"And that is the flesh of my flesh that I know and love speaking with. You like the game. And politics is all game of the purest sort. You'll be able to cause all kinds of trouble. I have no doubt."

"I very much plan to," said Alessandro.

"So where does our 'dear friend' Salvatore fit into all of this? I can't think of a less useful running mate." Angelo chuckled. "Or maybe the genius is convincing him to run against you."

"Ha! Now, that's an entertaining idea, but no, my interest in

Salvatore Martello has everything to do with the families and with Jimmy Martello. Nothing to do with him."

"Do tell," Angelo said. "I'm sure I will find all of this highly amusing."

"You don't take Jimmy Martello half as seriously as a threat as I think you ought to, Papa."

"I see no reason to. The boy's wet behind the ears. He's weak. He didn't even have the *testicoli* to avenge his own father. No, I do not take him seriously as a threat because he is not a serious person," Angelo said.

"Did you ever stop to consider the possibility that Jimmy was the one who pulled the gun on them?"

"A power play, of course. Ambition is a thing of beauty in the right people. But yes, I thought about it and dismissed the idea," said Angelo.

"I look at him. I watch him making moves, and I think he's trying to take over."

"Ah, taking over. That's young man's talk. But you find out as you get older that the effort isn't worth it, and it is better to have good neighbors than to always be looking over your shoulder, aware that someone is trying to bring the king down. The only way to become the king is to kill the king. That knowledge is enough to destroy a lesser man. The more you enjoy life, the more you *want* to enjoy your life rather than waking up every day wondering if it will be your last. Let me offer some wisdom of the years, *figlio*. When you're young, someone always seems to be trying to take over. The idea even appeals to you, and for a fleeting moment, it seems possible. Seductive. You want the power that comes with it, but you learn that to be the King of New York is a curse, not a prize. We all learn that, or we die before the lesson takes hold in our reckless minds."

Alessandro said nothing in return.

#

Sale sat counting his money.

There was an irony to the act, of course. So many times, he'd complained about how much he hated counting the money, because, of all things, there was so much of it.

Now he hated counting the money because there was so much less of it than there had been the week before, and the week before that.

His profits were on a steady, and alarming, decline. And the worst part was, he couldn't for the life of him understand why.

Kids had been falling over themselves to move his product.

They were banging down his door for dime bags, eighths, quarters—desperate for anything they could get their hands on and get out onto the street. Now, he couldn't get anyone out there for love or money. No one wanted to work on the streets. Too many of his corner boys and runners had been busted by the cops or taken out by rival gangs. He didn't have the protection for them, and no one was silly enough to take his dollar when it was going to get them killed. People weren't that desperate.

It had been nagging him for a while. There had to be a rat in his operation. Someone selling him out. Trouble was, he'd been so careful making sure no one knew all of his plans, there simply wasn't one person who could have betrayed him so successfully. Little people had little bits of the puzzle; no one had the whole thing.

He'd been clever with his setups.

So, how could his enemies know what he was doing?

Not just know, but know so quickly they could counter and collapse him before he could even think?

No way were the law or those BMF gangster rappers clever enough to figure all of this out and make counters to his strategies. But someone was, and they kept hitting his distribution network, taking his gear, and killing his people.

Part of Sale knew that in this game, nothing was fair, and no one owed him anything.

But at the same time, it was driving him out of his mind that he couldn't get ahead.

He was supposed to be ahead.

He deserved to be ahead.

And it wasn't happening because someone was to blame.

There was only one person who could destroy him so righteously, and look so innocent doing it. Jimmy. That little runt had done this to him. He didn't know how he'd done it, but he was goddamn sure that little wannabe don of a nephew had done it to him, and loved doing it.

The more he brooded, the more Sale filled up with rage.

Sale was old school. His worldview was a power dynamic more suited to the Mafia of the 1920s than the 2020s. Guns were his weapons of choice, along with blackmail, intimidation, and fear, but in a fight between a gun, the dark arts of the internet, and the sheer volume of information out there to be traded off and built on, a gun was worth nothing.

He had a phone when he got out because he thought he ought to have one, to call people, to make connections, but he barely understood it, let alone the apps and other functionalities. He had no idea it could be used against him, never mind that it already was.

Meanwhile, across town, the BMF were taking tips about everything he did, and using them as the foundation to rebuild their own empire.

Sometimes they shot the kids who were working for Sale; sometimes they recruited them.

It paid to keep everyone guessing.

Trust in Sale broke down, and before long, he wasn't as welcome as he had been.

Ironically, as the money dried up, so did the friendliness. No one wanted to deal with a loser who left their people exposed to the cops, or worse, rival crews.

Piece by piece, everything he'd tried to build began to fall apart.

It was like entropy. Once the cracks were there, the collapse was relentless and inevitable.

When he called his friends, they told him not to worry about it.

"Sometimes you win some; other times you lose. That's just business," they said.

There was no comfort in those platitudes.

"You have to help me get back on top," he pleaded.

"You'll be right where you're supposed to be," one of them

promised him.

Sale didn't want to think about what that might mean.

But part of him knew. Part of him had always known. Everything that was going wrong was going wrong for a reason. Jimmy. That cost him a lot of sleep.

After another week of dwindling money and no answers, he gave up and phoned Alessandro.

"Ah, my young friend, might I pick that very clever brain of yours?"

"Of course, Don Martello. How can I help you?"

Sale drew in a deep breath. He really didn't want to admit how badly he was failing, but he needed Alessandro to understand how serious the situation was, and the threat Jimmy Martello posed.

"Well, I'm sure you've been hearing whispers, but the truth is, I've had a run of bad luck lately," he began. "And I find myself wondering if there's any way it might not be bad luck, after all, but rather someone working against me. Someone with insider knowledge of my operations."

"I'm sure you've already thought about who has access to that information," Alessandro said.

"Naturally," Sale agreed. "I've been so careful about who knows what, and limiting it, so I'm the only one who knows enough to actually betray this operation, and, well, unless I have had a psychotic break and developed multiple personalities, I'm not selling myself out . . . but someone is. This can't be a coincidence."

"Then the most likely explanation is that your system has been compromised," Alessandro said.

"What do you mean?"

Alessandro thought about it for a moment. "You do all of your business on your phone?"

"Yes," said Sale.

"Then I think your phone has been compromised. Hacked. Bugged. I don't know. But if they are ahead of you at all times, then it is the logical weak spot in your op."

"It looks OK," Sale said, shaking his head.

Alessandro sighed heavily "Looks have nothing to do with it. You want to throw that phone in the river and get yourself a new one. Get two. Have a secret phone you only use for business, and one you use for show."

"And you think something as simple as changing my phone might solve my issue?" Sale asked with cautious optimism.

"I think there's a very good chance it will."

#

Travis was listening for the research and development department, enjoying Sale's cluelessness. The man was a moron. He was almost certainly going to get himself a replacement handset from the same company as before. He might even be dumb enough to use the same number. But even if he was smart enough to avoid the most obvious pitfalls, he would leave the phone on his office desk because that was how sloppy the man was.

Thinking about it, it might be just as well to let him have a good week, let him think he was winning, before they dropped the hammer. Just keep watching, biding their time until they could get on with ruining him for the boss.

As jobs went, it was one of the more entertaining things he'd been paid to do.

#

Jimmy regretted having arranged to be the courier. There was nothing but a glass door between him and the surgery where the donor was about to be divested of a viable chunk of her liver. Despite being at a distance, he knew he was going to be able to see more of the operation than he wanted.

The donor couldn't have been more than twenty-two.

Her eyes were big and solemn, but she seemed very calm.

First impression, they'd drugged her already, to make her pliable, but that made no sense. It would damage the organs. So, if it wasn't drugs that made her malleable, then what? Was it that she believed in the people who were using her like this? Or was it some sort of repayment, a family debt being cleared? Or, seriously long-term planning, with her having been born to act as a sort of body farm, like Nicky had suggested? That thought, looking at her now, in the flesh, was the sickest of all alternatives, because she wasn't just a bag of bones and organs. She was a living, breathing person with hopes and dreams and a personality and everything that went along with being human. Whatever it was, she was calm, and there was a mercy in that— for him as much as her. Jimmy wasn't sure he could have stood by and watched as they forced a screaming, terrified child onto the table to cut.

Again, he found himself back in that study, back in his father's final moments, and it was all so viscerally real. It was a grim reminder that he was doing the right thing, whatever the cost to his psyche.

It wasn't like the donation would kill the girl.

Some future donation might, but that wasn't on him. It wouldn't be his ghost to carry with him.

The medical team was masked. He couldn't have picked them out in a lineup. They were incredibly calm as well. They must have done this sort of thing every week, if not every day.

He watched with interest as the girl was sedated and they went to work on her.

Every move—not just the cutting—was slick.

He watched the nurses pass tools to the surgeon, saw blood on latex gloves as the cutting began, everything happening with such precision and pace. He was struck by the similarity to a butcher's shop or a meat factory. There was no indication they were taking a girl apart for money, even if it was a lot of money. This looked like a regular surgery . . . even if it was the very essence of irregular. It was the kind of stunt he couldn't afford to pull off too often without ramifications.

When the liver came out, it was dark red and glossy, and visually not much different from cow livers he had eaten during certain family occasions.

That was his cue to go in with the cooler and get moving.

Jimmy knew he had twelve hours at most to get that liver safely into Sazuki Kazu's body, or everything was for nothing.

He'd cashed in one of his owed favors in the form of a loan of a Gulfstream G550 and a pilot for the trip to Hawaii.

The people behind the favor had their own reasons for

agreeing beyond their debt to Jimmy. They knew the benefit of an in with the Sazukis, anyway, so it was more likely than not, he'd be able to cash in again down the line if push came to shove.

When Kazu had gotten sick, his family had moved him out to their Hawaiian retreat so that he could have peace and, ultimately, to remove the temptation of work. Admitting to his location was an act of trust on Haruto's part, and Jimmy knew exactly how important that was in terms of acknowledging his own standing.

Everything was set up.

Kazu would be in his own hospital, already being prepped for surgery.

Given it would take over ten hours to fly from New York to Hawaii, with a stop for refueling along the way, there would be no wiggle room. So, instead, he'd made arrangements to collect his liver from Los Angeles, which greatly reduced the flight time.

Wheels down, Jimmy was met by Haruto on the tarmac and was ushered into the back of an anonymous black car, which took off at Mach speed.

"Please accept this token, a viable liver for your father," Jimmy said, handing the cooler to Haruto, "as a sign of peace and friendship from myself and from my family."

"You'll come with me to the hospital," Haruto said.

It wasn't a question.

Haruto said very little until his own doctors had examined the liver and confirmed that it was indeed human rather than a pig liver or some other cross-species variant, and a match for Kazu.

Surgery followed quickly.

It was only after the surgeons had confirmed the success of the operation that Haruto spoke to him again.

"*Arigato*, Jimmy. I will not forget this. Come to me when you want your favor. It will be my pleasure to repay you with pride. You are a man of honor. I, too, am a man of honor. I owe you my father's health and life."

\#

QUATTRO

Stephanie had sent a lot of photos of Chiara to Jimmy. His research and development team forwarded them to him, along with what details they had.

Jimmy had to contain himself the moment he saw Chiara. He'd heard of love at first sight, but love at first photo? It felt irrational, especially since Jimmy had spent his entire life just accessorizing girls. Sure, he had dates, but never relationships. He was mainly concerned with who could possibly understand his family. The girls in other crime families were spoiled, yet they craved a wild, secret life, despite the watchful eyes of their fathers. He wanted none of that, but for this woman—this woman he'd never met, yet felt a gravitational pull toward—he was willing to risk it all. He didn't know her life, but he wanted to give her the best one he could. That started with rescuing her from chaos.

He spent a while just looking at her—familiarizing himself with her face. She was pretty. More than pretty. In a lot of the photos, she was smiling for the camera, and no matter what she was doing, she had a warmth about her. A life behind her eyes that he prayed was still there. In most of the pictures, she was with girlfriends—all of them pretty in their own ways, made prettier by money, but none were a match for Chiara, he thought.

The notes on her made for interesting reading.

Chiara wasn't Russian by birth, but Sicilian.

His heart skipped a beat when he read that, though there was no logical reason why it should matter to him. Then he noticed that her middle name was Anna—his mother's name. That felt significant too. Jimmy didn't believe in fate. But his mother was a huge believer in signs, and these were signs that, in her world, might as well have been neon.

The more time he spent looking at her pictures, the more he felt it, this irrational bond between them.

She could be anywhere in the world.

That posed the most obvious challenge: How was he supposed to find her? He couldn't just put a tracking app on her phone.

And, should he somehow succeed in the impossible and find her whereabouts, how was he supposed to rescue her? He didn't have his own personal army, a Navy SEAL Team he could dispatch to bring her home.

This made the deal with the liver seem painfully simple.

Rebuilding BMF supply lines had been child's play compared to this.

Could he do it?

For the first time since he'd taken over the Martello family,

Jimmy had doubts, and it was the absolute worst time to be having them.

And for the first time since he'd started this plan, he was faced with something that felt more important than his own vengeance.

He wanted to rescue Chiara.

He wanted to be a better man for her.

A hero in her life.

He didn't care how independent modern women were, or how capable of saving themselves they were. It wasn't about the female of the species. It was all about him and what he needed, and he needed to be something *good*.

The first challenge was getting her father to admit she was in trouble.

He could try and circumvent Popov, go behind his back, but that risked the Russian mobster thinking he was involved in her abduction. The same was likely if he simply cold-called with an offer to help solve his problems, a favor for a favor. A lot depended on why Chiara had been taken in the first place, and what Popov knew.

He sent an email to his research and development team, asking them to dig up what they could on Popov.

Did the man have debts?

Enemies?

Was this ransom or revenge, essentially, or a means of control? Keeping Popov in line.

Figuring this out would be a good start.

He didn't have any contacts in the Bratva who weren't themselves connected to Popov in some way, direct or indirect, and what connects he did have to the Russian mob were from the construction side of his own business. Legit. He needed to go to the dark side.

Somewhere over the last few days, it had stopped being about earning a favor from her father and became all about bringing Chiara home safely.

When Daniel checked in later that evening, Jimmy assumed it was going to be about Chiara. It wasn't.

"Well, boss man, I've got some juicy news for you. We're talking federal investigation. You're going to like this," Daniel said.

"Popov?

"Nah, Indie's looking into him as we speak. This is the sweet, sweet fruit you find when you hack into federal emails, boss, believe me. This is next-level insider world. I'm talking your angle into the Latin Kings."

It took Jimmy a moment to remember he'd tasked Daniel into

looking into the Kings. Not everything was about Chiara, even if that was how it felt inside his head right now. Bigger picture, the Latin Kings were vital to his plan. "Tell me more."

"Raul Cabrera has made some serious mistakes by the looks of it in this email chain, boss. He was pulled over on a ride to Milwaukee, two days ago, with ten guns in the car. Serious heavy-artillery stuff, not licensed handguns. Now, he might have managed to get off the hook, except for the fact the cops have been looking for a way to get to him for a while. They're investigating his arcade on the South Side of Chicago, assuming it's a front to trade weapons, semilegit or at least untraceable—no records, no licensing. Thousands upon thousands end up on the streets every year, bought legit, purged, and sold, that wind up in crimes all across the United States."

"And you think that's true?" Jimmy said.

"I know it's true. And if I can find that out, you can bet your ass that the cops know. What I don't know is why Raul isn't running at least some kind of legit gun trade. It's easier to hide things in plain sight. Running guns illegally out of gambling arcades isn't smart. Not with his reputation."

"So, he's heading for a fall?"

"Racing toward the edge of the cliff. They're going to slap him with a RICO charge. Raid the arcade, get the guns to prove the whole thing is a front, and they've got him. He won't be coming out to see the sun for a very long time. And inside, he's a dead man. We don't have a lot of time to take advantage, though," Daniel said. "They're gearing up to take him down in the next week or so. I can monitor chatter, but whatever you're going to do, you have to do it soonish."

Jimmy considered this new information.

Up until now, he'd been approaching people to see how he could help them—what they needed from someone out in the world, even if they didn't know it, and then delivering on that need.

If he made contact with the Latin Kings first, they could just as easily act on the intel without him, and he'd lose any sort of leverage his forewarning gave them. But if he acted without their explicit approval, he ran the risk of ticking them off, and the whole thing could very easily blow up in his face.

Time to take a gamble.

Thinking fast, he told Daniel, "I have an idea, but, dare I ask, how good are you with paperwork?"

"I assume you're thinking something properly filed and in the system like it's been there for a year already?"

"You're reading my mind," Jimmy said. "A hard copy I can hold in my hands."

"Of course," Daniel replied. "Why do I get the feeling you're going to play this for dramatic effect?"

"Because you're learning," Jimmy smiled.

If he played this right, it would do wonders for his reputation on the streets.

If . . .

#

Jimmy felt the cold steel at the tip of the gun's barrel kissing his forehead.

It was not a pleasant experience.

"You know what?" a garbled, deep voice echoed in the background. "I think you need a better view."

The gun then lifted from his forehead and moved into the space between his eyes.

Sale. It had to be Sale.

It could only be Sale.

Surely.

He couldn't see the man's face; he didn't need to. The more he focused on the voice, the surer he was. Even masked, it was unmistakable.

So, his uncle had finally grown some gonads and taken matters into his own hands.

Of course, Sale was too much of a coward to pull the trigger himself.

"There, that's better," the phantom voice continued. "Now, you have a front-row seat to the big show."

The pressure had left a ghost of pain on Jimmy's forehead, in the shape of a third eye.

He made a grab for the gun that should have been at his hip, his hand grasping at nothing.

The move earned a husky chuckle in the semidarkness. "Tsk, tsk, I have your gun, Jimmy boy. This is your last shot. *This* one right here." He jostled the pistol's tip and started laughing some more. In the unlit room, the only thing within Jimmy's line of sight was the gun itself. He couldn't even make out much about the hands holding the grip or the trigger finger.

It felt so familiar. The words felt so familiar. Like he'd lived this moment before.

He couldn't dwell on it.

Jimmy threw himself toward Sale in one desperate leap.

He expected to feel the bullets punch into his body.

It didn't matter.

He was going to die like a man, on his feet and fighting back, not on his knees begging for mercy.

He felt no fear.

The scene dropped into slow motion as Jimmy spun to see the surprise on his uncle's face.

Sale had expected surrender.

He was unprepared, like he always had been.

A gun is only a weapon if you're willing to use it.

Sale hesitated.

Jimmy punched him in the face.

Bang!

The bullet traced a searing line of pain across his ribs.

Life did not flash before his eyes. Instead, Jimmy saw Chiara, tied to a bed and weeping. If he died here, he couldn't save her. Two people died, even if only one of them was in this room. She didn't even know his name, or that he was coming to save her.

"You can't escape from me, boy," said Sale, only this time, his words had taken on a thick Russian accent. "Say *Спокойной ночи.*" It was good night. He knew it was good night, even if he had no idea how he knew, or why he suddenly understood Russian.

Jimmy heard the click of the trigger, and then . . .

Bang!

He woke up with cold sweat clinging to his clammy skin, more angry than afraid.

His phone rang. It was the noise that had dragged him from the dream. He'd made the switch from "Volare" as his ringtone to a standard siren, as the song still haunted him from the last good morning he'd had.

For a moment—the silent millisecond between heartbeats—he had the irrational hope that it was Chiara trying to reach out to him.

Shaking off the last remnants of the dream, he reached out for the phone and saw Nicky's name on the screen.

#

"You only have to look at the figures to see something has changed," Enzo said. "It's always in the numbers. The truth. Numbers never lie."

Getting accurate figures for Sale's exploits wasn't easy, but even within the limitations of their surveillance work, it was obvious that life had gotten a lot better for Sale recently. And that bugged Jimmy. He was certain their dark-web activities would lead his uncle right to the edge of despair and face a reality of going out of business.

The plan he'd been working on with the BMF had been going well.

So, it made no sense how Sale was getting ahead again.

And he hated things that went against reason and evidence.

It made him feel like an idiot. There was room for only one of those in his life, and that was Sale.

"Have we heard a peep out of Big Capo? This ought to concern him," Jimmy asked. His first thought was that their deal had gone sour, and the music man hadn't bothered to tell him.

"Last I heard, he was back on top and declaring peace with the families," Enzo said, shaking his head. The same thought must have occurred to him when he checked the numbers. "If there was trouble from him, we'd know about it."

"So, then, what's changed? What aren't we seeing here?" Jimmy was good with numbers and pattern recognition within them. It occurred to him that there was only one reasonable explanation, and that Sale must have found new territories for deals. He said as much. "You hear anything to suggest he's expanded into new markets?"

"Not a peep," said Enzo.

"So, a deal with the fucking devil, then, but you don't just develop a better business model or discover the genius of quality control like this. Improved his marketing? Getting the word out to the more desperate? Hitting up the twenty-four-hour party people?"

Jimmy laughed at the prospect. Sale was no businessman. He'd been lucky before. Was this another rich vein of luck, or was there something behind it?

"I thought we had him," Jimmy said, struggling to keep the

disappointment out of his voice. He tried to think. His research and development team watched Sale's every move. Nothing got past them—or at least, nothing should have. "Give me a minute, Enzo, I need to talk to some of my people."

He rang their office and got Travis.

"What can I do for you, boss?"

"Quick question: You notice anything unusual from our mutual friend lately?"

"Not much of note," Travis said. "He's staying at home more, ordering more takeout, but that's about it."

Jimmy swore quietly. "Thanks, Travis."

He hung up and turned his attention back to Enzo.

"Well, I think I know what's going on. He's regressed about twenty years and returned to conducting business face-to-face," he said, thinking it through. "He's leaving his phone at home, and when he calls for takeout, he's actually calling for someone to come and get him in a car we don't know and aren't tracking. Meaning, he's onto us. Even if he doesn't know exactly what we're doing, he's worked out that technology isn't his friend."

"That would explain everything," Enzo agreed. "If it was anyone other than your uncle, I'd buy it, but I don't think he's clever enough to think up something like that. Plus, doing better business by showing up, that's not Sale. He lacks . . ."

"People skills," Jimmy said.

"That's one way of putting it," Enzo said.

"OK, so he's got help. A partner in this. Someone far smarter than him?"

"Again, that would explain everything, except for the small question of why someone that clever would have any interest in getting into bed with a weasel like Sale," Enzo pointed out.

"You're right," said Jimmy. "So, what can this clever person see that we can't? Who the fuck benefits from working with Sale? Not someone from the gangs, so, someone else. But no fucker with half a brain trusts Sale, not from any of the families . . . so who does that leave?" A thought occurred to him then, a dark one. "Russian mob?"

Enzo shook his head. "You're chasing ghosts. You can't second-guess this shit; it'll make you paranoid. We know something's changed, but that's the only thing that we know. That change in the landscape means he's raking in the money again. Everything else is just guesswork."

"Maybe, but I think I'm right about this," Jimmy said. Maybe not the Russian mob, but someone who wanted to hurt the Martellos. Someone with a grudge against him, personally?

That could be any number of people.

He knew there were plenty out there who didn't like how he

was doing things.

Maybe they saw Sale as a route to him?

Was Sale going to invite someone to Sunday dinner and have them shoot Jimmy?

It wasn't like he didn't have form.

Or maybe Sale found himself a partner who was all about the green?

It never occurred to Jimmy that Alessandro could be the one helping Sale. Why would it? Never in a million years could he have guessed Alessandro's motives, how he was driven by reputation and connection, or that the only thing that truly interested Alessandro was building himself up, cementing his name in the minds of the families as he made his move to become King of New York. Reputation could get a lot done in this city. Alessandro had his eye on the kinds of money and power and influence only a truly corrupt politician could want. That was the real power, the true crown he intended to wear.

But neither Jimmy nor Alessandro knew the figure lurking in the shadows behind Sale.

Even Sale himself had no real clue what he'd gotten himself into.

#

It took his team two days to make contact with Popov. Another to arrange for a call.

Jimmy felt a certain amount of nervous trepidation when he dialed, and that was something he wasn't used to feeling. He didn't particularly like it.

"Jimmy Martello, is it?" said a low American voice.

"It is indeed," Jimmy said, thrown because he'd expected an '80s-movie thick Russian accent. "Am I talking to Ivan Popov?"

"You are," said Popov. "I don't know why you're interested in Chiara, but I am willing to talk."

Jimmy thought it was interesting that the man didn't automatically assume Jimmy had his daughter and was looking to negotiate. He decided not to pull any punches. Once they were through with the niceties, he made his play.

"Ivan Popov, I think you know who has taken your daughter. Am I correct?"

Jimmy heard the long sigh from the other end of the phone. "Chiara cannot be helped. I thank you for your concern."

"Do you mean it would be impossible to help her, or do you mean that *you* can't be seen helping her?" Jimmy pressed.

"I cannot help her," Popov said. "And I cannot hire you to

help her, if that was your plan, as tempting as it might be."

"There doesn't have to be payment, nothing to show I was working for you in any way. Could you owe me a favor?" Jimmy asked. "I'm not sure what the rules you're playing to are. There would be nothing to tie me to you."

There was silence on the other end of the phone for a little while.

"What a fascinating suggestion," Popov said eventually. "I can't imagine what sort of favor you think I could do you that would be worth the risk, though. Something related to your construction firm, I suppose? Smoothing the way with permits, helping you win some competitive clients? Hm, well, that kind of favor I could conceivably offer."

"Ah, it won't be a difficult favor, whatever it ends up being. I can promise you that much," Jimmy said. "I have no interest in holding you ransom over this. Ask around. People will tell you that isn't my style."

"I have done my due diligence before making this call," Popov assured him.

That raised a smile. He was dealing with a cautious man, not a stupid one. Good. "What can you tell me about the people who took her? What do they want?"

"They work for Lev Volkov. A very powerful man, very

clever, a spider of a man, with a web of influence that runs across the entire world. He cheated me, put me in a compromising position, and stole my daughter to make me work for him in return." This was the version of the story Popov had come to believe, neatly neglecting the details of his own shortcomings in the situation, including his inebriation and how, even in the cold light of day afterward, he had been willing to sell Chiara to save his own ass.

Jimmy heard what he wanted to hear—a family man in need of help.

He was particularly gifted when it came to not seeing things he didn't want to see.

"Do you have any idea where he might have taken her?"

"Volkov has bases in Siberia, London, Paris, and Tunisia that I know of. Probably more that I don't."

"That's a lot of ground to cover," Jimmy mused, thinking over the logistics, then smiled. "But it's a considerably narrower search than the whole world, so that's something."

Popov almost laughed.

Almost.

"There's nothing to say she is hidden just because we cannot see her," Popov noted. "I still know he wants her alive for the time being, and that he will keep her alive if I do as he says. He also knows I would do anything for her, and wouldn't for a second do anything that might risk her life, so he won't expect me to come after her. That could be to your advantage."

"Perhaps. If there's anything you can think of that might help me, you can reach me through my team. You have their details. Otherwise, you won't hear from me until I have your daughter somewhere safe."

"It won't be enough to get her out. You realize he will come after you, and keep coming after you," Popov said. "She will have to disappear. A new name, a new life. She may never be safe. You may well need to do the same, if he ever learns who you are. Lev Volkov is not the kind of man capable of accepting the kind of theft you are contemplating. You do this, and he will hunt you both for as long as you live."

Jimmy shrugged, though the gesture was lost on the phone. "If everyone did that when they said they would, there wouldn't be a single crime family left on this godforsaken planet," he said. "So, I think I'll take my chances."

Popov barked out a bleak laugh. "I like your attitude. It's going to get you killed, but that doesn't mean I don't like it."

#

By the time the plane landed, Chiara was beyond exhausted.

Despite everything, she'd fallen into a restless sleep a few times, but she kept waking up in a panic as her frightened mind took control of her dreaming one. It was so hard to stay focused, but she had to be alert, primed, ready to take any chance to escape, slim as it might be.

There could just as easily be none.

No one was coming to save her.

It stood to reason this was happening to her because of her father, so he wasn't going to come rushing in like a white knight, and she didn't have the kinds of friends who could launch a rescue mission.

From the plane, they bundled her into a car. There was nothing within view to assist in knowing where she was. She could have landed anywhere in the Western world, and the only reason she could guess that much was because the road signs were in English. It didn't help much. But, if she got out of here, it dangled one hope in front of her: She would be able to make herself understood. She just had to get away first.

She couldn't see the driver's face, and he didn't speak.

He was big and bulky, broad across the shoulders and bullish across the back of his neck. The man in the back of the car with her was also big and mostly silent. "Don't make this hard for yourself. It doesn't need to be," was all he said to her.

She heeded his advice.

She tried to think like them. What did they stand to gain from taking her? What did they hope to achieve? Her best guess was leverage, a way of making her father pliable.

Would he have agreed to them holding her as collateral if he thought he could keep both of them alive that way? Yes, 100 percent. He was a practical man, more than capable of making the best of a worst-case scenario.

But how far did this branch of worst choices spread?

Sex?

Because that was what made huge parts of the world go round, not money.

Was she meant to perform for some rich man, a prisoner in his house? Or was it broader and more debasing than that, with her ending up in a brothel on Herbertstraße, in the De Wallen district, or somewhere equally tawdry?

Both options horrified her but in completely different ways, even though part of the reality they represented was very much the same.

If it was about to become her reality, she needed to be clever about reshaping it.

The question was, *How?*

How could she take control of that bad situation?

Resisting wasn't going to work.

She harbored no illusions about what would happen to her if she put up a fight.

So, how could she take any sort of control? How could she still cling onto a part of her soul and not be utterly broken long before that single opportunity of escape arose?

By being the best whore she could be?

Was that even possible?

Could she do that to herself in order to survive?

More importantly, did she have a choice?

There was a difference between being given to some billionaire and being put to work on her back in a brothel—not just in how she'd be used, either, but in the reality of how hard it would be to find a way out. She was under no illusions. She had no passport. She couldn't just hop on a plane out of there. Every aspect of her life was in their hands to crush.

So, to survive, she'd need them to think she was something worth preserving.

She'd been an expensive girl her entire life, so maybe—just maybe—she could keep being just that, now that her life probably depended on it.

Before they got out of the car, the man in the back seat put a coat around her shoulders and pulled the hood up over her head.

The two of them stood her into the street and ushered her toward a building.

She couldn't be sure, but it was as though they were trying to hide her face. Security cameras?

Working on instinct, she succeeded in shaking her head momentarily free of the hood, turning her face right and left, praying that any camera in the vicinity would register her. Of course, that little rebellion would be worth nothing if no one was looking for her.

The two men led her down a side alley between two towering buildings. There were dumpsters and trash bags and other rubble, with a third building hidden behind them. Seeing it, she changed her thinking immediately. The place had an air of venerability about it, an impressive architectural gravitas that was both old and absolutely European. Not Bavarian, not Nordic. This was London, white-stone facades begrimed with soot and exhaust fumes.

The big, heavy door opened in front of her.

Now, from that next step until whenever she ran out of a future, everything she did had to be focused on survival.

#

The call came unreasonably early in the morning.

Jimmy scrambled to get it.

Daniel.

Jimmy had never been good with mornings. Usually, it took him a while to get moving. Not this morning. Adrenaline had him firing on all cylinders.

They had a plan in place. It was solid. Not that he wanted to be trying to make his moves half-asleep.

Before noon, he and Nicky were on a flight to Chicago.

Raul Cabrera was the corona of the Latin Kings.

As a younger man, he'd built himself a rep on a foundation of armed robberies and several particularly daring heists. The man was a thrill-seeker. He got his rocks off on the drama of a holdup, the rush of breaching vaults, and although he was arrested a couple of times, the cops had never been able to get much to stick. He was a slippery serpent. He'd done a few months in jail here and there, but his rap sheet was nothing close to what it should have been. Age brought a kind of wisdom to Raul. The attraction of selling guns began to outweigh the pleasures of using them. That was the tipping point. He was smart enough to know he was slowing down, and on a hot date with a box six feet under if he didn't change focus, so he turned his mind toward business—making bank off other people doing the heists and the killing.

The Latin Kings operated out of the backs of arcades, billiard halls, small dance halls, and barbershops. They had a good setup. Young foot traffic, hotheaded and full of anger that needed to get out of their systems. And if it didn't, well, the Kings had a way of helping with that too. Several of his customers served as guns for hire—hit men with very specific demands when it came to the tools of their trade, which kept life interesting for Raul, trying to source their wants and needs.

Amateurs might spray bullets from automatic weapons they barely knew how to use. But a professional who came to Raul would be looking for a single untraceable piece to take out a single target, then dispose of before they took their next commission. As of late, there had been high demand for a kind of bullet called a cop killer. Raul didn't care who did the dying from his trades, as long as the bank kept rolling in.

Jimmy and Nicky approached the Lucky Loot Arcade.

The pair were dressed in sweats for the first time in over a year.

In a peculiar way, it felt like coming back to himself, but it was a version of Jimmy that he didn't recognize. Now, it took effort to walk like someone wearing street clothes. It was an act, where before he'd been faking it whenever he'd walked into a club in a tailored suit.

Nicky had grown into his role of the unofficial capo of the Martello clan, too, but he looked more natural in the old uniform.

Once inside, they walked through the dimly lit arcade, with random lights flashing from every angle, alarms, bells, chimes, and so much other noise. A bunch of kids were hopping around on *Dance Dance Revolution*, and across the floor, another bunch clustered around a fake driving rig, playing *Need for Speed*.

No one paid them any attention.

Reaching the end of the machines, they spotted a tall man with a pencil-thin mustache and striped suit. He sat at a table outside of a small door. He was the only thing in the room that looked out of place, and weirdly at peace with it.

They headed straight for him.

He saw them.

One hand dropped beneath the table.

Jimmy could feel the gun pointing at his heart, even if he couldn't see it.

"We're hoping to get a few minutes with Raul Cabrera," Jimmy said.

"Why?" the man barked. One word full of dismissal.

"I'm not about to tell the doorman, but you can tell him I've come into possession of something that I think would prove most beneficial for him," Jimmy said, holding up a file folder containing information that the research and development team had put together for him.

"Guns on the table. Both of you. I'll see if he wants to talk to you. Names?"

Jimmy and Nicky put their pieces on the table and gave their names.

As the man opened the door behind him, Jimmy saw that Raul was playing a game on his phone. Jimmy found it amusing that the man was surrounded by state-of-the-art games, yet he preferred to hunch over his Android, tapping at the screen while trying to squash an elusive piece of candy.

Raul's man said something they couldn't hear.

Raul looked up. "Sí, I find myself curious. What do you want with me?"

Jimmy laid the file folder at Raul's desk. "I'm Jimmy Martello. My family has influence in New York City."

"I know who your family is. What they are."

"Good. That makes things easier. I want you to accept this as an offering of goodwill, from my family to you."

Raul flipped open the folder and found himself staring at confidential information about his businesses, legitimate and otherwise, including falsified trails that legitimized the more suspect nature of things. The FBI transcripts were buried in the file. His puzzled expression was a thing of beauty.

"How did you . . . ?"

Jimmy stopped him. "I know the cops are coming to you tonight. They're looking to hit you with a RICO charge and shut down your entire operation."

"How could you know that?" Raul shook his head.

"The world has moved on. I have some talented cyberattackers in my operation," Jimmy explained. "Knowledge has always been power, but the knowledge that is out there now, waiting to be tapped, that is god-level."

"This paperwork? Where . . ." Raul stammered.

"Trust me, it's genuine and not merely a good-looking fake. Thanks to my friends, it looks to all the world like you've been legit for years."

"Impressive," said Raul. "But why are you doing this? Not simply to impress me; I assume you want something in return."

Jimmy gave his favors speech.

"Well, I've heard some weird shit in my time, compadre, but you're something else, for sure," Raul said. "I guess we see what happens, and whether you're full of shit."

"Oh, they'll come knocking. I promise you."

The timing couldn't have been better. The last word was fading to a loaded silence between them as the feds came slamming in through the front door.

Raul bristled. Then turned to his doorman. "If this goes sideways, shoot these fuckers in the head," Raul said. Then he headed out to meet the cops with the research and development team's paperwork in his hand.

#

For the first hour, it had been a regular Wednesday night at the club—a little flirtation with the waitresses, a new cocktail to sample to appease the mixologist, a little time with a *cugino*.

Just the way Jimmy liked things.

He was starting to unwind when a very gray-looking man sidled up on his left, and a much younger, blonder, muscular guy posted up on his right. A third burly man stood in the distance.

Mattia—his bodyguard for the night—made eye contact, looking for guidance. Jimmy nodded to say it was OK. For now.

"Comrade Martello," said the gray man. "A pleasure to make your acquaintance."

"You seem to have me at a disadvantage. Alas, I don't think I know who you are," Jimmy said. "Tell me, how can I help?"

"Oh, we were merely curious, my friend and I. We were curious about your interest in Russian business."

Jimmy laughed like it was the most ridiculous thing he'd heard in months. "Ah. My new friend, believe me, I'm interested in *everyone's* business, because that's how I mean to do my business."

"That is a dangerous game to play," said the gray man. "People do not like having outsiders digging too deeply into their family life, if you understand me."

"I'm a family man myself," said Jimmy. "I understand well."

"Let me speak plainly, then, family man. What specifically spikes my curiosity is why a young, seemingly intelligent man like yourself would want to make an enemy of Lev Volkov? It makes no sense to me."

"I'm not looking to make enemies, comrade. Not my style, ever. Ask around. Everyone will tell you I'm interested in making friends."

"How incredibly charming." The gray man shook his head. "And naive. Believe me, it's easy enough to see what you're up to, Mr. Martello. You said ask around. We have. You're getting quite a reputation for doing people favors. So, we hear your people are asking about Ivan Popov, and that trips alarms for us. Now, this could all be very innocent, but equally, it is very likely that Lev Volkov isn't going to like what you are doing. And you wouldn't want to be the source of his displeasure. Believe me. So, I ask you again, why are you so willing to make an enemy of this man?"

Jimmy stood up. "Well, this is all very tedious, I have to say, and quite disappointing."

The big, blond muscle made a grab for him, but Mattia intercepted the move, then threw a punch that had the guy sprawling back across several tables, with drinks spilled and glasses smashed before his bulk hit the floor.

The club's security spilled in.

Given a choice of shooting or running, the two Russians still on their feet made their retreat, while the third was thrown through the door and onto the street before he knew what was happening.

No one disrespected Jimmy in his bar.

#

Alessandro had a girl with a camera following Jimmy around.

The fact that she was female was no coincidence. It was a

gamble based on ego. If Jimmy noticed her, there was a good chance he was arrogant enough to assume she was looking to go home with him, and not make much of it. In the time he'd been watching, he'd seen enough women come onto Jimmy to know it was a viable explanation for her presence. And Mya was more than pretty. She had a way about her that made lesser men weak while she was entirely ruthless.

Alessandro had used her before. He knew she could be counted on for discretion. She was a pro. One with expensive tastes.

Mya got him some decent shots of Jimmy talking with the Russians.

She'd done well. There were several that looked like a far more convivial conversation than she said had gone down. He recognized the older man, Bogodan Yakovlev. Alessandro had run into some drama with him some years back and hadn't forgotten the experience. The man dripped menace. The muscle's name didn't really matter, not when Yakovlev was with him.

He showed Sale the photos, laying them out on the table.

"This is why we cannot trust Jimmy Martello," Alessandro reasoned. "Yakovlev is the worst of the Russians, believe me. He's the kind of Bratva that other Bratva are afraid of."

"This is not a good look for us," Sale agreed, staring at the gray-haired man in the photographs. "What the fuck is Jimmy boy playing at?"

"I don't know, but I ask you this, Don Martello: What can Jimmy say to these people that they want to hear? What can he offer them that they want to buy?" The unsaid part: *How can this be anything other than a threat to his own people?*

Three hours later, Sale was puffing on a cigar and drinking Angelo's cognac as he repeated those lines.

His delivery was stilted, but he got the message across, taking credit for Mya and Alessandro's detective work and passing it off as his own.

"I've had business with Yakovlev, many years ago," Angelo said, "though it is hard to call it business. Three men died, and another two could not work again after what he did to them. Their children work for me now, because I am a man of honor, and grieve still for their loss. They will always be taken care of. Yakovlev is unpredictable. He collects finger bones. If Jimmy has made friends with him, that would be a cause for concern, yes, but for Jimmy as much as us. As I said, I know him. He doesn't make friends. Whatever else is happening here, Yakovlev is using the boy to get to the rest of us." He was thinking to himself, nodding. "I think it would be wise to avoid any family gatherings for the time being."

Sale agreed with him, and let him have some of the photos.

A few days later, Angelo had his own little chat with Louie Graziano, and passed a few of those photos along.

Word got around, and the families agreed that no large gatherings were to be had where Yakovlev might be tempted to turn them into a massacre.

After a couple of days, Sale took the last of his photos to Jimmy.

"These must be fake," he said, as he handed a photo over. "Tell me these are fake, *nipote*."

Jimmy shrugged. "Mattia had to haul this thug off me. It turned ugly fast." He looked at the photos. "Not that you can tell from these photos. They might look friendly, but I promise you, it wasn't."

Sale shrugged in return. "You're out there being friendly with so many people these days, my boy. It's hard for people to be sure where your loyalties lie." That was an attempted jab, though Jimmy metaphorically bobbed and weaved.

"Well, *people* should know," Jimmy said, fighting to control his rising anger. "I'm a Martello. Family first. Always. It is not open for discussion."

"I hate to be the bearer of bad news, Jimmy, but no one seems willing to tell you the truth to your face, so I have to *yet again*. People doubt you. And these photos don't help. The families are growing concerned. We don't get into bed with the Russians. Ever."

Sale enjoyed the moment. He had the upper hand. He knew Jimmy cared about the family, and more so what the family thought of him. Doing anything to tarnish his blessed corpse of a father's memory was a knife to the heart for the little prick. That made it all the more entertaining, turning the family he so adored against him. It was almost as good as being in charge, Sale thought. In the meantime, he would continue to chip away at the image of his nephew, and at some point, he'd do enough damage that Jimmy would be out—or dead. Then it would behoove him, a better man, to step in to fill the power vacuum.

#

Jimmy made a point of gathering with the family as often as possible, and always on a Sunday afternoon for dinner. There were, of course, times when he couldn't make it because his business had a way of intruding with the larger family gatherings, so on those occasions, he made sure to visit his mother and *Zia* Rosaria during the week to make amends.

He worried about both of them.

Today would be especially difficult for his mother. It was

one of those landmark dates. A day full of grief. Her wedding anniversary. He bought her a bunch of white roses and a box of her favorite chocolates, though neither would make up for what he couldn't give her—yet.

"You're a good boy, Jimmy." She smiled softly, taking the flowers from him. She headed for the kitchen. Four steps away from the sink, she couldn't resist. "No matter what anyone else says, I know you're a good boy."

"A lot of things are being said, Mamma, but there's no truth to them. I need you to believe me. I'm not selling the family out to the Russians. I'm not doing business with them. Nothing like that. It's gossip, and it's meant to cause us pain."

"Ah, people always talk, Jimmy. It doesn't matter what you do, or what you don't do," Rosaria said. She was stirring a pot of sauce on the stove that smelled of fragrant herbs. "People like to make up their own truths. We call it gossip, but it's more than that. They'll say all sorts of things about you, because that's what they want to be true. I've had my share of it; I can tell you."

"I only worry, because any rumor about me reflects badly on Mamma."

"Don't you worry about me, son. You make me proud every day. People don't understand what you're doing, and that's just fine, because you do, don't you?" Anna said.

"I do," he promised.

"There you go, then. Let them worry, and then let them talk to each other and worry each other."

"Why can't you just tell us what this secrecy and running about is for?" Rosaria asked, without looking up.

"Ah, in time, I promise, but right now, everything depends upon no one knowing what I'm up to. Well, Nicky and Enzo know, of course, and they're with me totally. All I can tell you is, it will go some way to making us whole again, after everything that's happened. Our loss . . .."

He looked at both women in turn, still struggling to speak to either of them about the men they had lost.

"I can't see how that works," Anna said. "But I don't need to."

He breathed deeply, thinking about saying nothing but decided they needed to know something was happening, that their men hadn't been forgotten. Someone was still speaking for them. "I think I know who was behind it," he told them. "I don't know how to prove it yet, and it's . . . delicate. So, nothing happens until I can prove it. Sure, I could have put a bullet through his brain a year ago, but that's not justice. That's anger. We are better than that. My father was better than that. My uncle was better than that. So, truth above anger. I want people to know what really happened in that room, what led to it, and why. The truth is more than a bullet. And that's what I'm working on. Trust me. It's best if you don't know any more than that."

"You know who killed my Italo," Anna said slowly, "and you never told me?"

"I *think* I know, Mamma, and that's not the same. I want a confession to give to you," Jimmy said. "I want to hear him admit it. I want *you* to hear him admit it. I think you should both have that."

Tears shimmered on Anna's cheeks, but she was a tough woman. She kept a fierce grip on her emotions. "You're right," she told her son, nodding once. "I want that. I need that. I need to make sense of this, after all this time. I'll never forget what happened, but I think if I understood, I could make my peace with it."

Jimmy put his arms around Anna and held her for a moment. Neither of them spoke. It was a difficult day for both them. "I only want to give you that, Mamma, believe me. Everything I am doing, it is for that moment."

"I never regretted marrying your father," she told him. "Not ever. Find a girl you can love like that, Jimmy."

Jimmy wanted to tell her that he knew who she was; he just hadn't found her yet. But anything that came out of his mouth would be admitting to the crazy. How could he admit to such strong feelings for a woman he had never met, whom he had never seen beyond a photograph, and had never so much as heard her voice? That wasn't the kind of infatuation you admitted to your mother. What sort of man even pretends to himself that a girl like that is just waiting to be saved so she can fall in love with him?

And yet . . .

It felt like fate.

And that was the kind of thing his mother could easily love and believe in fiercely enough for both of them.

#

The research and development team had a hand in the design of their office space, and had taken measures to ensure that surveillance by conventional means was useless. They'd set up hidden cameras in the corridors so they knew if anyone was outside. They also had disruption devices running on frequencies that interfered with listening devices. They swept the room for bugs every morning and scoured it for signs of new technology in the most unlikely places.

They weren't taking chances.

"You should do this for my office too," Jimmy noted, after Daniel walked him through it.

"Sure thing, boss," Daniel replied with a smile. "Although from what I see on the cameras, your biggest issue is our mutual friend hanging about in the corridors, trying to get close enough to whisper his poison in your ear."

Jimmy laughed at that. Sale always had something he wanted to discuss, something that was so important, it couldn't wait. And when he heard it, it felt, if not abject, then at least pointless. Jimmy guessed it was more about his uncle trying to keep an eye on him in the hopes he'd let something slip rather than trying to prove his own usefulness. Which, as far as Jimmy was concerned, amounted to a big fat zilch.

"Still bugs me that he manages to be such a nuisance, given how much time he spends hanging around here like a bad smell."

"Not working alone," Indie said. "Only answer."

It was rare Indie said anything in their meetings. "We can't prove it, though," Daniel agreed. "But from what I can source, I'd say his MO has changed radically as of late, so I'm with Indie on this."

"Enzo is seeing the same thing, insofar as he can access any figures. What we do know for sure is that Sale is spending a lot of money at the moment. He can't help splashing out. It's a compulsion, and he's making a point of showing off his merchandise, so we get some sense of his income from that," Jimmy said.

"I can't see why anyone clever enough to stay hidden would want to work with Sale," Daniel remarked.

"We're all in agreement on that," Jimmy said. "Now, far be it from me to make the obvious connection, but there aren't many groups content with being invisible power brokers where drugs are concerned. So, the question is, which cartel is he in bed with, how deep, and how long before they cut him down and replace him with their own man?"

"Wishful thinking, maybe," Daniel said, stroking his furrowed brow. "But there's something to the idea. Maybe . . . He'd have a hard time advancing his little empire of drugs if he wasn't dealing with one of the major players, and we know it's not the BMF. Someone like the Sinaloa Cartel could be a decent candidate, but I didn't think they were that active here."

"But this is what they do, export business. Like a pyramid scheme where the aim is getting everyone high enough, they keep trying to crawl up each brick until they are on the top and the only thing left is to fall . . ." His hatred of drugs and the trade that preyed on vulnerable and addicted people wasn't exactly hidden. "The structure of the pyramid can make it hard to tell who they're working with, but if Sale's into cocaine, he's got to be dealing with them, even if only indirectly," Jimmy reasoned.

"I've been looking into the people he was in prison with," Daniel said. "You said he claimed that was where he made his key contacts?"

"That's what he always says," Jimmy confirmed. "He made his connects on the inside. *S fucking B.*"

"Well, for all the digging, I couldn't find any major players locked up at the same time and place. They're all small-time, the fall guys."

Jimmy nodded. "So, if there was no one in there to connect with, how the fuck did he come out with so many useful contacts? Because that motherfucker has been able to get ahead despite pretty much everything we've done to screw with his trade."

"Someone in there recruited him. They supplied him with the contacts as part of his work for them."

"But, again, no one is going to pick Sale for his smarts," Jimmy said.

"So, there's some kind of gameplay here, way bigger than the drug deals Sale has been making. It's the only obvious solution to all of the questions. There's another player behind it all, with their own agenda."

"And Sale is their useful idiot," Jimmy finished that line of reasoning.

Daniel nodded.

"Judas," said Indie.

"I wondered about that too," Daniel said. "I guess the good news is that whoever these people are, getting you killed isn't high on their list of priorities right now."

"Small comfort, assuming they even exist." Jimmy smiled. "This is all speculation."

"It is," Daniel agreed. "But I'm very good at what I do; that's why you pay me the big bucks, and I'm prepared to stake my life being right. Or, more accurately, I'm going to stake *your* life on that."

Jimmy laughed.

He knew that was true.

#

Don Pasquale Genovese was ninety-two when he died.

He'd been long retired from his family business, even before he'd shuffled off his mortal coil.

He remained an impressive man to the end.

Despite all the anxieties about Jimmy, there was no way they could not have a funeral for Don Pasquale and not expect every significant family man in the country to pay his respects, including Jimmy Martello.

The whole situation might have been awkward, but he'd already booked a flight to Europe for a few days, so he delegated Nicky as his capo to take Rosaria and go in his place. He would make his own pilgrimage later, upon his return. All that mattered in terms of the families was that the Martello clan had shown their respect in sending their capo. There was honor in that. For now. But not to make his own pilgrimage later, that was an insult. It was a fine line to walk.

"They're scared of you," Sale said in a corridor ambush the day the funeral was made public. "They're scared you're going to try something crazy with your Russian friends."

"I have no Russian friends," Jimmy replied stoically.

"I told them that. They've been watching too much *Game of Thrones*. But there you are. What can you do? Still, I think it would be better if you didn't show your face."

"I think you're right, Sale," Jimmy said.

It was a win-win situation for Sale. If Jimmy showed up, then Alessandro would spend the entire time trying to persuade people Jimmy was making a deal with someone other than them.

If Jimmy didn't show up, Sale would present himself as the de facto head of the Martello family. The eldest male. He didn't consider Nicky to be a real underboss. He was as wet behind the ears and wasn't formally made. It wouldn't take much to convince them it was insulting that Jimmy hadn't cut his business trip short, the way they had for Italo's funeral, even if everyone knew that none of them wanted him there.

As far as Sale was concerned, it was a plan that couldn't fail.

And, given there was a funeral, there was bound to be a repast, where connects could be made and cemented.

Sale imagined himself in the company of powerful men—where, as far as he was concerned, he belonged, by birthright. They would recognize him as one of their own. He'd talk with them, share a few jokes, offer insights, and all would have a good time.

The funeral plan had been Alessandro's, but Sale had forgotten that already.

He was too busy thinking about how clever he'd been and how much fun the funeral would be to even consider that young Alessandro was manipulating him.

Alessandro had seeds to plant and ideas he wanted the dons to consider. Sale was barely more than just a mouthpiece to parrot them, convinced all along they were his ideas, his genius.

Sale's greatest weakness was that he thought he was clever, and that made him easy to manipulate.

He had no idea who was really setting him up.

#

Siberia, London, Paris, and Tunisia.

Jimmy had allowed himself only a couple of days in each place. He had picked Novosibirsk as his Siberian city, quite simply because it was the largest one there, not because there were any specific leads or connects. In Tunisia, it was the capital, Tunis. In both cases, he had no idea where Volkov maintained his base of operations, if indeed it was even within the city limits and not somewhere far outside the scrutiny and jurisdiction of local law.

He'd had Enzo find family members for him to visit.

London and Paris were easy enough. The Martellos were victims of their own diaspora, like so many Italian families, so it didn't take long to find *cugini*, even if some were so distantly related to him and the gene pool was so diluted that they'd almost miss the link under sequencing.

Enzo had found him one contact in Siberia who was willing to meet in Novosibirsk, and someone in Tunisia from a family they'd done good business with through the years.

In his head, Jimmy was just going to step off the plane, roll into one of these places, bang on a few doors, and voilà, see Chiara standing there. Or maybe she'd be crossing a road with a goon too close for her to risk running, and he'd step in. Everything would be perfect in that fairy tale.

Life wasn't that, though. Especially not his.

The slaughter in his father's study proved beyond any doubt that he didn't live in any sort of a fairy tale.

Outside of the fairy tale, what he needed to do was firm up his contacts and find out about Russian activity on the ground. His main hope was to gather enough intelligence to give his team a chance at finding her, but that was a huge ask. The problem with being outside the fairy tale was that that was all they had.

Jimmy wasn't ready for Siberia.

He thought New York winters were cold, but the air in Novosibirsk made his lungs shrivel and his bones freeze; it was that cold. Enzo had organized a translator, but that made everything slow. Poking around asking was dangerous. This was their home turf, and every single Russian could have been working for Volkov, assuming Volkov was in the pocket of one of the oligarchs, and in turn in the deep pockets of the FSB and

Putin's goons. It was a different world. And he didn't like it. Surrounded by signs he couldn't read and people speaking a language he didn't understand, Jimmy felt alone and lost.

His main hope in all of the time he spent there was that Chiara was somewhere else, because if she was in this icebox of a country he'd never be able to find her.

Tunisia was a relief after that, even if it was only due to the fact that it was so much warmer and his contacts spoke English, even some Italian, as well as several other languages. It removed the need for an interpreter and made conversation relatively easy, even if he needed to fumble through a few languages a couple of times to find a way to make himself understood. Yes, there was a Russian presence in the city. Yes, they believed there was a base near Tunis and quite possibly a smaller one farther over in Sudan. No, the man they called the Great Bear hadn't been seen for a long time. But, seen or not, there was a massive house on the outskirts of the city, more akin to a compound than a mansion, and the place had been locked up tightly for the last few months.

Locked up, but not abandoned.

There was a security guard on duty at any given time, day and night. It was never more vulnerable than that.

The Tunisian *cugini* had a gift in that with their smiles and charm, it felt like they could get just about anyone talking. Of course, the cigars and high-priced liquor they brought with them didn't hurt. They did their thing, and in less than half an hour, they had convincing assurances that no one had been at the place for every bit as long as Chiara had been missing. Now, that could be taken one of two ways: either cross it off the list, because there wasn't enough security for the protection of a prized asset, or underline it because the fact no one was coming or going—even if there was an armed guard on the door 24-7— meant there was something inside worth protecting.

He resisted the temptation to make a move too soon and headed for Paris, acutely aware that he could have been leaving her behind.

He knew Paris from previous visits, and although his family there was distant, he'd met several of them before when they'd visited America.

There were four of them, and he was never quite sure which one was which—they were all de-aged versions of him with their white, tight-fitting T-shirts and designer shades. They went out of their way to make sure he was aware they had turned over every stone looking for Russians in their fair city and had several locations where the Russians liked to drink. One, they hoped, would prove fruitful.

It took them a few tries to find someone willing to talk, but enough Stoli eventually loosened a few lips. Yes, Volkov owned a number of properties in Paris. Yes, sometimes he brought in girls. Yes, sometimes they were stolen from his enemies, rivals, or fools who owed him money.

No one recognized Chiara from the photos.

They didn't let that deter them. They took her photo to some of the brothels, asking about fresh meat.

No one had girls who hadn't been there for months already, and none that matched her description.

Jimmy wasn't sure he could rule out Paris, either, as it ticked so many of the boxes, but every one they opened was empty, so he moved over to London, sticking to his original plan.

He'd suspected it was London from day one. That was the most frequent location for where the girls were trafficked, based on his research. Nothing thus far had changed that feeling.

In his first few hours in the city, he saw five women who, at a distance, he was sure must be her, but they turned out to be complete strangers. He humbled himself when he realized that Chiara was also a complete stranger to him . . . for now.

His connect, Marvino, took him on a tour of Russian brothels, first online, scrolling through page after page of "Meet the Girls" portraits before they went knocking on doors in person. He saw a lot of very young girls—some very pretty; others striking or different, veering into the fetish territory—who tried desperately not to appear frightened or sad.

He couldn't save all of them, so he did his best not to think about how they got there, or what their lives were like, as toys for the lost and the lonely.

As much as he wanted to sympathize, he needed to focus on finding Chiara.

By the time he flew back to New York, he had one decent lead.

Rumor had it that Volkov's people had brought a new girl in recently, but they weren't putting her up for sale just yet. She was, so the whispers went, special.

"They do tests," Marvino explained. "Medical first, because a clean girl is worth more. A virgin is worth even more. They'll auction off her virginity if they can, and that takes a while to set up the auction itself. It isn't like they can just walk up to Sotheby's and say the next lot is a ripe twenty-four-year-old piece of ass. It doesn't even matter if she's not; there are a lot of sickos and pervs out there who will pay big money to live out their darkest fantasy. I've heard whispers that the best money they ever took was on a dark-web auction with some BDSM psycho wanting to make his own snuff film. No idea if it's true, but such stories are the foundation of a man like Lev Volkov's reputation."

#

The funeral was a tense gathering, and the repast was even worse.

You only had to look around the room to know that everyone assembled had at least one concealed weapon.

No one wanted a war.

No one wanted to start something.

But if something started, they were all ready.

No prisoners.

No backing down.

Take it to the afterlife.

Alessandro could feel the threat in the air, like the constant screaming of distant sirens.

His body buzzed with adrenaline.

If he played it right, today could work out very well for him.

It was a gamble, but somewhere along the line, he'd become a gambling man.

Still, if he was wrong about Jimmy Martello, this could all go to hell in a heartbeat.

For all that Alessandro had been saying about how Jimmy was a dangerous man, he didn't think it was true. It was just too . . . unlikely. Alessandro was good when it came to thinking about plots and moves, the idea of puzzles and following the through line, ignoring the noise to find the truth. And nothing he'd seen in any of it came close to a reality where an interfamily shootout was in the cards. It wasn't a Michael Mann movie. From where he was, it seemed fairly obvious that Jimmy was angling to improve his standing. He might have ideas above his station and truly think being King of New York was his destiny, but it felt far more likely there was another set of objectives at play. He was using information, turning people into pieces, but he didn't seem to be amassing genuine support or actual power. If it came down to it, Alessandro thought he could win more of the families over because he had more to offer. That was how they operated.

He had a lot of conversations that day.

Quiet conversations, where he very gently seeded ideas, and let people think they'd come up with them on their own.

Why were they taking so much time and effort bribing politicians, which was a crapshoot, when they could get their own people into those positions, and loyalty would never be a question?

Alessandro wanted to be *that* man, and made no bones about it. He talked about his own ambitions and his care for the family. He had one goal, prosperity, though not his own. Everyone's. He was committed to the family. He wanted to share some of his ideas, things he'd try to implement if he got the votes, but he didn't get the chance.

An explosion of noise shattered the air.

People screamed.

A hundred hands reached for guns.

They were all on edge, spooked and looking for the silhouette of Jimmy Martello to rise up, starting something, here, now, of all times, all places.

An entire room full of people looked at one another, looked for the threat, the source of the noise, trying to figure out where it had started and what was really going on.

For a few seconds, no one moved.

"It's fine! It's fine! Stay calm!" Alessandro shouted into the quiet of the room, looking to take charge, to placate people even before they knew what had happened.

He'd seen it.

It wasn't Martello.

It was a clumsy server girl.

People made space around him, and as they moved back, they

revealed the poor girl who'd dropped a massive glass bowl.

Food and glass had scattered across the floor, hence the explosion of noise that had sounded eerily like a bomb going off deep in the heart of the building, taking out the windows.

"It's all good. No real harm done, unless you're a glass bowl, that is," Alessandro called out again, and in that moment, felt the wave of relief as the tension ebbed.

A few people laughed, even if it wasn't funny.

He gave the girl a gentle smile. "Best get it cleaned up," he said. "Someone could get hurt."

She returned his smile shyly.

She'd done well. He'd gambled on the broken bowl not leading to actual shots fired, and the bet had paid off. Each and every one of them in that room had seen just how jumpy the other great men of the families were right now. But more than that, what they'd also seen was how cool and alert he'd been, handling the situation calmly, a gentle wit as he got control of the situation before an itchy trigger finger caused a fatal problem.

The day had been everything he could have hoped for.

#

Jimmy felt the cold steel of the tip of the gun's muzzle kissing his forehead.

He'd been waiting for this.

One of Volkov's men, maybe, or someone Yakovlev had sent.

"You know what?" The words were sinister and familiar. He didn't recognize the voice. "I think you need a better view." The pressure lifted from Jimmy's forehead and moved into the space between his eyes.

He'd lived this moment a hundred times before, but it was different every time, just as much as it was the same.

How many enemies had he made by now? They outweighed friends at this point.

For every favor he had owed to him, he'd probably drawn as much if not more ill will.

Any number of people could have put targets on him.

Jimmy felt an overwhelming sense of exhaustion coupled with resignation.

He'd put so much of his life into this plan that he couldn't back out now.

He had to keep going, had to make it work.

It was the most important thing in his life.

"There, that's better," the phantom voice continued. "Now, you have a front row seat to the big show."

He wondered if it would be a relief to die.

"You don't have a gun," the voice said. "You're going to die by the gun, just like your daddy. You couldn't save him. You can't save yourself. You can't even avenge him properly. You are weak. You are nothing. You are such a disappointment. I pity you, Jimmy boy."

"Why would you care?" Jimmy said. He had nothing to lose. A guy who hadn't made the kill by now wasn't intending to pull the trigger. Too much talking.

Bang!

It would be so easy to die.

And yet somehow, he was awake, and shaking.

The tremors were violent.

Convulsions.

Jimmy reached for the light, but it was daylight already.

He remembered his *nonna* calling him a vampire, and wondered if that was how he'd stayed alive this long.

Maybe Sale hadn't thought to get him staked through the heart.

#

The first photo was out of focus, but he could see that one of the figures, caught midmovement, had a hood pulled over their head.

However, as the series of shots progressed, the hood came off, and a face was exposed. Still blurry, and blown up too large for the resolution to hold from the security camera footage. Chin at a defiant angle, or maybe that was his mind adding the details it wanted to see.

Jimmy's heart fluttered.

It was her.

It had to be.

It could only be.

Chiara . . .

How many times in London had he thought he'd caught a glimpse of her, only to get close and realize that the woman in question didn't look anything like her.

It could be Chiara, though.

There was a similarity to the features that his mind kept filling in. But the last of the photos made him wonder. The massive brute of a man with her forced the hood back down over her head, like he really didn't want her seen. Not by anyone or anything.

"Don't ask me what I had to do to find these," said Daniel.

"Is that a subtle way of saying I should be paying you more?" Jimmy asked, still flicking through the images, staring at her face.

"Now, that's a question you should consider, but I can help with the answer, which is obviously yes. I'm worth every cent." Daniel laughed.

Jimmy was paying him a lot, but he'd more than earned it, not just with this stuff. The real worth in what his team was doing came through helping the family open up new markets and ways of working online.

"Do you know where she is?"

"I've got a best guess, and it's a very good guess, I should admit," said Daniel, and he started explaining what he'd been able to put together from the images. They were all from a similar angle, obviously a security feed, and they showed very little in the way of landmarks, but he'd written a short piece of code looking for places within Google Maps that matched all of the significant landmarks within a five-hundred-mile radius. He'd managed to narrow it down to what he was 99 percent sure was the right door. There was a partial reflection of shop signage that was distinctive. There was the spire of a church in the distance, along with two skyscrapers. And then, stuff like the positioning of the sun—which against the time stamp allowed him to work out the orientation of buildings and the relative position of the church against the shop name. Once he narrowed this down to London, he was able to narrow it further to fifteen close matches, with one that was considerably more compelling than the others.

Jimmy nodded like he understood.

The team hadn't gotten very far with the translation software because the Russians were using a relatively complex code language that required a cypher to decrypt, but they were working on it. They'd decoded a few messages, though, or thought that they had. There had been a little guesswork in places, like an ad promising, "Exciting new vodkas in stock" meant they had just taken a delivery of new girls. "One night only, wet T-shirt contest. Are you thirsty?" was a promise they were going to auction off a virgin and give customers time to get in their bids. Another message they'd succeeded in deciphering promised that they'd passed their health and safety inspection and had just received hygiene certificates. Very clean. Food safety assured, along with the health of the new girls in the brothels.

"It was the frequency of the food inspection messages that tweaked my Spidey senses. Way too regular, meaning something else had to be going on. Then, thanks to the wonders of our online translation, one sicko replied how much he loved food safety inspections, and I knew I was onto something," Daniel explained.

"And Chiara? Is she on the menu?"

"Ultimately, I'd assume so," said Daniel. "A lot is going to depend on how she handles herself, the fight she puts up, or if she's pliable. If she fights, then they have to resort to drugs and other means of breaking her and assuring her compliance. In that case, she's not looking at a pretty future. But, if she's good, works hard, makes men happy, then she'll stay there, or be moved somewhere better."

"And if she tries to escape?" He didn't need to hear the answer from Daniel; he already knew.

"It won't go well for her."

Jimmy needed her to be clever enough to figure this out.

The idea of what she'd have to endure to survive was sickening.

But the idea of her dying was worse.

"I'm getting on a plane tonight," Jimmy said.

It wasn't up for debate.

"Give me the street address for that door."

He had his phone out and was already scrolling through last-minute flights to all London airports.

#

Alessandro brought his gun up against the young woman's temple.

He could feel her shaking against him. Tears made her mascara run.

"Please," she said.

It wasn't clear what she was begging for.

"This doesn't have to go badly. I just want you to phone your boss and tell him to come down here, easy as that," Alessandro promised, speaking softly. He didn't want her doing anything stupid. "Just pick up the phone, and tell him he has to come. Do that, and I promise you, hand on heart, nothing bad is going to happen to you. I need you to believe me when I say that. I don't make promises lightly. Do you believe me?"

"Yes," she said. "I'll need to get my phone out of my bag."

"You do that, nice and slowly, and keep your hands where I can see them. That's a good girl. Almost home now. No heroics." Not that she looked like she was capable of any desperate measures. He wasn't taking any chances.

Apparently, the receptionist felt the same way.

She opened her bag and gently tipped out the contents onto the counter.

She didn't have a gun in there. That took the tension out of his body.

"Good girl," he said. "Very good."

Her hands were shaking as she handled the phone. She had him up front on her contacts, so it only took a couple of touches to the glass to call her boss.

He could hear Jimmy's repl. "I'm sorry, Aileen, I don't have time for this. I've got a plane to catch. Take it to Nicky if it's urgent. Otherwise, I'll deal with it when I get back." He started to click off as she begged, "Please."

Alessandro kept the gun pointed at her.

#

"It's urgent. I swear. And only you can deal with it. Please Mr. Martello."

"No can do." Jimmy killed the call.

The last thing he heard before the line died between them was the unmistakable sound of a gunshot. There isn't a sound like it in the world.

His gut lurched beneath him. In his mind's eye, he saw Aileen lying in a pool of her own blood.

Could he have saved her life with something as simple as the word *yes*?

Nah.

That kind of thinking was ridiculous.

The sort of guy who'd shoot a receptionist was going to do that regardless of whether he took a moment to listen to whatever he was demanding or not. She was doomed the moment he'd walked into reception and demanded she call Jimmy. He felt a pang of grief for her, and guilt, but buried it down deep. He needed to get on that plane. He couldn't think about what a madman with a gun was doing in his office right now.

But he learned something about himself in the minutes that ensued; he couldn't just turn it off and walk away. It wasn't him.

#

Jimmy used one of the side doors to get into the Martello Construction building, keying in the alarm code so it didn't trip the siren in warning, and made his way from there to the front desk, moving slyly through the connecting passageways that ran behind the scenes. It wasn't much, but knowledge of the terrain gave him some small advantage.

He assumed that whoever had shot Aileen was staying at the front desk, waiting for him.

They could just as easily have gone deeper into the building and put down his people one by one, though.

He knew he'd only get one shot, two at max, to deal with this. Guns weren't his jam since the day his patriarchs died. He felt horribly out of his depth, but everyone in here was his people, and they were counting on him to keep them safe. The Martello name assured some of that, but now that a gunman was inside their sanctuary, the name counted for nothing. That was a lesson his father, his grandfather, and his uncle had learned at a cost.

He came through the last door, covering the angles, heart hammering.

"Glad you could finally make it," Alessandro said.

He was sitting on one of the reception sofas, looking entirely relaxed. There was no blood. It looked for all the world like they were just keeping an appointment, business as usual.

"What the fuck?"

Alessandro gestured with the gun. "Say hello, Aileen," he told the girl.

"Hello," Aileen said nervously.

By the sound of it, she was on the floor with her back pressed to the desk. The sudden surge of relief was like a tidal flow of adrenaline through his body.

"Are you OK?" he called to her.

Alessandro smiled, like everything was going according to his grand plan. "Go ahead, answer any questions. It's fine. We're all friends here."

"I'm OK, Mr. Martello. I'm so sorry about this. I tried—"

"None of this is your fault," he cut her off. "Don't even begin to think that way. This is family business, and it was never part of your job description. All that matters is that you're safe. We can take it from here." To Alessandro, he said, "Why don't you let her go? I'm here now."

"How many of your employees know that this whole thing is a fraud? A front? I mean, does darling little Aileen here know that her charming boss is really a mobster?"

It was reasonable to assume none of the employees on the legitimate side of the business had a clue what they were a part of, or hadn't until now.

"There are more ways of ruining someone's life than spraying bullets about," Alessandro said, still eerily relaxed. "I've been watching you, Jimmy. And you know what I find fascinating? There are at least a hundred ways in which I can get to you and mess you up. You start anything, and I will finish you. Is that clear?"

Jimmy was shaking his head. "I don't know what you think I'm starting, but you've got it wrong. You are the one who walked in here with a gun."

Alessandro chuckled. "I had a point to make. I'm hoping that I made it. Otherwise, next time I might be forced to shoot something more important than an acoustic tile. Of course, I've had time to wonder how you intend to handle this. Now, I mean. Do you pay Aileen off, or will you shoot her yourself now that she knows too much about who you really are?"

From beneath the desk, Aileen whimpered in fear.

"You came here for a reason, so say what you've got to say. Then get the fuck out of here," Jimmy said.

Alessandro smiled coldly.

"You would never make it as a politician, Jimmy boy, you know that? Far too impatient, far too blunt. No room for subtlety and artifice. It's time to reel in the ambitions. Stop getting ahead of yourself. There's only room for one king, and that's not going to be you. That's my message. Consider it delivered," Alessandro said. "Whether you take heed or not, that's very much up to you. But if you don't, this is going to end ugly."

With that, he got up and walked out of the building.

Jimmy kept his gun trained on Alessandro's back long after the door was closed and the man was well away. His finger itched to pull the trigger and put several slugs into his back, stitching a line from his ass to his neck, but if he did that, he *would* be starting something, and that would just play into the ill feelings toward him right now. He'd find himself facing a war of the families.

He couldn't afford to do that.

"Please don't shoot me, Mr. Martello," Aileen said. "I swear I won't tell anyone what happened . . . I don't care who you are . . . please." He looked down at her sympathetically and gently helped her up off the floor.

#

Jimmy only had carry-on luggage.

He rushed through the airport, sprinting through Customs with seconds to spare and was in his seat, the last man on the plane, before they locked the doors.

He had no idea what the hell Alessandro was thinking, pulling a stunt like that, but it had gotten his attention. It was hard not to worry about the long-term implications.

Some days it felt like he was juggling far too many things, some of them sharp, others on fire, everything never more than a fingertip from being dropped.

But this was the life he'd signed up for.

It was how his father had lived, and his grandfather, and

down the generations before them to their roots in the old towns of Sicily.

He slept the sleep of the damned on the plane, only waking when the vibrations through the toughened glass of the window shivered him back to consciousness. Jimmy touched down at Heathrow, ready for whatever the United Kingdom had to throw at him.

His friend Bryan met him outside the terminal. He was waiting in a low-riding sports car and had offered to put him up for a few days.

Jimmy had warned him, "I'm here on business," meaning, "Things could get messy," but his old friend had simply delivered a wry smile.

"Bring it on. I could do with a little excitement in my life."

He'd always had a "live fast, die young, and leave a beautiful corpse behind" attitude, which was at odds with Jimmy's more cautious worldview. Right now, that was exactly the kind of man he needed on his team.

"Are you ready to party?" Bryan asked, as he navigated the streets at high speed.

"I need to check out some Russian brothels," Jimmy said, raising an eyebrow from his friend in the driver's seat.

"Russian girls always look so sad," Bryan said. "Now, Polish girls, they're a whole other issue. I know some great Polish places. Beautiful girls. Fun, fun, fun."

"I'm looking for class rather than fun," Jimmy said. "And it has to be Russian."

"Whatever floats your boat, my brother. Who am I to criticize?"

To get the revels started, Bryan took him to a couple of bars in the heart of the city and, with a little encouragement, got very drunk indeed, making a show of himself. Jimmy pretended to be every bit as drunk, but he wasn't drinking. He needed his head clear. They staggered in and out of a few places, flashing money around, asking for spectacular girls, and making sure the right people knew they were looking and what exactly they were looking for. Someone new. Someone different. Over the course of the evening, they scoped out and ruled out some places, and checked out a lot of young women in the process.

The sheer number was disturbing, and barely scratched the surface of what was nothing more or less than a human-trafficking operation. It was as ugly as it was lucrative to the men behind it, and as soul-crushing to the girls trapped inside it.

Jimmy needed to stay alert the whole time, even as he was making his grand "drunken" gestures.

He couldn't be sure if anyone was paying attention to him, but if they were, word would get back to the right kind of people who were always just a shot away in the darkness beyond the bright lights.

The risk was that he'd make himself so noticeable, Volkov's people would be suspicious. Someone somewhere would connect the dots between the man making a scene in a London dive bar and the man who had been talking to Popov.

He couldn't afford for those dots to connect too quickly, though, not if he wanted to hit the house and get Chiara out through the door his research and development crew had found for him. It was such a stupid idea, marching up to the front door, banging on it and demanding to be let in, that he kept telling himself it just might work.

He was becoming an accomplished liar whenever it meant lying to himself.

"A friend of mine told me I needed to visit, and made a point that I should ask about food safety inspections?" Jimmy said at one bar, leaning in conspiratorially to breathe heavily in the barman's face. "Dunno if I'm the butt of a joke here or what, but this is me asking. I've got the money . . ."

"Sounds like your friend has a very odd sense of humor," the first barman said.

But the second time he asked, he got a different answer. "I hear the doctors haven't looked at her yet, but soon."

"Ah, good, good. That's good. If I grease your palm, how about you let me know the moment she gets her certificates?"

"Well, my friend, for the right price, you can get a text message as soon as the bidding begins," the barman said. "You're sure you want to play? It can be a rich man's game."

Jimmy paid.

He hadn't considered what he would do if he won the bid, and it wasn't Chiara.

He couldn't very well save everyone, could he?

#

"So, you're back in London again?" Enzo was on the phone. He didn't sound happy. "How long are you away for this time?"

"I'm not sure. As long as it takes," Jimmy admitted.

Enzo sighed deeply, making no attempt to hide is displeasure. "I know you're not an idiot, Jimmy, and I know I don't need to tell you this isn't good for business, but I'm going to tell you, anyway. There's a lot of nervousness in the families right now. A lot. They're all on edge. The balance is precarious. I've got a bad feeling about all of this."

"I can't be responsible for other people's imaginations," Jimmy said. "Let me ask you something now, because you know how much I value your wisdom in all things, Enzo: What could I do right now that wouldn't be interpreted as a threat?"

Enzo went quiet for a moment. "You know, said out loud, that's not a bad question, Jimmy. And I hate to admit that I'm not sure I know the answer. There's trouble brewing here, and I'm beginning to think that maybe all we can do is try to ride this tiger."

"Which means it makes no sense for me to come back early," Jimmy said. "So, I think I should stay in London until I find Chiara."

"I don't mean to be a Debbie Downer, but at what point do we consider that it might not be possible? Can we at least be pragmatic about this, and set some limits?"

Jimmy didn't want to hear it.

He needed to believe that he could find Chiara, and that his plan was going to work. Too much was riding on it, not just bringing the girl home and playing the hero, which was an admittedly delicious prospect, but only gravy. The real meal was in getting the Russians in his pocket.

He knew in his heart that this was a long shot.

"A lot of people owe me favors. That side of the plan is

working. It's just one more . . ."

"Yes, sunshine, you've made some good moves, especially when it's been your own game and you've been able to dictate the plays," Enzo agreed. "But you aren't the only player now. It's no good being the best pitcher in the world if you're on a tennis court with balls whizzing at your head. You feel me?"

"Yeah, I get that, I do, and I appreciate the concern," Jimmy admitted. "But I'm not blind here; there's no blindfold across my eyes. I might not know who I'm up against, but I can see their moves as they shuffle their pieces around. That's something."

"But is it enough, Jimmy? From where I'm sitting on the sidelines, I'd remind you that all you can do is play your own game. But if you don't keep an eye on what other games everyone around you is playing, you're going to be left playing pickups while someone smarter walks around the court and puts a bullet in your head. You know that. You can't afford to be so focused on your own plan. You need to be aware."

"Just let me get this current situation figured out," Jimmy said, almost like a willful child digging in his heels. He refused to be wrong.

"I've said my piece, son. You know I'll watch your back as best I can. You don't get to be as old as I am without learning a few things. I'm absolutely sure the current unease is down to

Sale's stirring. The thing that has me concerned is that usually no one takes him seriously. This time, they are. Which has to mean there's something else going on here, and I don't know what it is. I hate not knowing. But moves *are* being made."

"I hear you, Enzo, and you know I respect you," Jimmy said. "I appreciate you telling me these things."

"I don't want your respect, my boy. I want you alive. I owe your old man that much. Wherever this tiger is taking us, I will see you through it," Enzo promised him. "You have my word."

#

Jimmy couldn't sleep.

It was a curious mix of jet lag and the buzz of the hunt.

He took cabs, cruising around the city, looking for that one face, that sweet, familiar face he'd never actually seen before. He walked the streets around the Russian clubs and brothels, listening, looking, knowing that at some point, he was going to have to go up to that door and bang on it, real hard.

That idea drove him mad.

"You look like shit," Bryan said when they met up for lunch.

Jimmy didn't have the energy to bat it back at him.

"Cheer up, my man. I may have something for you." Bryan

cracked a smile. "So, I have this cousin. Well, I say he's a cousin, it's complicated, but he's like a brother to me, you know? Same as you're my brother from another mother . . ."

Jimmy waited because he knew there was no point trying to make Bryan get to the point.

"Anyway, this guy, who is sort of my cousin but not my cousin, he's dating this Italian-Russian girl. She's one hot piece of tail, let me tell you. She works in a club not far from here, you know, Russian clubs, the kinds of places we've been going to. Although this one is pretty exclusive, doesn't have signage outside, very much a case of you need to be invited along, lots of discreet money being splashed. Well, the way my cousin tells it, she's spending a lot of time babysitting this new girl. American, but with Italian blood, and I'm thinking, What are the odds that we're out banging down metaphorical doors looking for this woman for you, and lo and behold, our Russians have themselves a new girl who just so happens to fit the description I keep hearing you put around. Coincidence? I think not."

Jimmy could hardly believe his ears.

"They've been checking her out, all the usual health 'tests' that are basically just ways to see if they can make more bank on rare meat. But yeah, my cousin's girlfriend has been helping her out, buying clothes and getting her set up. They're about the same size, and this other girl isn't allowed to go out yet, but from everything she's saying, the Russians are spending a lot of money on making her look the part before they put her to work. They don't do that unless they expect to make serious bank from selling her."

"Do you think your friend would help us get in?" Jimmy asked.

"She might, but you know what she'd be risking, putting herself out there like that. The Russians aren't exactly famous for being forgiving," Bryan said. "I'll text her and see if she'll meet up."

It was fate, Jimmy thought.

It was meant to be.

He didn't want to think about anything else.

#

First impression, as she walked through the coffee shop door, was how much Nicola looked like Chiara.

Not twins. But there could easily have been some sort of familial link.

It unnerved him.

"What?" she said by way of an introduction when she saw

how Jimmy was staring at her.

"This is my friend. My cousin, well, sort of a cousin . . . You know how it goes. Families. Complicated things," Bryan said. "He's trying to find someone."

Nicola watched as Bryan went to get coffees for them all.

"You're the guy," she said to Jimmy. "Bryan was pretty vague."

"I'm the guy," he agreed. "Can I ask you something? The girl you're babysitting, does she look like you?"

"She looks so much like me, it's uncomfortable," she said with a nod. "She's a little bit shorter and a foot size smaller, and I've got more moles, slightly different cheekbones. The odd angle is different, but face-forward, it's unnerving, like looking at a clone being shaped out of silicon."

It was quite the image. "Do you know her name?"

"They're calling her Eva. Doesn't mean much, though. All the girls have short names like that. None of them use their real ones."

"And she hasn't told you her real name?"

The woman shook her head.

He nodded.

"I think she could be the kidnapped girl I'm looking for. That being the case, I want to get her out of there, and home, but I can't do it alone. Will you help me?"

"These aren't the kind of people you mess with," Nicola said. "The club where I work is owned by Lev Volkov. You know the name? He's a heavyweight Russian mobster. He's the kind of man who pulls Putin's strings. He scares me. So no, I won't help you, because I can't be on the wrong side of him."

"I understand. I wouldn't ask you to take any risks," Jimmy said. "I wouldn't ask you to endanger yourself, but I need to find a way to get to her out of there and back home. If it was you in there, you'd be praying there was someone like me—someone like you—out there trying to find you . . ."

She nodded but didn't commit.

"I'd owe you a huge favor," Jimmy said. "Ask around. Jimmy Martello is a good man to have in your debt."

#

Rosaria always liked to go to church on Sundays.

Nicky wasn't so keen on church himself, but he knew those four walls gave her comfort. He liked to see his mamma dressed for the service. After his father died, she stopped going out and took less pride in her appearance, so this weekly ritual took on a new level of importance.

Nicky joined her when he could, or picked her up afterward.

She had something on her mind today—he could tell when they were walking to the car. She didn't say anything at first, which in and of itself was a sure sign something was on her mind.

"Do you want to go for a coffee, Ma? Maybe get ourselves a nice slice of cheesecake?"

As she'd gone to the afternoon service, there was no hurry getting back for lunch.

"I'd like that, but how about a nice gelato? It's so warm out."

"Sure thing, Ma."

"How are you and Jimmy?" she asked.

Nicky thought about this. There were so many ways he could interpret the question, and each had a very different answer. "We're good. Haven't seen so much of him because he's busy, but he texts me most days, keeping me up to speed, and we're working together fine."

"You aren't worried about him?" Rosaria asked.

"Ma, trust me, he's just fine. I know there's a lot of rumors flying, but like he said to *Zia* Anna, none of it is true. And believe me, I should know. I've been his right-hand man for everything he's done."

"You know, some people are starting to say he was the one behind your father's murder."

"He wasn't. Those people don't know shit," Nicky said hotly, then made a face because of the vulgarity. His mother didn't appreciate his language. "I was there, remember? Because I'll never forget that day as long as I live. He had nothing to do with it. You have my word, Ma."

Rosaria reached over and touched his arm. "I know it must be hard for you, too, the things people say about what happened to us."

"You don't believe it was Jimmy, do you?"

"I don't know what I believe anymore, or what he's doing. But I worry about you, Domenico. I worry about what kind of trouble he's getting you into." Rosaria was the only person in the world who called him by his given name. The name he shared with his dead father.

Nicky smiled. "Ma, I don't need to tell you what I am, or what my father was before me. Ours isn't a desk job. There are always going to be risks."

"Sometimes I wish it was a desk job," she admitted.

"I'm going to take good care of you, and help Jimmy take care of our whole family," Nicky said. "That's what this is all about. Soon now, the truth will come out, and we will have vengeance for Papa."

"It's so unfair how much of this is just chance. You were

born a few years after Jimmy. That doesn't make him the better man, any more than your father being younger than his father means anything about who you are."

"But this is how the family works," Nicky said. "And honestly, I don't mind at all. I'm happy with Jimmy running things. Let me be his unofficial capo. I'm not ready to be made yet. I'm happy here, learning, for when the day comes."

"Sometimes I wish you were more ambitious," Rosaria said wistfully.

Nicky took his time answering. He wasn't sure where this was coming from, and he didn't want to risk losing his temper with the old woman for no reason, but there was an undercurrent to her words. "What are you saying?"

"Oh, nothing really . . . only . . . if something happened . . . if you were in charge, I think that would be better."

He shook his head, not wanting to understand. "If something happened to Jimmy?" Nicky said slowly.

Rosaria gave him a small smile. "Something could easily happen to him. He's taking a lot of risks, making a lot of enemies."

"Maybe so, Ma, but let me be absolutely clear here: I'm not one of them," Nicky said. "I'd take a bullet for that man."

She changed the subject abruptly, redirecting to talk about the church service and whether she should buy a new dress for the christening next week.

He indulged her and offered to take her clothes shopping.

Nicky had a lot on his mind when he drove home.

He didn't like it that his mamma was talking this way.

Where had this come from?

It didn't feel like her words, or her way of thinking.

She'd never said anything like this before. The idea of betrayal, of betraying blood for gain . . . That wasn't him. It wasn't his father, and it had never been her . . .

Had someone been talking to her?

And if so, who?

Who would she trust enough to listen to them and start to think it would be a good idea for Nicky to betray his *cugino* and leader, and make a play to take over the Martello family?

There was only one man to whom family meant so little.

Sale.

Had he gotten his mother's ear?

If he had, that wasn't good.

But if he hadn't, and it was someone else spreading poison, that was worse. Deceitful strength in numbers.

#

Alessandro had been following Jimmy like he was some sort of religion.

He knew where Jimmy liked to eat, and what, he knew which gym he went to, and who his personal trainer was. He knew Jimmy's favorite cocktail bars and his preferred drinks, even which waitresses liked him best.

Alessandro was good when it came to talking to people. He had charisma, without coming off as offensive when he pressed. He had a gift for getting what he needed out of them without getting too much of their attention in the process, so he wasn't immediately memorable.

He asked questions and got people chatting.

It helped that Alessandro had the kind of mind that could make big pictures out of little details. For him, it was akin to working the edges of a jigsaw puzzle to get a sense of the shape. Right now, he was collecting pieces of a picture of Jimmy Martello and trying to fit them together.

But it wasn't quite fitting.

All of the people who worked for Jimmy or served him in clubs seemed to like him. Some men—like his father—could be gentlemen with anyone they thought worthy, but treated employees and little people like dirt.

Angelo thought that made him look powerful.

It was a very old-fashioned view of the world.

Once, maybe, but not anymore.

Was it an act with Jimmy, or was he genuinely a nice guy?

Alessandro considered that.

The other angle was that Jimmy was clever, so maybe he was clever enough to want people to love him and be loyal to him rather than be scared of him, and understood the new, more modern dynamic the families needed.

There wasn't anyone who worked for Angelo who would take a bullet for him out of love, only fear, and they would almost certainly be half a second too slow to make a difference and save his life. He had the feeling there were a lot of people who would jump in front of Jimmy Martello to save his life. That was a very particular kind of power. And it made Jimmy a fascinating conundrum he wanted to solve.

What would happen if a man with Jimmy's charisma started making friends with people who worked for a man like Angelo?

Now, that was a question, wasn't it?

And what would happen if a man like Jimmy wanted to kill a man like Angelo?

That was an even bigger one.

How loyal would Angelo's people turn out to be?

Or would they simply let Jimmy walk in somewhere he

should not be to end things quietly, deliberately not checking him for a weapon?

He could imagine it.

If Jimmy pulled a gun, none of them would throw themselves in to save Angelo's life. Not fast enough, even if they reacted. All those people his father had shouted at, bullied, and threatened over the years—what would they do if someone who had been a friend to them, shown them respect, treated them well, stuck a knife in the head of the Massino family?

He wanted to believe they'd care, that they'd take Jimmy down, but even as he thought that, he realized, in truth, he wasn't even sure *he'd* care. And that was as damning as anything.

He didn't enjoy working for his father. He didn't particulate care for his company, and he wouldn't have shared a Cohiba and cognac with the old man out of anything other than duty. Angelo didn't respect him; he put up with him, but he thought of his son more like a yapping pup running around his ankles getting in the way of the future of the family. And that was where the challenge of stepping into his shoes would be one he'd relish, because he knew deep down, the old man hated the idea of ever giving up his choke hold on the family.

That led to another line of thinking: Did Jimmy really mean to take out the other dons? It seemed such an enormous affront to the families, the arrogance of the youngest family head gunning for the rest of them, bloodshed in the name of the crown . . . The phrase "heavy is the head that wears the crown" came back to him as he thought about Jimmy killing his father. Was he capable of it, if it moved him closer to the throne?

Now that he'd met the man properly, across a battlefield, he wasn't so sure.

Jimmy had come in ready to kill, expecting to see bloodshed, but he hadn't retaliated, he'd reasoned.

He was a different kind of mobster.

The final question that occurred to Alessandro was: Did that make Jimmy Martello the kind of mobster he could benefit from?

Alessandro might be the future of the Massinos, but he wasn't ready to usher that future in with a bullet. Yet that didn't mean he wasn't more than capable of embracing a future where someone else pulled the trigger.

And if Angelo Massino died, could Jimmy Martello shoulder the blame?

Alessandro didn't particularly like the idea of wasting lives, or needless violence, but there was a time and a place for everything.

And that time felt like now.

#

The day Carlito Fermin was released from Rikers back into the real world, he came walking down the cage, expecting his boys to be waiting for him at the other end.

He had no idea what had been going on with the Trinitario clan while he'd been inside—because they had been too scared to tell him in case he lost his mind and took it out on them. The reality was the Martello family owned them now. They'd made a deal with the devil that was Jimmy Martello, which allowed them to stay alive and keep all of their body parts. In return, they went along with whatever Jimmy asked of them, and that included letting him know Lito's release date and not showing up to take the man home.

Jimmy had other ideas.

Raheim Perdomo, Franklin Casper, and Hector Castro had been taking orders from Jimmy from the moment he found out what they had done, and taking his orders was better than the bullets they deserved.

They weren't the most honorable of souls, and the paid lip service to omertà for them was more about having the easy, green lifestyle to waste on hookers and blow. They didn't give a shit what Jimmy had in mind for Lito as long as they were well out of it themselves.

Prison had not been kind to Carlito Fermin.

He wasn't as strong as he used to be. No amount of trigger skills were worth a damn to a man when he couldn't get a gun.

The deal he'd made to kill the Martello family had gone sideways.

Word had gotten around that his boys screwed up.

They'd left two of their targets standing.

After that, he had nothing to trade.

All around him were bigger, stronger men, good with their fists, handy with knives, and able make weapons out of just about anything they could lay their hands on in a pinch.

He had to take on the worst jobs just to stay safe in lockup.

His saving grace had been finding a couple of boys who needed help with reading and writing. They made his life easier, though for the man he had been to see the man he had become . . . he would have been disgusted with himself.

The only thing that had kept him going was the idea of getting out and seeking revenge on Sale.

In Lito's mind, his own bad luck was 100 percent on Sale's head.

He couldn't blame his boys for what happened; they were

good boys, but they weren't properly prepared. Sale had described the youngest two as a couple of no-account kids. Weak. Frightened. Not two men who could handle themselves and put up the fight of their lives to protect their kin.

Sale was a fucking idiot.

Raheim, Hector, and Franklin had shot at people before. They'd worked a number of armed robberies in their time, nickel-and-dime stuff, not armored cars or that kind of thing—corner stores, grabbing the cash from the register and all the booze they could carry. Gas stations. Isolated, easy targets where people weren't likely to fight back.

They'd killed in a showdown, not in cold blood, though not a hit, and that was a very different sort of job.

Sale had been so sure they could do it, and that the good times would flow for Lito and his boys.

But Sale had shit for brains.

Lito wasn't smart enough to figure out what had happened, but he knew he'd been fucked somehow. Sale was the most obvious candidate for the fuckery, so Sale was the one he wanted to hurt. Badly.

When the sleek black car pulled up, Lito didn't recognize it.

Two massive brutes emerged from the rear door. He didn't recognize them, either. He assumed they were here for someone else who was being released.

"Carlito Fermin?" one of them asked.

"Yeah?" he said, uneasy.

"We're here to pick you up."

Lito's choices were to get in the car, or get in the car with a few fresh bruises, as far as he could see.

He got in the car.

The brute got in beside him, and he was soon between them, a rose between two thorns. He smiled to himself. It was a nervous smile. He was not in control here. He couldn't see much of the driver or the man in the front seat.

The car rolled away from the gate.

Life, he knew, was about to get a whole lot worse for him.

"Hello, Carlito," said the man in the front seat. "I don't think we've met before. I would say it's a pleasure, but it really isn't. You might not recognize me, but I'm sure you've heard my name. I'm Nicky Martello."

Carlito swallowed hard.

Of course, he knew the name.

Little Nicky, Sale's nephew, one of the marks his boys had failed to kill.

His prospects of getting out of the car alive had taken a nosedive.

"I'm going to go ahead and guess that you want to live. In fact, I'm reasonably sure that you would do anything to save your own skin. Am I right, Lito?" Nicky said.

"Absolutely," Lito replied, not missing a beat.

"I do so like being right," said Nicky. "OK, well, I'll make it easy for you; for now, I'm not expecting much from you. All you have to do is be good. No trying to escape; no trying to contact anyone. No making problems for me, and we will get along just fine. We'll take you somewhere nice; you'll be comfortable. Play the game, and you'll be just fine. Fuck me off, and you are dog food. Understood, Lito?"

"One hundred percent. Fuck around, and you might as well call me Cesar or Alpo. Got it. Whatever you say," Lito replied. They needed him alive, and right now, that was music to his ears. He was a survivor. He would do whatever he needed to keep it that way.

#

Sale phoned for Chinese takeout.

They'd delivered him to the usual meeting spot, pumped him with half-decent fake whiskey. All things considered, it had been a half-decent day too. Life was on the up. He was on the rise, once again.

His plans were coming together, business was booming, and he could feel the crown on his head, because he sure as hell felt like the king.

So what if his family hadn't turned him into a made man?

He was going to make himself, and they could all carry on burning in hell.

He had been thinking too small. That was clear now.

Far too small.

The trick to prosperity was ambition, and he was feeling ambitious.

All those years when he'd dreamed of himself as head of the Martello family, that wasn't true, naked, raw ambition. That was small. What were they, really? A family? One chess piece in a bigger network of organized crime? *Martello* wasn't a name to be reckoned with. Outside of New York, no one had heard of them, outside the tragedy of a couple of dead leaders, and that had been his doing too.

He was meant for bigger things.

Better things.

And now, he had the right team behind him. It was obvious, really.

He should have seen it from the beginning . . .

All he had to do was start a war.

It wasn't hard to get the families feuding; they were always beefing about something, and deep down, they distrusted the crap out of each other. There was so much bad blood in the old blood. They all hated one another. Peace was only ever uneasy. Ramp up the jealousy, feed the resentment, encourage the suspicion, and the knives came out.

He could make that happen.

Then, once they'd beaten each other down, he could pick up the pieces.

Easy as that.

It was such a simple plan. It was amazing to him he hadn't come up with it sooner.

Not that he'd come up with it at all; Sale wasn't sharp enough to see when someone was feeding him lines. He couldn't tell when Alessandro was setting him up, and he certainly couldn't tell that his drinking friends were playing their own game.

As far as he knew, they were a couple of helpful guys he'd met in prison, good guys who felt him, who knew what it was like to be SB, and had stayed in touch after they got out.

They'd been great for the connects. They knew a world full of people he didn't and were always more than happy to make the introductions.

He owed them big-time.

He knew that, and he appreciated that they weren't in any hurry to make him repay them.

They'd talked about that debt as recently as today, even.

"I should get everyone together, explain to the families how Jimmy has sold us out to the Russians," Sale said.

His friends had agreed with his reasoning. Yes, that was what he should do. A family gathering, caterers, champagne, big cases of flowers, maybe a string quartet, that kind of deal. Because this was a big deal. This was Sale's time to shine. Didn't he want the families to look at him and see a readymade replacement for Jimmy?

"I have no idea how I'd find a string quartet in this city of heathens."

"Oh, we can help you with that, no worries. And a florist. You know, we have a friend, very handy with an ice pick, does the most incredible ice sculptures. They're to die for," they promised him.

"How can I thank you?" Sale asked. "You've already done so much . . ."

They had a laugh about this. His friends never really wanted anything much in return for all the things they did for him.

"Thank us? We don't need thanking. All we really want is front-row seats so we can watch you finish Jimmy Martello."

"Goes without saying, but I'll say it, anyway: Best seats in the house for my good friends. Done deal," said Sale.

#

Life had been good to Chiara. She had spent most of it enjoying the finer things and the doors her father's money opened.

That couldn't help her now.

There was always her body; it was a weapon in most instances, though now it was mainly employed in self-defense. There were men out there who would pay good money for the opportunity to break her, like some sort of prized stallion. It was never about pleasure with those men. But knowing them, and what they got off on, she could use that. Maybe. Or at least fool herself into thinking she had an element of control in this new hell she called life.

Getting people to like her?

She wasn't sure how much use that would be, all things considered. To pity her, perhaps, but then for everyone that felt sorry or a twinge of guilt over her situation, another would be stroking his meat and relishing it.

For the last five years, she'd almost succeeded in convincing herself she was well adjusted, fun, untamed, and that people—the right kind of people—would be drawn to that. She wasn't, of course. She was every bit as broken as the rest of her generation, especially those with money and no understanding of the worth of anything against the dollar number on the price tag.

But she was a fast study and whip-smart.

Her situation was bad, but none of the people forced to babysit her were the enemy. They were in their own situations, with their own survival instincts to follow. They weren't responsible for her. They hadn't ordered her kidnapping. And the more time she spent around them, the more she came to believe that they didn't wish her any harm. Being kind cost her nothing, even in this awful place, but maybe it bought some little goodwill.

She hoped so, because she needed any small advantages she could get.

Chiara hadn't always been a spoiled rich girl.

She could still remember life before Ivan Popov had swept her up and made her his daughter. No one had ever told her the full story about her mother, or what had happened to her, but she knew the woman was a very good person who had ended up in a very bad place. She felt a kind of empathy for that now. As a child, Chiara had made up all sorts of fanciful stories about the woman who had given birth to her—she was a princess from a distant land, of course. They were on the run from evil people, obviously. She waited for fairy godmothers, talking animal friends, and handsome princes to show up and save her.

As she grew older, she worked out a different reality; her mother had almost certainly run away from her biological father and eventually left her behind too. The sensation of ever-present danger chasing them had loomed overhead since she was born.

Ivan Popov was not Chiara's idea of a fairy godmother, and his version of salvation was not exactly Disneyland fairy tales.

But in he'd swept, just the same, offering a world of ponies and pretty dresses, ballet lessons, and anything else her childish heart desired to win her affection. And trust.

She wanted a lot.

Popov promised she would have all of it, but more than anything, he swore to her that she would finally be safe and happy.

Chiara had endured a lot of being cold, hungry, and scared. The idea of a normal life was seductive. She wanted to be a normal child.

When Ivan first arrived in Sicily, he spoke enough Italian

to get his point across. She'd listen to him talk in his broken variation of the language, hear his promises, and think that Popov was going to rescue her mother as well. But he hadn't, and to this day, she still didn't know why. There was never going to be salvation for her mother. So, as a child, he'd come to her, with another gift and another cherished smile, and told her she had to choose. This life with him, with the gifts and the love and the horses and the rest of the fairy tale she'd craved, or her mother.

It was no choice for a girl to make.

She went with Popov to be his daughter and never looked back. She learned her mother died shortly thereafter.

It hadn't been a difficult promise to keep, in the end. With all the glamour and indulgence Popov had to offer, she did miss her mother often, and when she did, it came in waves. Eventually, she became the spirit guide that she spoke to when she needed advice. Her North Star. Her compass. She asked her mother from the heavens if she would be OK in this instance, and she strangely felt reassured, even if destruction awaited.

In these last few weeks, Chiara had nothing but time to think about her life.

It had occurred to her a long time ago that her biological parents had somehow become entangled with the Russian mob, and that Popov was almost certainly another person her mother had been running away from all along. How could it not have been, given the life he led, the people he called associates? But what was the reason? Was it money? Was it another branch of the illegal activities that permeated throughout her adoptive father's mob? And was there a world in which this mess was not Ivan Popov's fault? Did her biological father cause this chaos, to which her mother had to make that initial exit? It was all so much to process.

She could have created a thousand new stories in the prison of her mind, inventing them to stay alive.

She couldn't stop thinking about it, and yet her mind always returned to this: Her mother was a victim of human trafficking and perhaps Chiara herself was now next in line. The only conduit was the same man who promised her ponies and pretty things, whom she eventually called Papa.

Because she kept coming back to the same thing. For all that he professed to love her, she had no reason to believe a single word that had come out of Ivan Popov's mouth.

There was no evidence that her life was anything but a story he'd convinced her was worth believing in.

And that scared her deeply, because there was only so much power to lies, and they always, eventually, fell to the truth . . .

Did she want to know the truth?

#

Sale was halfway through a massive slice of cake when Alessandro walked through the door.

Sale came here every Monday afternoon, a creature of habit, sad discipline, and greed. Alessandro often found him here. It was a quiet café run by a middle-aged Polish couple with no underworld connections who would have probably chased him out of the shop with a broom if they'd known what he did.

"I don't know how to pronounce it, but it's very good. You should get yourself a slice," Sale said, as Alessandro joined him at the table.

"No need. Just coffee for me." Alessandro forbade indulgence. He was a disciplined man.

"I wanted to invite you to a party," Sale said around a mouthful of diminishing crumbs.

"A party? What's the celebration?" Alessandro asked, the wheels spinning behind his eyes, already wondering how to turn this to his advantage.

"I'm going to finish Jimmy Martello once and for all," Sale explained. "You were right, by the way, that it's better to ruin a man and keep him alive to suffer the humiliation."

Alessandro smiled. "I'm always right, Don Martello, but I'm glad you see things my way," he said. It wasn't that he wanted Jimmy alive so much as he didn't want Sale starting a war they weren't ready for. Sale shooting Jimmy in cold blood didn't fit with Alessandro's plan. But Sale provoking Jimmy Martello into drawing down . . . that could work.

"I want to get everyone there, all the families. I want them to see him crushed. That's important to me," Sale said, with a wry smile. "After all, what's the point of humiliation if no one is around to savor it? A tree falls in the woods, and no one gives a shit."

"Indeed."

"So, I know you're invested . . . So I thought . . . maybe you could help me with that?"

"Happy to," Alessandro promised him.

"Thing is, people have been nervous about big gatherings, on account of Jimmy. So, we can't tell them Jimmy is going to be there," Sale said.

"I see the logic, but at the same time, the families need to see that you have Jimmy under control, that you are the natural leader of the Martello family. So yes, we need to play it just right," Alessandro said.

"I knew I could count on you to understand things," Sale said. "I've got proof now. I've got a witness who is coming, one who will swear to the truth of it and has undeniable proof that Jimmy has sold us out to the Russians."

"I'm impressed," said Alessandro. "Dare I ask how you pulled that off?"

"I can't reveal my contacts, obviously," Sale said, waving his hands dismissively, like a stage magician. "But you know I am a very well-connected man. Prison days . . . business . . . I know people who know people. They came through for me."

Alessandro nodded.

He was surprised that Sale had found a lead to connect Jimmy to the Russians, given it was almost certainly bullshit, but that was Sale, a gift that kept giving in the most unexpected ways. It was a shame that he would almost certainly die before this was through. He was beginning to see the man's not-so-deplorable side. Still, Sale could have his moment in the sun, bask in the glory, and Alessandro would turn his attention to other things, like how to turn the party into a full-scale brawl.

"I've got a lot of plans for this party," Sale said, as though reading his mind. "I'm getting ice sculptures, a water fountain, a chocolate fountain, and some kind of big thing with flowers. Hell, I'm even bringing in a string quartet. Can you imagine? A string quartet. It's going to be an event . . ."

"Isn't that something," Alessandro agreed. A string quartet and ice sculptures? Had Sale been bingeing Martha Stewart *and* Pinterest? "Classical, or jazz?" he asked.

"For what?" Sale replied, before digging back into his cake.

"The string quartet," Alessandro said.

Sale waved a forkful of cake at him. "I don't care what they play, just as long as everyone is impressed."

"Well, either would be sophisticated," Alessandro said.

No, he thought, this was not Sale's idea.

Someone had sold it to him.

So, who, and why?

He needed to know the other players in the game. Otherwise, he was going to make mistakes when it came to entering the endgame. Sale was a simple enough creature, emotionally fragile, ego-driven, bitter, but Sale with someone else pulling his strings was a whole other matter.

"So, what have you been up to? You got any news for me?" Sale asked.

"Chasing ghosts and rumors mostly," Alessandro admitted. "I know the Russians have an issue with Jimmy, but it didn't take long to find out that those photos of him with Yakovlev aren't a fair representation of what happened." Sale shrugged and finished off eating his cake. "I had a little chat with one of the doormen. Turns out that they had to throw out Yakovlev and his muscle. My photographer left before it got to that, so it wasn't clear what we were seeing, but we weren't seeing all of it."

"Looked pretty friendly to me," Sale said.

"That was the whole point of getting the photos," Alessandro said. "They served a purpose, but we don't want to be lying to ourselves, Don Martello. There's more here. I've been trying to find out why a man like Yakovlev might be pissed with Jimmy."

"Oh, you know the Russians are born angry," Sale said, like it really didn't interest him. Those few words were a perfect demonstration of why Sale would never amount to anything alone. He was the sum of the people manipulating him.

"Well, it turns out that Jimmy has been asking a lot of questions about a business associate of Yakovlev's—a man called Volkov."

Sale shook his head. "Like I said, those Russians could start a fight if they were alone in inside a McDonald's bag. Jimmy asks a lot of questions. So what? That's him. All talk and no action."

Alessandro was painfully familiar with the bipolar way Sale vacillated between thinking Jimmy was the devil incarnate and talking about him like he was a useless petulant child.

It had very little to do with Jimmy and a lot to do with whether Sale felt like he was winning. And that's when he realized Jimmy hadn't called a hit on him at all. It was a performative act by Sale to further his manipulative tactics. Smart, yet pathetic.

#

There was no time left for Chiara. Her fate was sealed. She was going to be sold for money, for whatever purpose the highest bidder desired. They had been plumping her up like a lamb to the slaughter, with clothes bought to appeal to the pervs: lingerie, jewels, subtle shades of makeup, and everything else that would ultimately create a broken doll version of herself.

She dressed but couldn't bear to look at herself in the mirror. She didn't want to see what they would see. She didn't know how they would do it—like a cattle market where she was paraded around a ring and men barked out prices, or as a photo on the dark web along with a countdown clock while the auction was open. Would it be silent, with masked bids, or like eBay with them spiraling before their eyes, dollar signs scrolling? Some other way? Would a man just turn up at the door and say, "You are mine," like a twisted version of those old fairy tales she'd loved?

It didn't bear dwelling on.

She sat in the chair for the girl to apply her makeup and do her hair.

The girl leaned in so close, her lips brushed against Chiara's ear and whispered, "It's going to be OK."

"Unlikely," she said, without anger.

"Someone is coming," the girl said softly. Chiara watched her eyes darting around though the backward glass of the mirror. She was trying to look everywhere at once, like she couldn't trust they weren't being overheard. "Trust him. He's going to get you out of here."

It was a good dream.

#

Nicola came through for him.

She had a different address. Not the door they'd hurried Chiara through when she'd first been taken, but a dirty hotel in Shoreditch where the auction was going to take place.

Nicola had swiped one of those little cards they gave to members, meaning he could walk in through the back door, no questions.

"I hear there's new merchandise, and I want to be in on the auction," Jimmy said.

Nicola had told him some of the numbers her paymasters had commanded on previous auctions, and they went beyond anything even his wildest nightmares had imagined. But it seemed the Russians had worked out exactly how much a life was worth in retail.

"Come with me, sir," the man behind the desk said, happy to steer him toward where he needed to be.

Jimmy greased his palm with an excessive tip.

The man dipped his head in thanks and pocketed it.

There were a dozen men in the room, all of them staring at a blank screen that dominated the largest wall. A man in a suit stood beside the TV. Once Jimmy had taken his seat, the man walked among them, offering each a small signal-locked phone that contained a single app that would allow them to make their bids.

"You will need to input your details for the bank transfer, which will be drawn at the end of the auction. If you cannot pay, we will move onto the next highest bidder, and so on. But do not waste our time or yours. Anyone who cannot pay will not be welcome at our next sale."

It took a few seconds to set everything up, but once it was, the man turned on the TV, and the image of a girl on a bed somewhere in the hotel filled the screen.

She was unmistakably the one he'd been dreaming about all this time. She looked proud, defiant, and undeniably beautiful despite her circumstances. There was no fear in her face. She was dressed in a tiny red leather skirt with a slinky black tank top and chunky heels. Her eye makeup was dramatic, and her dark brown hair fell below her waist.

She had no idea she was on camera.

"If you would like to start the bidding," the Russian said, and a moment later, numbers were appearing on the screen, the amounts tied to the devices they had been issued. There were no names. Nothing to tie them to the activities beyond the ultimate bank transfer, from offshore, for the winner, who would take it all.

One thousand became $30,000 in a matter of seconds and showed no signs of slowing as the men around the room leaned forward intently, studying Ivan Popov's little girl. Thirty became $70,000 and topped the $100,000 mark before Jimmy made his first bid.

One by one, bidders around the room dropped out, their high bids turning red on the screen as they ended their participation, until, with her worth already commanding a cool quarter of a million, there were only three of them left to fight for her soul. A Saudi—one of their endless royal family no doubt; a Nigerian—who had almost certainly profited from endless scams where he masqueraded as a prince looking to fleece the gullible; and Jimmy, who had still to place his opening bet.

Jimmy watched her a moment longer. He'd been wrong. She *was* scared, but her bravery was more than a match for the fear. He was looking at a survivor.

The Nigerian dropped out at $275,000.

The Saudi looked at the number, then at the auctioneer. "If he isn't going to bid, I'll take my prize." He nodded toward Jimmy.

Time to shit or get off the pot.

He punched in a number. It was a chunk of the family's liquid assets, and to be honest, he wasn't entirely sure the transfer would clear, since they hid more money in assets than they had readily available. If it was flagged, there was no way on God's earth Enzo was letting it through. It was more than twice the Saudi's offer.

The other man reached for his handset, typed something, and Jimmy's heart sank in the second before the lower bid turned red. The Saudi was out. "Too rich of a purchase for my blood. Enjoy your pussy."

The auctioneer came across to where he sat while the others left the room.

He took the handset off him. "Now, just the little matter of settling up your winning bid. Congratulations. I hope she gives you many hours of pleasure."

"I'm sure she will. Where is she?"

"Aleksandr will take you through to her while we wait for the transaction to clear. You won't be allowed to leave the building with her before then, but we have no problem with you examining the merchandise."

"Take me to the river."

The Russian didn't seem to understand the reference, which was just fine by him. Another goon took him deeper into the hotel, down a number of paint-peeling back corridors to a service elevator, which rattled and shook as it climbed up the floors before the door opened on a landing with six more doors. The goon pointed toward one.

Jimmy went in alone.

She was still there and perched on the edge of the bed.

Her eyes were full of challenge.

She didn't say a word as he closed the door behind him. He had no idea if the camera was still relaying images of the room to the big screen downstairs, but he had to assume so.

He sat down on the other edge of the bed, though he measured his proximity to her so she remained comfortable, while letting the cameras believe he was ready for action. He was ready, but not the kind of action the auctioneers had hoped for.

He tried to picture the camera angles from memory and position himself so that no one could read his lips before he whispered, "I'm taking you back to your father. I won't hurt you, I swear. I'd be grateful if, in return, you didn't hurt me, either." He managed a ghost of a smile. "I'm Jimmy."

Jimmy's coat had deep pockets.

In them, folded down small, were a pair of ballet-style shoes, a silk blouse, and a skirt. He felt like one of those stage magicians with their endless scarves as he pulled them out of their various concealments. Silk had been Nicola's idea, too, because it would fold small and still look good.

He stood facing the camera for a moment, looking for the hidden lens. It didn't take long to find when you knew where to look, and a single dime blinded it, stuck in place with gum. He kept his back to her while she stripped out of the red leather skirt and put on the clothes he'd brought with him.

She didn't put on the ballet slippers, pointing to the heels she had.

He shook his head.

"Trust me, those are no good."

She nodded and made the switch.

When she was ready, he gave her an envelope from his inside pocket.

"There's a passport in there and plane tickets. For today's flight, as of now your name is Kimberly Finamore."

Chiara opened the passport to reveal a photo of herself next to Kimberly Finamore's name. She smirked as she remembered the exact photo that was used for the fake documentation. It was a selfie of her with Maryum and Stephanie on their girls' trip to LA. She realized her girls had called this mystery man to rescue her, which only built up her animosity toward her father. But who was this guy, anyway? Who *did* her friends call, and could she trust him? She saw him scaling the room at every corner for safety. Beyond his breathtaking good looks, she was disarmed by how skilled he appeared in this rescue mission. But was it a rescue mission? She still wasn't sure. All she knew was that she was drawn to this new potential friend . . . or potential enemy.

Jimmy checked the door to make sure the corridor was clear. It wasn't. The goon stood by the elevator door. He gestured for the man to come over, and as he did, he stepped back slightly as though to allow him through, only to slam his head in the door repeatedly until he was on his knees. He had the geography of the place in his head, and assuming Nicola hadn't sold him out at the last hurdle, knew the room beside hers had what he needed. He kicked open the door, crossed the room, ignoring the couple on the bed—the man in lingerie, the woman in leather—and led Chiara by the hand to the window. It was a huge sash thing that worked on a little rope pulley that took him a second to understand. Then he had it open and was helping her through.

"There's a car at the bottom. Don't stop for anyone. Get in it, and get the hell out of here," Jimmy urged. "You have to be on that plane."

"What are you going to do?" Chiara inquired, sounding concerned for her savior.

"Make sure you get on the plane."

He hit the fire alarm and followed her down the metal stairs outside, not looking back.

Wild steps echoed and clanged.

Shouts chased them.

By now, the Russians had probably discovered his money was no good. This was always going to be the most dangerous part of the plan, with his back exposed to a bunch of pissed-off

Russian mobsters to whom he owed over half a million.

Halfway down, gunshots rang out.

With two flights left, one careened off the metal rail inches from his hand.

He stopped holding the handrail.

Every muscle in his body burned. He wasn't used to moving like this. She was five steps ahead of him and hit the street first, but froze because there was no sight of any waiting car.

Jimmy panicked before he heard the roar of an engine gunning and saw Bryan's low-riding sports car come surging down the tight alleyway. He'd been parked up by the mouth of it, with a view of every way in and out of the place, and hadn't committed to one until he'd seen them clattering down the fire escape.

He threw open the door, and without thinking, Chiara climbed inside, over the back of the passenger seat, to perch on the narrow back seat.

Jimmy was in the passenger seat two seconds later and slammed the door as more Russian goons came surging out of the service doors. They started shooting up the street as Bryan slammed the stick shift into reverse and powered out of there in a shriek of rubber.

"So, are you really saving me or just kidnapping me from my

kidnappers?" Chiara asked as the car sped toward the airport.

#

The whole business with the ice sculptures and string quartet bugged Alessandro.

Like Sale had ever listened to a string quartet in his life.

So, his puppeteer wanted this big family gathering.

Alessandro could think of several reasons someone might want that, but couldn't prove any of them.

He tried asking Sale indirectly, on the pretense of helping him get things set for the big event, but didn't learn much.

The one thing that wasn't a lie was that without him vouching for everything, there was no way Sale was getting all of the families under one roof. They were way too edgy for that, and nervous Mafia men were not something you wanted to be around.

He could smell the blood. He just didn't know from which direction the bullets were going to start flying.

He weighed his options carefully, and then did the only thing that made sense.

He phoned Jimmy Martello.

"Consider this an anonymous tip-off," Alessandro said.

"Alessandro?" Jimmy said. He sounded amused.

"Don't try and be cute, Jimmy," Alessandro said. "Your uncle, Salvatore, is making his play. He's planning a big family gathering. Everyone there. He doesn't want you to know about it just yet, but he is going to make sure you show, because you're the main attraction. He says he's going to expose your dealings with the Russians."

Jimmy laughed.

"He wants all the families there to see him destroy you. I don't know if he means to kill you. He might try."

"This is not news," said Jimmy.

"Maybe not, but there's more to it. I don't think this is his idea. I think someone else wants this gathering, and they're using him to get to you. So . . . look do what you will with this. I don't care if you live or die, Jimmy. I just don't trust that snake, and I know he's been poisoning the well around your name, so . . . just be aware. OK?"

"Consider me aware. All the families, you said?"

Alessandro confirmed this.

"Right. Do whatever you gotta to make it happen," Jimmy told him. "I'll be there, and if there really is someone manipulating him, I'll be ready for them. If you're right, I'm going to owe you one."

"I have thoughts about this, and exactly the kind of favor I'd want you to owe me, Jimmy," Alessandro said. "When shit goes down, I want to be center stage. I want everyone to know where I was in all of this."

"I'm sure we can figure out the finer points, assuming you want to be seen helping me?"

"Well, I sure as hell don't want anyone coming out of this to think I was working for Sale," Alessandro said.

"I can't argue with that," said Jimmy. "Who knows? *You* might have a career in politics yet."

#

They were walking through the old neighborhoods where they'd hung out as kids.

They'd both dressed down so as not to draw attention to themselves.

Nicky swigged his Moka Drink.

"What's on your mind? Speak up, cuz," Jimmy asked.

"Something's going down," Nicky said. "I can feel it."

"Something's always going down."

"Not like that. I think someone's been trying to play my ma. She's been spouting shit. Disloyal shit. Not the kind of thing she's ever said before."

"How so?"

"Just whispers, you know, insidious little whispers, making her think I should be in charge, not you. Don't be cross with her, Jimmy. She's fragile these days. It's not her; she'd never sell you out."

"I don't want you to worry about this, Nicky. Not about me, and not about your mamma. But believe me, I'm more grateful than you could ever know, because you just turned a paranoid theory into a fact. That helps me."

Nicky stopped walking and turned to face Jimmy. "So, there is something."

"There is," said Jimmy. "And it could be big. The problem is, it's mostly guesses right now. But if one by one my guesses are proving right, this could play out well for us."

Jimmy told him about the families gathering. It was the first Nicky had heard of Sale's big shindig, but that wasn't a surprise.

"*Cugino*, I know you're not an idiot and you don't need me telling you this, but you have to know this is a setup, right?" Nicky said.

"One hundred percent," Jimmy replied. "Only not for me. At least, not if I get this right."

"I'm all in," Nicky said. "Whatever you need. *Famiglia*."

Jimmy smiled at him.

He'd had to do a lot of thinking lately, about whom he could trust and who would betray him, and the one thing he knew for sure was if Nicky turned on him, he'd never survive this.

But if he couldn't trust Nicky, he couldn't trust anyone.

#

The smile when he shut the phone with Haruto was a match for any knife slash. The retired Yakuza boss Sazuki Kazu was doing well with his new liver, and Haruto was keen to repay the debt.

"Is that really all you want?" he asked Jimmy, curious and a little surprised that it wasn't more.

"It would mean a great deal to me, Sazuki-san" Jimmy said.

"Then I will do as you ask," Haruto promised.

Jimmy had a long list of people to contact. One by one, he set about calling in the favors owed to him.

So far, no one had found any of his small requests to be unreasonable or problematic, and all had assured him they would come through.

The way he figured it was, if after the event, they felt he'd asked too much of them after the event, he'd probably be dead anyway, and it wouldn't matter.

He was gambling everything on this one play.

It wasn't smart, but it was the only way he could think of that, if he won, he was sure to take home the big prize.

"Hey, Capo, my brother," Jimmy said when he finally got through to the BMF offices. "You know that favor we talked about?"

#

Jimmy didn't call Ivan Popov.

That was a favor he meant to ask for in person.

He'd given Chiara a few days to recover from her ordeal. After they'd touched down back in the States, he'd booked her into a luxury hotel under her fake name and told her she couldn't go back to her own Brooklyn apartment yet. Volkov would have people looking for her. After all, he's lost his new prized girl and was out the promised half a mil for his trouble.

There was a safe house Popov had set up. Jimmy was taking her there now. That was where he intended to make his ask.

It was about 6:00 p.m. when they finally arrived in Brighton Beach, pulling up outside the address Popov had given him.

He texted to say it was them before he got out of the car.

The door opened. Popov stood back in the shadows.

He told Chiara it was safe to get out.

She stretched and turned to face the door, seeing the silhouette of her father in the doorway.

"моя дочь," Popov said, tears streaming down his face as he rushed out to embrace his daughter. "Can you ever forgive me?"

"I'll need certain reassurances," she said, but she was smiling despite her voice sounding so cold. She hugged her father.

"Of course, of course, anything you need. I will make it so, my girl," Popov said.

She nodded. "OK, well, if I'm going to set foot inside that house, Father, I need you to promise me you're never going to let another girl be taken. "

Popov hung his head. "It's over now, as of today," Ivan said.

"And you, Mr. Martello, please tell me your family isn't into that shit, either," Chiara said.

"Nope, the Martellos are ordinary decent criminals." He smiled. "We're all about fraud, but moving into internet gambling." Jimmy turned to Popov. "I promised you I would bring her home. I am a man of my word."

Popov nodded. "I am in your debt, Mr. Martello. You wanted a favor, if I recall? What can I do? If not money? Construction contracts? Help with zoning, permits? You name it. I will do everything in my power to repay you."

Jimmy explained what he needed.

#

It was all going to plan.

Better.

The world was there before him, waiting for him to claim it.

The ice sculptures were works of art.

Alessandro had come through with his promise and persuaded most of the dons to come. Two of the clan heads took a moment to seek him out and compliment him on the string quartet. "Such a wonderful addition," they said, which he took as affirmation of his good taste. For the gathering itself, Sale's friends had sourced a vast courtyard in the shadow of a luxury hotel. Walking around now, he felt like he owned the world.

Jimmy turned up late, looking worried and underdressed.

Sale was content.

It would all come out now. This was his destiny. Here, among the families, he would smile and be gracious and take their compliments as he ascended to take the throne.

Sale approached the mike.

He looked around at the faces. It didn't even matter that

they weren't all looking at him. He breathed in deeply, tapped the mike twice and leaned in. "Is this thing on?" He chuckled self-deprecatingly. Everyone could hear him. "Our guest of honor has arrived." His smile was genuine. To anyone who didn't know, he looked like a man taking great pride in his family. "Jimmy Martello. Jimmy, Jimmy, Jimmy . . . what have you been up to, you scamp? Obviously, as host, I want to say a few words, but first, I think we should hear from someone else . . . someone with insider knowledge, and you know what they say about knowledge. So, without further ado, a word from our sponsor."

At that point, Alessandro was supposed to appear with whoever the witness was.

It was all carefully choreographed.

Sale could see Alessandro approaching, but to his horror, he realized he knew the man following behind him.

This was no surprise nail in his nephew's coffin.

It was Carlito Fermin.

The same Lito he had paid to have the men of the Martello family killed.

Sickness clamped like a vise around his guts. He felt the pressure around his heart. This couldn't be happening. This was supposed to be *his* moment. It would be, though not in the way that he imagined.

Sale froze, unable to make sense of what he was seeing.

Was Carlito Fermin the one with evidence of Jimmy Martello's Russian dealings?

It was only then—turning and turning about, the mike still in his hand, clutched like a weapon he thought he could use to beat and batter his way out of there—that Sale realized his audience was considerably bigger than he'd expected.

There were a lot of unfamiliar faces out there in the crowd.

More people showed up in the courtyard.

Several looked to be foreign, an international crew. Good. Good. He smiled, thinking these were the people his friends had wanted to invite to the party.

That smile froze on his lips as he saw most were openly carrying.

In that moment, he understood that everything was out of his control, and always had been.

"Friends," Alessandro said, his voice carrying clearly over the PA. "Some of you will remember Carlito Fermin, I'm sure. We're lucky to have him with us. Blessed, even. As he has only recently been released for time served, but he thought it was important he tell you a story. One that you should have heard a long time ago, but now he is going to put things right."

"It's all lies!" Sale shouted, panicking.

A few faces turned his way.

He shook his head, backing up a step.

There was nowhere to run. He'd put himself above them all, standing on a raised part of the stage, but with people crowding around it, he was cut off from any avenue of escape.

There were dozens upon dozens of them, all gathered close, ignoring the show. They only had eyes for him.

These were all the people who owed Jimmy a favor, and they had come to pay their debt.

Such a small thing.

Such a simple one.

Strength in numbers.

Of course, they were all delighted to honor their debt to him and return the favor.

Jimmy walked through the crowd and climbed up onto the stage beside his uncle. He took the mike from Sale's hand with no resistance. "Friends, family, my thanks to each and every one of you for being here today to hear this truth, and of course a heartfelt thanks to Alessandro Massino for making it all possible. To those of you who are here to repay favors you owe me, consider the debts repaid. Your presence is much appreciated. It was important for me that you bear witness to what is said here today. That is the power of the truth. There is a blood debt being settled here, now. And while every word you will hear from Lito's mouth is true, I am making it known that I have no intention of starting a blood feud with the man or his kin. He's giving us the truth, and in doing so, I consider his wrong against the Martellos made good, understood?"

There were murmurs. Of course, no one understood. Not yet. But they would.

"Carry on please, Lito."

Jimmy gave Lito the microphone and stepped away.

Lito cleared his throat. It was a nervous tick. Unsurprising, given there must have been four hundred crowded into the courtyard. "My name is Lito. A few of you know me, I think, better than you would want; one I know better than he could dare fear. I was in prison with the man who was so eager to bring you all here, Salvatore Martello, though I knew him as SB. I think most of you know him as Sale? He was not a good man, but few of us in there are. We do our time, we get out, we keep our noses clean, or we don't. But not SB. He was thinking big. Dreaming. He came to me in my cell one day, and he had this idea . . . He said that if I did this thing for him, he would see me and my people well looked after. And as head of the family, he'd make sure we were paid—and by paid, I mean a lot of money—if I could arrange a contract killing for him. It was just business. I hold nothing against any of you. And, hand on heart, I regret ever being taken in by this man . . . He isn't what he claims, not even close. There is no honor in his body. He is a snake."

There were sounds of shock from those who knew the Martellos. Murmurs of discontent. Of surprise. Disgust. Because they could read between the lines. They knew whom the targets of the kill order were. They'd called them kin. Family. This was a betrayal of the worst sort. Blood on blood.

Lito carried on with his speech. "Three of my boys took the job. They went into that house that Sunday with express orders from SB. They shot Italo Martello Sr. and his sons, Italo Jr. and Domenico. He'd ordered the deaths of Nicky Martello and Jimmy Martello as well. The women were to be spared, but the male heirs were to be taken out, leaving the way open for him to claim the seat at the head of the table. But things didn't work out that way. Jimmy Martello returned fire. He stood his ground, and along with his cousin Nicky, drove my boys out of his family home. This, I swear to you, is the truth. On my life, *mi madre*'s life, and *mi padre*'s eternal soul."

Jimmy nodded. "I believe you, Lito. I was there." He turned to Sale. "So, *Zio*, are you man enough to admit that you called the hit that took the lives of your father and your brothers?"

"This is all lies! All of it. Disgusting, filthy lies!" Sale screamed, red in the face and dripping sweat. "You're scum, Jimmy boy. You're in bed with the Russians. I've got proof! You paid off this contemptible piece of shit to lie for you. It's all lies. Every fucking word of it. I am Martello through and through. Martello blood flows through my veins. This is my family!"

"And yet you had them murdered. Some family man you are, Sale."

"Shut the fuck up, you filthy-mouthed fucking liar!"

No one moved.

The favors stayed in place around the stage, cutting off any and all lines of escape. The families stood back, watching the final act of the tragedy of the Martellos play out.

Just then, Nicky hopped on stage, holding a recorder. He grabbed the microphone. He played the recording for the crowd, audio recorded from under Sale's desk, revealing all plans . . . including Sale's previous failed attempts to murder Jimmy. Collective gasps bounced around the room.

"You don't think I'd just accuse you without proof, do you, Sale? I'm not like you," Jimmy said. "I'm not stupid. I've spent years now gathering evidence, undeniable proof. Everything from DNA linking Lito's boys to the murder scene to proof of payments from your accounts, siphoned out of the family's banks. I've got hours upon hours of recorded transcripts from your phone. I've got tracking that puts you at key dates and times in meetings about deceit, and on and on. Witnesses, everything, and it's all there for anyone here who wants to see it. Justice needs to be served, now, for my father, for my uncle, and my grandfather—"

Jimmy saw the gun in Sale's hand.

He had no time to think.

He reached for his own gun—a weapon that was not there, despite the admonishment of Enzo to always carry because the game around him had changed. The gun was in the lockbox at home. He'd rushed to this meeting, and he'd forgotten his own weapon. Death in the shape of the hollow muzzle of Sale's Glock lifted toward him.

Salvatore Martello had never been man enough to do his own dirty work before.

Never.

He was, above all things, beyond all things, a coward.

But more, he was like a fucking cockroach.

He clung onto life desperately.

He'd have said he was a survivor, but that was wrong. He wasn't. He was a parasite.

He pulled the trigger.

Bang!

And an echo, a split-second behind the first gunshot.

Bang!

Jimmy knew he was dead. He felt the sting of a bullet, though his mind refused to admit it. Instead, he spiraled, and the world slowed down impossibly. He felt himself spinning, the world lurching away around him, as the sound of gunshots ricocheted around the confines of the courtyard, louder than they had any right being. The men of the families moved for their own weapons, but the favors simply stood there, between them, calm, making sure that no one did something they would regret.

This was Martello business.

Jimmy saw Sale's arm swing wide, the look of manic glee transform into one of confusion before he fell backward, a third eye opening in the middle of his skull.

The bullet was an immediate killer. It fragmented on impact, the exit wound through Sale's face left him unrecognizable in death.

Sale fell.

The second shot, the echo a fraction after the first that had been meant for Jimmy's head, had whistled wide as the impact of the kill shot threw Sale's arm off, saving Jimmy Martello's life.

Sale couldn't even do that right.

Jimmy was on his knees, a trickle of blood running from his temple where the bullet only grazed him as he scanned the gathering for the shooter. His mind was struggling to make sense of the situation. The first shot hadn't been Sale's. There'd been a fraction in it, but such small margins saved and cost lives.

He saw her walking toward him, the gun he'd left in the lockbox in her hand.

Chiara.

The favors melted away to allow her through.

She climbed up onto the stage, standing over Sale's fallen body. He could see her thinking about putting another bullet in him, just to be sure that he was dead. But Sale wasn't getting up from that head shot, mainly because he didn't have much in the way of a head left.

"You saved my life," Jimmy said.

"I'd say that just about makes us even. I hate owing people. So, how about we call that my debt repaid? Here." She pressed a silk scarf into his hand and made him hold it to the head wound. It was the first time they had touched. Skin on skin. The sensation was electric.

Jimmy stood there, surrounded by family, but the only person he cared about in that moment was walking away, led by her father through the crowd.

He wanted to rush after her but knew it was more important that they got her out of there, and gave the families time to get their stories straight and explain the bullet in Sale's head. Because that was what it was all going to come down to when Detective Mulligan and his cronies turned up looking to dot the *i*'s and cross the *t*'s. Jimmy had spent months making them his pets to the point of compliance. Who knew they would finally acquiesce to Rico Suave? But they, too, were in on the plan. They knew Sale was the behind the murders, that Jimmy had legitimized the Martello business, and that justice had to be quietly served. It wasn't a basket full of pastries and wine in exchange for silence; it was the truth. Partially. Now, they just needed a story that they could put in their reports and forget about.

It was a good story too. Believable. Especially with so many there prepared to say they'd heard Salvatore Martello unmasked as the killer of his own kin and, shamed, watched as he took the coward's way out, a bullet in his own head, rather than face the consequences. Everyone, including the police, knew that wasn't true, but if everyone said it, then it *was* . . . in the book of record.

#

The speech was the cue for Sale's unseen friends to crash the party.

Alessandro had been right to be suspicious.

The friends Sale had made in prison were no friends to him at all. Everything they'd given him had a price he couldn't possibly ever repay, but that was the point. They owned him. He'd been useful to them, far more useful than he'd ever suspected. Their foot soldiers rolled in, piling out of two big, anonymous vans, locked and loaded, and ready to gun down entire mobbed-up families in that moment.

A slaughter.

If Sale hadn't died moments earlier, he would have then. Little did he know, but his fate had been sealed long before he set foot inside that courtyard with its fancy ice sculptures and the echo of violins cutting and spiraling through the night air as the string quartet played on.

Alessandro was a little disappointed that "Don Martello" would never know he was the one who had sold him out to Jimmy, but he had enjoyed delivering Lito to the party. The look on Sale's stupid face as he tried to untangle his thoughts and catch up with the reality of what was happening was, like the old Mastercard ad said, priceless.

Similar, in point of fact, to the expression of the masked

men as they drove their vans into the sweeping arc of the parking lot, thinking they were going to unleash carnage only to realize they'd driven into their own trap and it had sprung.

Their first inkling had been nothing more telling than glass catching the light up above: the scope from a rifle. They recognized it for what it was and quickly made at least two others, though they missed more. The hotel was booked out by Jimmy's favors, with shooters covering the main approach and courtyard from the windows up above, and with men on the ground armed to the teeth. And not just family men. Every manner of enemy was in that space waiting to greet them as they came spilling out of their vans. Made men, family foot soldiers, Yakuza, gang boys from the BMF, Latin Kings, cold-blooded Russians.

This wasn't the peaceful family gathering ripe for slaughter that Sale had sold them.

This was a war party.

Taking on all of them would have been suicide.

The vans didn't so much as slow. They accelerated through the sweep of the lot and gunned their engines as they made their escape.

While Alessandro never found out who they were, he knew that he'd made the right call throwing his all in with Jimmy.

Now for Jimmy to make sure everyone knew that he'd played his part well. He wanted people to think well of him when it came time to enter the polling booths.

#

There were photographs of the interior, of course, but Jimmy wanted to remake his father's study from memory rather than copy every detail. There was something special about a child's impressions of his father's sanctuary. So much of the original room had been destroyed during the murders. But sitting in the chair that was so like his father's chair, Jimmy truly believed these four walls held the spirit of the old room, and more importantly, the spirit of the family.

That morning, Jimmy had taken his old suit out of his wardrobe, and he'd sent it to be cleaned. It was a symbolic act—he wasn't going to wear it again, but he did not need to keep his father's blood as a reminder of what had happened anymore.

There had been justice for the family, finally.

Together, he and Enzo lit the candles.

"You've done well, my boy," Enzo said, then corrected himself. "A boy no longer. You are a man now, in this, forged in the crucible of grief. Wherever he is, your father is proud of you.

I know that with all of my heart."

Slowly, the men of the Martello family gathered in the room. Nearly two years had passed since Sale's execution. Jimmy had crystallized his place as the King of New York, known for mobilizing crime families across all sects. It was bold and it was brave, and it had become Jimmy's signature. His only bit of violence during his short reign thus far was having Volkov annihilated execution-style, derailing his whole sex-trafficking business and removing the target from the Popovs' backs. Today was once again his birthday, and in true Jimmy fashion, he would be gifting someone else.

Jimmy remembered how his father had walked behind the desk and pulled out the humidor from inside the desk drawer, how there were Cohibas lined up like soldiers. Jimmy did that same thing now.

He had the bottles of Martello family wine as well, and enough small glasses for everyone to raise a glass to the dead.

Nicky came in with Chiara—the last two people he'd been waiting for.

Jimmy took a slow breath. He'd thought about nothing other than what he was going to say now, here, because this was an important ritual for the family, and his first time doing it. And he was terrified of making a mess of it.

Enzo had taken him through the ritual more than once and insisted he was ready.

Everyone who gathered in that room knew what was coming and had given him their blessing.

"First, let's have a little vino," Jimmy said, smiling. In that moment, as he decanted a bottle of the family's vintage, he felt like his father was with him. It was the first time he had felt that in a long time. "We're doing something traditional today, but we're also doing something new. You have a powerful heart, you have a lion's courage, and in the moment that matters most, you aren't afraid to do whatever it takes."

Jimmy took out a prayer card. "Your middle name, Anna, for Saint Anne."

He turned the card so everyone could see it.

Nicky passed him a knife.

This was the life they had chosen.

The life of the knife...and the gun.

They made eye contact for a moment.

Nicky would be next. Jimmy would see to that.

Enzo passed him a gun and nodded to him with respect.

"Give me your hand, Chiara."

She put her hand in his, her eyes bold and defiant. Jimmy pricked the tip of her finger with the knife and squeezed a few drops of her blood onto the image of the saint.

Nicky brought out a lighter and set one corner of the card aflame.

He was calm today, his hands steady.

He and Jimmy both remembered how he'd nearly dropped the card when Jimmy was being made. Things were different now. They passed the card between them until finally it came into Chiara's hands.

Jimmy turned to face her. "Chiara Popov, while you aren't Martello by blood, your descent is Sicilian, and you have earned your place in this family if you want to take it."

"Yes," she said, looking at him. "I want that."

He smiled gently, as though those three words were the happiest thing he had ever heard.

He put the knife and the gun into her hands. "You live by the knife and the gun now. And that is how you will die. We all will one day."

She returned the smile. "I'm not afraid to die, and I'm not afraid to live first, either."

There was laughter, and conversations started up around the room. Glasses were raised. He heard Nicky calling out a toast. Jimmy leaned in closer to Chiara. "Will you be my Queen of New York?"

"I'll have to think about it."

The smile on her face was all the answer he needed.

#

Jimmy felt the grip of the gun's handle as he jostled the barrel against the other man's forehead.

He remembered this dream even as he revisited it.

Things were different now.

He knew he was dreaming.

No one was going to make him kneel in the dark with a gun at his temple.

In the dream now, lucid, he had his gun pressed against Sale's forehead, or maybe it was Lev Volkov's. He couldn't really tell, and it didn't really matter.

He didn't pull the trigger.

Right now, in this moment, he didn't need to.

The kneeling man was irrelevant. A ghost.

Jimmy knew he was in control.

Around him, his family sang one of those church hymns he'd never bothered to learn. He wasn't religious. He'd never cared about it before, but now he let the words wash over him. He didn't believe in life eternal, or life after death. He was much more of a pragmatic soul than that. But he did trust the evidence of his own eyes, always.

He could see his father, his grandfather, and his uncle, gone to join in this choir of ancestors all singing together.

After the violence and struggle of their lives, it all felt strangely peaceful.

"I'll look after the family now," Jimmy promised the dead. "And I will spend every day trying to be the man you raised me to be. Go now, rest. This is my time. My burden. I will carry it as my duty. That is my solemn vow. My oath. I am and will always be a family man. I live by the knife and the gun, but I am ruled by my head and my heart, always, in all things."

He woke with a feeling of contentment that he had not felt in a long time, in no little part because of the woman who lay sleeping beside him.

The dead were gone.

They were missed.

They would always be missed.

But the time for mourning them was over.

Now, it was time for him to focus on the living. There was a whole kingdom out there for them to explore together.

La fine . . . o l'inizio . . .